Jenny Forrester was a fine bit of stuff – and she knew it. She could twist men round her little finger – all sorts of men – even men like Ben McNulty.

And it was Jenny, provocative and remorseless, who was to blame when Ben progressed from a minor street-corner thug to a razor-slashing gang-leader, proud of his reign of terror, proud to be called a 'head-case'.

BILL McGHEE

Cut and Run

CORGI BOOKS

CUT AND RUN

A CORGI BOOK 0 552 08335 6

Originally published in Great Britain by
Hammond, Hammond & Co. Ltd.

PRINTING HISTORY
Hammond, Hammond edition published 1962
Corgi edition published 1963
Corgi edition reissued 1967
Corgi edition reissued 1984
Corgi edition reprinted 1984

This book is set in 10/11 Palatino

Corgi Books are published by Transworld Publishers Ltd.,
Century House, 61-63 Uxbridge Road,
Ealing, London W5 5SA.

Made and printed in Great Britain by
Hunt Barnard Printing Ltd., Aylesbury, Bucks.

Cut and Run

INTRODUCTION

It may seem pretentious to write an introductory chapter to a book such as this. Perhaps it is. But in doing so I am not trying to give an air of importance to my modest work. My object is to make certain facts clear, so that the reader can understand the story and the mentality of its characters, twisted and alien as it may well appear.

A number of publications on the same theme have already been slated by some of Glasgow's prominent citizens for giving a distorted impression of the city, for showing its citizens as foul-mouthed, razor-slashing gangsters or lazy, street-corner louts. Let me forestall any such criticism, and put the reader straight about any misconception which might arise from what I say. The story which follows has nothing whatsoever to do with the ordinary people of Glasgow: high, middle or lower class. These are mere spectators – and that rarely – of the kind of violence I describe. Indeed, in general, they are not even spectators, but only read about it in the newspapers.

But do not imagine that these furious and beastly outbursts of violence do not take place in Glasgow. Read a Glasgow evening paper dated to-day or a few days back, and you will read something which is so endemic and peculiar to Glasgow that it no longer rates a paragraph in the national Press. Is it possible that the English have overtaken us in the horrible – always downhill – race of delinquency? All I hope for is that the race will shortly be called off.

London, Paris, New York, Singapore, Tokyo, perhaps even Moscow: all these great cities have their seamy sides. You cannot kill the *fact* merely by saying loudly that it does not exist. Every orchard has its fruit in varying degrees of decay, and, when you crowd a million or more people in a relatively small area, you are bound to get quite a lot of decaying fruit.

However, there is one curious thing about Glasgow

gangsters which has always interested – and puzzled – me. The majority of the most notorious and hardened of them in the pre-War years made scarcely a penny out of their crimes. Not plain robbery, but 'breaches of the peace' and 'assault' were the usual charges. 'Religion' was normally the spur. Bigotry was bred in the bone, a condition which still becomes evident at certain football matches. When you got past your childhood, if you lived in a slum area, you belonged either to an Orange street or a Catholic one, you supported either Rangers or Celtic.

The War made some changes, as it did in many other walks of life. And the records are their to show that a lot of the former street-corner thigs died in the War – honourably.

There were those of course who would not soldier and indeed they had their counterparts elsewhere. These characters, who deserted permanently, or dodged the services by other means, and the younger element, then came into their own. Money became more plentiful, and a blackmarket existed in most commodities. Allied servicemen with bulging pockets visited the city, and the lads began forming 'grovet-teams' (strong-arm groups) to relieve them of the bulge.

But the real gang outbreaks come in phases. For two or three months certain crowds carry on a feud, then things quieten down considerably till a later date, when the trouble begins afresh, maybe in some other quarter. It is difficult to pinpoint one particular reason why adolescents should become street-corner hooligans, rather than live the ordinary life of their quieter neighbours. Some lads become involved through an unkind twist of fate. They 'cop a doing' from one group or another, and, with thoughts of revenge, become themselves members of a rival group. Others are initiated because of a misguided urge for excitement. But all of them seem to believe that notoriety, in varying stages, is a good substitute for the fame that most people would prefer, but are never likely to achieve.

One cannot possibly class these youngsters with the other ruffian, whose 'chib' is never absent, even when he has reached middle-age. It must be remembered that a large number of the city's slum, male, population go through the foolish hard-case phase, during the process of growing up, and, if everyone who had ever taken part in a gang fracas were immediately apprehended and imprisoned, the law would be unable to find accommodation, food and prison-clothing for them, even if all the present inmates were evicted. This may seem a terrible state of affairs, but it is not so bad as it appears. Most of the boys do not make the grade as 'chib-man' simply because their natures are essentially decent, and they have become involved in a destiny of violence they were never intended for. This is often proved in later life.

The really prominent 'chib-man', however, is a hardened criminal who spends most of his life 'inside', since he finds it necessary, each time he is released, to prove his underlings, and the world in general, that a 'wee bit time' has not softened him up. Although he manages to escape the consequences of many of his crimes, due to victims being too 'windy' to report the matter, or because of a mistaken code of honour, there are occasions when the law happens to be on the spot at the crucial moment.

Most of the lads spend a very short time in the company of the top-notchers. There are, of course, exceptions, such as the ambitious youth who appears on the horizon as a threat, picturing himself in the shoes of some well-known hard-case. Sooner or later one such youngster comes off best in the encounter, and the loser's career is on the wane. If it happens again the loser no longer carries the threat he did, and that is when the street-bookmakers and traders refuse to give him any money, and the publicans sop serving drink without payment.

But the ordinary lad's term of gangsterism is short merely because he is squeamish, and, although he may succeed in hiding this very human failing from the others, he himself cannot ignore it. Most of the blows he delivers with a weapon are motivated by self-preservation and fear: fear of carrying a 'chib-mark' on his face, through 'sleeping in the traps' and letting the other fellow get there first. I am not trying to whitewash these individuals, but nobody who has not experienced life in the Glasgow slums can imagine just how easy it is to become, for a time, one of the crowd. Only for a time.

For that squeamishness is the cosh-boy's worst crime. To be a success he must be prepared to 'take a liberty' when the

9

necessity arises. An old lady or a cripple should never be allowed to stand in his way. If he sticks to that rule he will thoroughly enhance his reputation. Behind his back others will refer to him (and what more could he ask for?) as a 'nutter' or lunatic. Another term commonly used is ... HEAD-CASE ...

Many gang-fights, through the years, have been caused by the girls who run around with the 'chib-men', sometimes carrying the offensive weapons which the term implies. They play off one group against another, carry tales, and generally cause the trouble that only such a girl could.

The American gangster's female, according to all reports, is his 'moll'. the Glasgow street-corner girl is sometimes known (perhaps because, unlike more respectable lasses, she never wears a hat) as a ... HAIRY ...

The dialogue in this book is often foul, and regularly features the local slang terms. But the people between the covers wouldn't be realistic to me without these characteristics of speech.

The story is fictional, inasmuch as the characters are composite. Yet near counterparts may be found in the slum areas of the city. The incidents which here are strung together in one single narrative have been repeated many times, in real life, in the history of Glasgow's slums ...

CHAPTER ONE

I have always tried to find excuses for Ben, even for those deeds of his which won't brook any excuse or forgiveness, and I still do so by laying most of the blame at Jenny's door. The general opinion was that he was just an incorrigible, destined from the very beginning to commit the almost unimaginable acts of violence and brutality that were chalked up to his horrifying score, but I hold to my contention that everything might have been a lot different if their paths had never crossed. Another marriage could have made another man of Ben.

Despite her country upbringing, Jenny Forrester was a born hairy if ever there was one. She was also a fine bit of stuff and knew it, and the constant admiration of men was meat and drink to her. She got it, too, and from all sorts of men. She knew she could twist them round her little finger, and spent her adult years doing so. Old or young, fat or thin, tall or short – as long as they wore a pair of breeks they were Jenny's meat. Despite the fact that he was a real hard case, she even succeeded in dominating Ben McNulty most of the time, and the odd thing about that is that she made her conquest of him before she reached the hairy stage at all, for the hairy is strictly a part of city life, and Jenny had never lived in a city till Ben brought her to Glasgow.

When they met, she was still living in her home-town of Blairgowrie, a bonny wee place in Perthshire. Ben and I went to the Blair area every year for the 'berry-picking', a seasonal occupation which provided a few weeks holiday, paid, for the poorer people of Glasgow, Dundee and stations between.

We always tried to arrive there along with the early birds around the seventh of July, so as to have the maximum time there, and it was on that day in the year 1941 that we pitched our tent just outside the town. There were huts available on all the farms, but they were mostly reserved for families, and the rest of us lived under canvas. Since I was due to report at Richmond in Yorkshire for military duty on the ninth of August and Ben was awaiting his call-up papers, we were determined to make the most of our last days of freedom.

The first week we didn't bother to go into the town till Saturday night, when we had a few drinks and, around nine o'clock, decided to do the jiggin', in other words, go dancing. There was a dance hall just off the Wellmeadow, the town square, and we made for that. A fair crowd was gathered there, and, although the dancers in most small towns are inclined to be clannish, at that time of year there were more Glaswegians present here than locals, and we had no difficulty in finding partners.

We had a couple of dances, and then Ben got his lamps on Jenny. She looked sweet sixteen. I don't know if she had ever been kissed, but if not a lot of country lads had been slow. That's what I told Ben when I saw his interest increasing, my intention being to put him off. Don't get me wrong. I'm just as fond of women as the next bloke, and nobody has ever questioned my virility, but my conscience compels me to deal with only the experienced, tenement-stairhead type when it comes to casual affairs. Maybe I'm trying to convince myself that the age of chivalry is not yet dead. Anyway, I have a thing about it. I said to Ben:

'Ah see you're eyein' up the wee finger. Wad yo no' be better diggin' up wan o' wur ain crowd? There's plenty o' them here.'

'You take your pick o' them, Bill,' said Ben. 'This wan'll dae me fine.'

'You're takin' a liberty,' I said, meaning that he was

12

taking advantage of a country lass, and at the same time feeling somewhat surprised at the extent of this knight-errant streak in me. He drew his eyes away from the girl and turned to look at me with that queer expression that sometimes appeared on his face. 'Aw, dry your eyes,' he reported. 'It's nane o' your bloody business.' I wilted under his gaze and closed my big mouth. You never could reason with Ben.

Just at that moment the band such as it was in a small place like this, struck up, and my pal crossed the floor to ask a dance from the girl we had been discussing. He never knew what he was letting himself in for.

Ben and Jenny tangoed, waltzed and jitterbugged for the rest of the evening, and in between one of these displays I was introduced to Jenny's china, a short-haired synthetic blonde of eighteen. Ben was obviously expecting me to pair off with her, but, trying to practise what I'd been preaching, I 'renegued' and kept my attention directed elsewhere.

Each time I caught sight of the other two on the floor, I could see that she was thriving on his admiration, which was not surprising. Ben was quite good-looking, his face as yet unmarked by the scars that were later to decorate it. Standing five-foot-nine, with a good square pair of shoulders on him, with a dark complexion that the girls seemed to like and jet-black hair wavy enough to give the impression that he slept with it wrapped in corrugated iron, he usually managed to get women to look favourably on him. He also had a good line of patter, which of course is half the battle.

Although he dressed in traditional fly-man fashion, his exceptionally long jacket and high-waisted stove-pipe trousers looked good on him, an achievement I now know to be no mean one, for nowadays when similar dress is called the latest thing for smart young yobs, some strange sights are to be seen. In those days his made-to-measure suits were considered unorthodox. In fact, Ben was something of a pioneer where clothes are concerned.

He danced in fly-man style: shoulders hunched, holding the girl close with her back arched so that her taut breasts strained against her dress. He took long steps with his knee between her legs, and I could plainly see that her thighs matched her shapely calves and ankles. No wonder Ben was so interested. That body and those legs, plus her perfectly featured face and Titian hair, were really something, and I have to admit that deep-down a certain amount of envy was stirring. And I had plenty of company. Half the males present, when their partners were too busy to notice, were having as big an eyeful as I was. Now and again some young buck would make overtures in Jenny's direction, only to be repelled by Ben's glower. He wasn't sharing with anybody, even for as long as it would take to do three laps round the floor.

Just before the last waltz, Ben and I went to the 'Houses of Parliament', and while there he came right out and asked me if I would take Jenny's pal, whose name was Ruby off his hands, as he wished to 'lumber' Jenny. I wasn't at all surprised at his intention to escort her home. In fact I was well ahead of him. I had already made other arrangements and told him so. Ben didn't look pleased.

'Look, Ben,' I said, 'Ah don't feel like lumberin' ony o' these young local burds. Better leavin' them to the locals.'

But I added hastily: 'Onywey – Ah'm walkin' up the road wi' that lassie, Pearl, that stays in the end hut at the camp.'

He was silent. I made a feeble attempt at laughing.

'Ah'm certainly among the jewel'ry the night – Rubies and Pearls,' I faltered. He looked at me for a moment, said, 'Ye lousy bastart,' and stalked angrily.

Pearl and I had a couple of miles to walk, but in such company I had no complaints. Out on the street there was no sign of Ben or the twosome he wanted to split, so presumably things had worked out for him. They usually did.

The girl and I had covered about half the length of our journey, and, as we strolled along the tree-lined lane with the River Errick on one side and the railway on the other, I was wondering how to steer the conversation into the proper channels, when Cupid, in the form of a small, flittering bat, gave me a hand. The bat flew straight at our heads as such creatures do, and next moment Pearl was in my arms, her warm body pressed against mine. Right then I felt like seeking out that bat and finding a fairy castle for it to inhabit. I can't say whether Pearl was really scared, or if she was just taking matters into her own hands because I was a slowcoach. I didn't ask. Just accepted my chance. And I'm not fooling about that bat and the fairy castle.

A little farther along the road was a cornfield which I made full use of, and so forgot for the moment all about Ben and his lumber. No normal man could have thought of other things while engaged in a love session with Pearl. And I'm more or less normal.

Ben wasn't around when we finally got back to the camp. The girl came with me to the bivouac tent he and I shared, but I soon persuaded her to move on to her aunt's hut, as I didn't want her around when Ben showed up. I didn't love her or anything like that, regardless of what I might have told her in the cornfield, but I had no wish to hear her insulted, and Ben would probably do just that, especially if he had been unsuccessful in his own ploys.

I needn't have worried. Ben still hadn't come back when I fell asleep, the last sounds I heard being when the night was stabbed by the whistle of a stoat and the squeal of a dying rabbit. The quiet peace of the countryside . . .

Next morning I awoke to familiar snores and found my pal lying beside me. Leaving him undisturbed, I

15

rose and joined a crowd of the other pickets at the communal tap. At last I managed to get near enough to throw some water on my face. As I stood drying myself, Pearl joined me. Her presence embarrassed me, and I broke away as soon as possible. I fried a couple of kippers and carried them, along with a cup of tea, to the tent, where I gave Ben a shake. He thanked me for providing breakfast in bed and got wired into it. It looked as if something had given him an appetite.

His mood had altered considerably since last night, and we bummed away amicably till the noise of a tractor outside the tent interrupted us. The voice of the 'grieve' was heard raised, and we realized it must be getting late when the gaffer was here. We should have been up on the field by now. We didn't answer, but quickly dressed. When he had gone, we followed him.

All day long I waited impatiently for the lurid description that invariably followed one of Ben's amatory adventures, but this time none came, and at last I asked him outright how he had got on with Jenny.

'Ah won a watch,' he said, and nothing more.

I knew from that that all had been well with him, but his reticence and the far-away look in his eyes when he spoke left me disturbed.

From that day onwards for the rest of our stay in Blairgowrie he left me to my own devices. During working hours of course we picked together, but then, after a meal, he would get 'brammed up' and, without saying where he was going, would 'blow himself'. There was no need for him to tell me whom he was going to meet and I didn't ask him. I knew, and he knew I knew.

I spent a few more nights in Pearl's company, and then, when we had tacitly agreed that the first fine gloss had worn off, I chummed up with two Dundee lads from another farm. When I wasn't playing pontoon or brag in the camp, I was having a drink

16

with these blokes in town.

On some of these visits I would meet Ben in the street, with Jenny hanging possessively on to his arm. When I approached, she always turned her head away, with her nose in the air, as if I didn't smell nice. It was as plain as the face round my nose that she didn't like me, and for my part it was eachy-peachy. Like her predecessors, she was due to back a deuce from her association with Ben, but she was so obviously a troublemaker that I began to wonder.

There was a lot of grief ahead, and my private crystal ball told me that Ben wasn't only dishing it out. He was on the receiving-end for more than his share of it.

CHAPTER TWO

Our original intentions had been to leave Blair together on August the seventh, but it came as no great surprise to me when Ben told me he had decided to stay a little longer. It was the sixth of the month, and we were having a smoke at the end of a row of berries, sitting on top of our upturned 'luggies', when the subject came up. Although the news was expected, I was yet a bit huffy about it, and let him know.

'Is it ower the heid o' this burd, Jenny?' I asked. 'Have ye fell for her?'

'Listen, Bill—,' he retorted, stubbing out the cigarette and getting to his feet. 'Ye know whit Ah telt ye already aboot interferin' in ma business. Don't stick your nose in too faur or Ah'll have tae cut it off.'

I'm rather fond of my nose since it's my best feature. I dropped the subject, and we continued picking till the end of the new dreel, then knocked off.

The following day, Ben, who was out doing a bit,

chucked it early in order to have a drink with me before I left. I had just packed my working clobber, and was making a pot of tea, when he came down the road.

'Ah'll gie ye a "butty" inty the toon,' he muttered awkwardly.

'Okay,' I agreed. 'Dae ye want a moothfu' o'tea furst?'

'Ah'll take a wee drap,' he said, 'an' get somethin' tae eat in bye.'

When he had gulped down the hot tea, he took a hold of my case and we left the camp, with the good wishes of my fellow-pickers, and a somewhat watery smile from Pearl, as we passed the fields. Around one o'clock we trudged into town.

In a wee pub round the corner from the railway station, we were standing over a pint, when Ben spoke a trifle hesitantly:

'Bill – Ah – Ah know ye – didny mean ony harm when ye were chirpin' aboot Jenny. Ah'm sorry Ah lost the heid.' He was rubbing the tip of his nose between forefinger and thumb. Not, as one might suppose, because he had forgotten to bring a handkerchief. It was a sure sign that Ben was ill at ease. I knew, better than anyone, that he was not in the habit of apologizing for anything.

'Whit's the strength o' it wi' you an' her?' I enquired.

'Well,' he mumbled, 'Ah fancy her strong.' He hesitated, then added, 'An' Ah think she feels the same aboot me,' looking a lot less confident than he now sounded. 'So she says onywey,' he finished with a shrug, after another pause. I could have ventured a fair retort to that but thought better of it, instead putting another question to him with a good idea what his answer would be.

'Whit are yese gaunny dae then?' I asked. 'Are ye anchorin' here?'

'Naw!' He paused uncertainly, and continued in a

18

thoughtful tone, 'Ah thinks she's comin' back tae Glesca wi' me.'

I was right. My feelings were mixed. I was pleased at my perfect powers of deduction, and dreading the thought of Jenny as a permanent fixture in the Calton. He looked at the expression on my face and said:

'Bill – although we've been chinas since the Pope wiz an altar-boy an' Ah've always liked ye a lot, Ah'm warnin' ye no' tae say a word oot o' place tae her at ony time.' I gazed fascinated at his long spatulate finger which waved in front of me, and tried to concentrate on his words. 'If ye dae,' he was saying, 'you're bang in trouble.' I must have been wearing a hurt look for he hesitated before continuing. 'Gawd stiff me!' he ejaculated, and I could see he was reluctant to impart the information that followed. Some compelling force made him say: 'Ah've already had wan needle wi' her ower the heid o' ye.'

It was now obvious why she acted so swivel-headed when I appeared on her horizon. I couldn't see for the life of me why I should be the cause of a tiff, and I didn't really care.

'Ah'm never likely tae see her again,' I said. 'Ye'll have scrubbed it by the time Ah get ma furst leave.' He was shaking his head.

'Nae danger,' he assured me. 'When ye see me, ye'll see her.' But he was still pulling at the knob on the end of his nose. Ben was still feeling uncomfortable, or maybe he was now, subconsciously, apologizing to himself for the trouble that his rashness was to bring, sometime in the future, upon his head.

At this juncture, the conversation took a more congenial turn, while we swigged a few pint-pots, and, when I caught the four o'clock bus for Perth, Ben was standing at the kerb, waving his hand, with a friendly smile on his face.

*   *   *

19

Three months or so elapsed, and I arrived in Glasgow at approximately eight a.m. on the twelfth of November, commencing ten days' leave, granted me on the completion of my preliminary training. My mother who, at that time, was a grass-widow, had been warned, by telegram, of my arrival, and had bacon and eggs prepared for my breakfast. I washed up and changed into my civvies, then unpacked some of my gear, including a pair of intricately beaten brass candlesticks, which I had won at cards. They hadn't cost much originally, but my mother was all tickled with them. We sat about the house yattering till the boozers opened at eleven, when I took her down for a half and a stout. An hour and several drinks later, I left for Stevenson Street.

At Ben's mother's house, I was told he had only been there once, and that only to collect some clothing and stuff, including a communication directing him to the Marine barracks at Chatham, and to arrive not later than the twenty-third of September. I had an idea that wherever he was Jenny was with him. Her name had not been mentioned to Ben's mother. It was obviously an illicit arrangement that I didn't make Mrs McNulty any the wiser. I wondered if Ben had answered his call-up.

The visit to the McNulty residence was not entirely fruitless however, as Ben's younger sister was present when I called, and she was worth going on a mystery tour to view.

Isa, Ben and I had been brought up together in the Calton. From the days when I had a constant drip at my nose, I had watched Isa grow alongside of me. I could remember her running around the streets barefooted, with her frock tucked inside her knickers, and how it used to embarrass me to have such intimate garments flaunted in my presence. Then, when she had stopped growing upwards, and began spreading outwards, in the right places, many sleep-

20

less nights I had spent after being in Ben's house when Isa was engaged in her ablutions. Her mother would reprimand her for standing at the sink, dressed in a slip that was many sizes too large, and was wont to reveal far too much of the upper part of her body. At the same time the garment had been shortened to such an extent that it was apt to creep up over her buttocks, and allow a glimpse of pink satin tights as she stooped. At those times I was both grateful to, and peevish at, Mrs McNulty, for stopping the show, but there's no doubt that my first mature thoughts were centred around that girl. When we had reached what was considered a reasonable 'winching' age, I had an occasional notion to date her, but found it difficult to kiss and fondle her, after our years of sexless camaraderie. Albeit she seemed keen enough.

When I called as a representative of the armed forces, I found it easier to make headway. The uniform made me like a new man. My line of attack was roughly that, since she was on the sick panel, by reason of anaemia, or some such young women's trouble, she wouldn't have much money, and would allow me to treat her to the flicks that night. Crude, I admit, but it proved successful.

The major part of that leave was spent with Isa, doing the pictures most nights, and, by the time I was due to return, we considered ourselves as 'winching' steady.

I was glad I didn't see the unpredictable Ben before I left. At times he could appear as a deep depression, changing fair weather to foul just by his presence, and my rheumatics told me that this could be one of the times when an umbrella might be needed. It was always hard to figure what Ben would do under any given circumstances, and his association with the Blairgowrie girl was, in my opinion, an added factor in this uncertainty of my friend's reaction towards his sister's suitor.

21

When I got back to Richmond, it was to discover that I had been placed on a draft, proceeding to Yeovil in Somerset, for gunnery training. I corresponded with Isa regularly, each letter becoming more endearing as the weeks passed. Yeovil, like all similar towns during wartime, had its quota of soldier-struck or sailor-struck girls. But the charms of the uniform-hunting women of that particular area were completely eclipsed in my mind by thoughts of Isa. I was crazy about the girl.

Christmas arrived and, trudging through the thin carpet of snow that covered the road to the Company Office, I found that there were three letters for Gunner William McGhee. Scanning the envelopes, I pushed the first two in my tunic pocket and gazed at the third, surprised. The others were more or less expected. My mother had written of course, and there was the usual epistle from Isa, but the one I now held in my hand, fumbling with the flap was adorned with Ben's unmistakable scrawl. The contents were short and sweet.

'How's it?' it said. 'I was wondering if you could wangle a leave for next week (Hogmanay). I'd like you to be my best man. I'm getting married to Jenny. Hope things are going alright with you as it is with me. See you next week – I hope – Your Old China – Ben.'

I stood gazing unseeingly at the words, a strange premonition nagging at me. The point I couldn't understand was that Jenny had forgotten sufficiently our incompatability to allow me to be male witness at her wedding. It didn't fit my ideas about her.

I entered the hut, flopped on my bunk and extracted the other two letters. I opened my mother's, like a kid with a sandwich and a chocolate-biscuit, keeping the tit-bit till the last. Mother's letter was the usual mass of well-meaning but, in so far as the army was involved, impractical advice, interspersed with admonitions to remember to write often. I laid it aside for future reference, and relaxed, to enjoy to the full Isa's honeyed words.

All that matters about Isa's letter, as far as this tale is concerned, is that it contained a note saying that she was to be best maid at the coming ceremony. I would have been prepared to go three rounds with our heavyweight champion R.S.M., while one of the Camp Police was cuffed to either of my wrists, just for the sake of seeing Isa. The letters I had received were the necessary thrust I needed.

I hopped from my bed forthwith and hurried back to the Company Office, where I applied for compassionate leave on the grounds that my grandma's rickets were troubling her, or some such unlikely reason. Wonders will never cease. The leave was granted next day. You never saw kit packed so quickly in all your life.

As the train sped northwards, expectancy mounted so much in me that I was unable to have my usual travel-nap, and the pretty WAAF who was pushed against me might well have chewed her gums in mortification at the scant attention her comely features got from me. My heart was beating like a triphammer and she must have been aware it was not on her account.

It's amazing how glad one can be to see the dismal smoke-begrimed tenements that tell you you're on the outskirts of Glasgow. Fighting my way past the jostling crowds, through the narrow gate at the end of the platform in Central Station, I reluctantly pushed Isa to the back of my mind for the present, since it was not she but Ben who stood there, searching for me with his eyes.

Out on Argyle Street we hopped on a tramcar, and, as it trundled through the early morning mist, we discussed a very important topic – finance. I opened that part of the conversation like this:

'Ah might as well tell ye,' I said. 'Ah'll have tae dae a

job tae get some cash for the weddin'.'

Ben laughed. 'Ah'm practically in the grubber masel',' he replied. 'Or ye widny need ony money. Ah'd pey for the lot.' To which I replied with some heat:

'Don't talk like a scrubber, man. It widny maitter if ye were loaded.' I was counting off on my fingers. 'Ah've got tae pey for the ring, taxi, floo'ers, an' Gawd knows whit.' Then I added indignantly: 'Whit kin'a best man dae ye think Ah am?' Ben was looking at me derisively. 'Anyway, Ah'll need booze money, an' Ah'd have tae buy the best maid a present, even if it whidny been Isa. Definitely – Ah've got tae have cash.'

'Ye can keep your heid an' Ah'll buy ye a bunnet,' Ben retorted with another laugh. 'An' by the wey – whit's the score wi' Isa an' you?'

This was it. This is what I meant. The deep depression was hovering, and there was no umbrella handy. Nothing to stop it falling on me if it decided to. I hesitated, then stammered out, 'Well, Ben, don't be surprised if there's anither weddin' soon.' He made no comment. I changed the subject.

'Ah think Ah'll screw that wee tobacconist's in the Gallagate,' I mused. 'It's always been good for a score onytime Ah done it.'

Ben chuckled condescendingly. 'Twenty quid?' he queried. 'If you're guan' screwin', you're as well gettin' hung for a sheep as a lamb.' I didn't agree with that. I don't fancy getting hung at all. This is why all my illegal ventures had been confined to petty stuff. The greater amount of money involved, the more risk attached, I say. I told Ben as much. He didn't bother to answer my arguments. Instead he said:

'Ah've got somethin' lined up masel', if ye'd like tae be rung in,' and seeing the interest I was unable to hide, due to my embarrassed financial state, he added, 'Ah'll tell ye aboot it the night.'

He got off the tram, and I went home to leave my

kit in the old wife's.

I hadn't let her know I was coming home. Sort of surprise, pleasant, I hoped. She was still in her kip and came to the door in her night attire.

'Hello, son,' she greeted me effusively, with traces of tears in her eyes. 'Ah didny know ye were comin' hame. How did ye no' let me know? Ah widda had a cup o'tea ready for ye.'

'Ah wantit tae surprise y, Maw,' I answered simply, smiling.

'Ye certainly did, son, ye certainly did,' she repeated, nodding her head vigorously. 'But how did ye manage it sae quick?'

'Ah worked a flanker on ma Company Commander, an' got a wee leave,' I answered. 'Ah've tae be Ben McNulty's best man.'

'That—' she was choking over her words. 'That – rascal?' she ejaculated. Strong language indeed for her. 'Ah thoaght the Army (she said the word with a capital A) widda kept ye oota that yin's road, son.' She laid her hand on my arm, emphasising her words. 'He's a bad yin that yin,' she said, tut-tutting, and shaking her head mechanically.

Dead shrewd, the old wife was. Tipped McNulty for a headcase since he had entered his teens. She started to deliver to me all her usual comments on his character and predictions as to his future, while I wired into the tightener that she had laid out for me, and more or less closed my ears to her rigmarole.

My teeth were sinking into a soda-scone filled with crisp fried bacon while she rambled on.

'An' lookit whit he done that night his sister wiz at the dancin' wi' 'im,' she was saying. I looked at her inquisitively, trying to recall her previous words, but she took no notice. I wondered if she had discovered that my affair with Isa was serious.

Her slightly plump cheeks inflating and deflating rhythmically with her words (that was the way she spoke in the morning before she had inserted her 'wallies') she continued.

'Jist 'cos the young fella asked Isa if he could see her hame, that yin Ben goes ower an' hits 'im wi' a razor or somethin'. Ese a bad yin.'

'Where wiz this?' I asked, while a feather was dragged up my spine.

'In the Brighton Public,' she answered, inadvertently showing her gums, then hurriedly concealing them again, as if the house were full of visitors.

I heard nothing more that she said. My mind was otherwise occupied.

When I had pulled myself together, I decided that Ben could go to hell, and that he would never frighten me off like that, no matter how he tried. And I was prepared to let him know that, I told myself.

Later in the day, I went round to the McNulty's house, where I spent a few hours, mostly talking to Isa, while Ben seemed to be ignoring us. But around seven in the evening he came over and spoke to me quietly.

'Are ye comin' doon for a pint, Bill?' he asked.

I nodded agreement, but as I rose from my seat I could feel my brow pores open to release some sweat, and a part of my brain, the cautious part, was saying, 'This is it. You've had it, chum. He just wants to get you out of the house to give you it.' Bravely, I thought, I pushed the qualms aside.

I could have died laughing, or something, when we got down on the street, and Ben began to discuss the job he had lined up. I gulped my heart back down my throat and listened, as he gave me the strength of it.

'It's a good thing,' he explained. 'That wee bird, Susie Divers, that steys up the stair fae the old wife put me on tae it. She works in the place, an' she says we'll get a coupla hunn'er' oot it.' I licked my lips and sucked the water from between my teeth, while he continued, waving his arms about like an excited tic-tac man as he spoke. 'She'll put us fly tae a wey in, an' where the gelt'll be lyin'.'

We were at the boozer's door, but he laid a restraining hand on my arm as I made to enter. 'We canny back a deuce, Bill,' he persisted earnestly. 'It's a Jew-boy's place ower near Paisley Road Toll, an' the cash'll be there for the luftin' on Saturday night.' He gave me a penetrating glance. 'Whiddye say?'

I hesitated for a moment, then nodded at Ben's beaming face. I was convinced. It is never very difficult to persuade me to join an expedition in search of money. I shoved my hands in my trouser-pockets and leaned against the wall.

'Jist the two o' us inty it?' I asked him.

'We-e-e-ell,' he mumbled ponderously. 'We could staun' splittin' it three ways, an' Ah'd like tae dig up a place nearhaun' the crib, where we could wait till it wiz time tae go tae the graft.' Engrossed as he was in the subject, it didn't prevent him from eyeing up two pairs of female legs which were passing just then. He turned back to me. 'Ah think we'll take a run ower there an' see if we can fin wan o' the "Tims" that says roon' that quarter.' I was cushy. I agreed.

We went along to Abercrombie Street and caught a number seven tram, which dropped us near a public house aptly named the *Crow Bar*. It was a hangout for half the rogues in the city. The other half were 'inside', mostly for crimes that were first hatched within the confines of its walls. On that particular night, surprisingly enough, the place was more or less empty, which fact not unnaturally dampened our spirits somewhat. We decided to have a drink anyway, in the hope that a likely candidate would appear shortly.

We emptied two pint-pots, and started on two more, before we spotted a possible 'hander' stepping up to the other end of the bar. We joined him, leaving our drinks where they were.

A small rotund man about forty years old who looked as if he were saving up for a razor-blade appeared glad to see us. 'Blaster' Brown, who had earned his title by indulging in safe-blowing activities in his youth, was in fact very glad to see us, witness the gleaming row of gums he displayed at sight of us. And when I strained my meagre finances to buy a gill of 'dadlum', his mouth split so much that the ends reached to his grey sideboards. Things were bad with him, and when the coins rattled on the wet bar-top his ears wiggled like a nervous rabbit's lugs.

He had left the 'peters' alone since his sentences began to be dished out a number of years at a time. These days he did a bit of small-time stuff now and again, but tried to stay away from the High Court.

He gobbled the rough wine like a fish in the Sahara, and I dug into my pocket and managed to buy him another.

I thought he ws going to fall around my neck, and Ben watched him disgustedly while he drank and talked about himself. Why, I don't know. He could see off the stuff, himself when he started, and that was often.

The whole point of the discourse as far as I could see, was that Blaster's life had been a series of ups and downs, and that his present financial status was but a temporary set-back. He knew that prosperity once more would shine its rays upon him, and meanwhile, with a childlike innocence, he faced his poverty, prepared to accept whatever came his way.

I knew Blaster had spent more money in a night than Ben and I had spent in a week. Like most of the screwsmen he couldn't get rid of his money quick enough when he was bang in the game; but, when he was broke, he was thankful for small donations.

While Ben was listening sardonically to Blaster, I happened to glance in the wall-mirror behind them, and there was Davie the Dummy seeing off one of our drinks. I'd known him for years. Knew he was a bit of a 'minesweeper', for I'd seen him at it with other people's drink, and he'd been barred from various hostelries for it.

I started to sweat. I wasn't worrying about the loss of a drop of beer, but there was no telling what Ben would do if he saw him at it. It wasn't wise to start anything in a strange district and the Dummy had bags of friends on this side of the city.

Just at this moment my head-case friend got his lamps on the mirror, and saw the other beer disappear. By the look on Ben's face, I knew that the trouble I had been hoping to avoid was now about to materialize.

CHAPTER THREE

Ben strode along the bar and grabbed the Dummy's arm as he turned to walk away. Ben swung him around. 'Ah'll have a pint aff ye, Dummy,' he said.

'We don't want ony trouble, Ben,' I interrupted, speaking over his shoulder in a low tone.

Without releasing his grip on the Dummy, he turned his head showing his near-perfect teeth in that crazy grin of his. 'Who disny?'

Some of the few customers present were edging away, and the bartender looked as if he didn't know whether to shout for help, or lay an egg. And I felt much the same myself.

The Dummy was grunting, and waving his arms about, trying to convey something to us, in sign language. Neither of us know what he was 'talking' about.

I looked at Ben and that crazy grin was still there. He was enjoying himself. In his element. But not me. I earnestly wished myself somewhere else, but it didn't work. My fairy godmother must be strictly union.

This was her night off.

Like most of his kind, Dave was quick-tempered, probably because of his affliction, and was inclined to be a bit of a nutter. He grabbed a pint measure from the bar, smashed it and jabbed the broken edge at Ben's 'coupon'. I could have told him not to try that. Too often I had seen Ben in action. Before you could say, 'How's your Maw for sugar?' Ben's hand darted in the direction of his handkerchief-pocket, and at the same time, he instinctively dodged the jagged glass.

The Dummy's weight was behind the intended blow, as he hit the razor with his cheek. Suddenly he was in possession of another mouth, at a slight angle to the original one. This new opening was spouting blood like rain from a broken gutter. He let out an unearthly screech, and I wondered if the noise could be coming from the cut, while he clapped his hands to his face as if to stem the flow, but the tighter his hands pressed, the more gore oozed between his shaking fingers.

Quickly we made for the door, but not quick enough. Three of the Hatchet (a local gang) were there before us, appearing as if from nowhere. The 'chibs' were out. They were all set for trouble. For a moment, while time seemed to stand still, we faced each other, neither group making a move. Then I realized there was nothing else for it, as I produced the 'malky' from my pocket. In his hand Ben still had his own, stained a bright red with the Dummy's blood.

One of the three, Hood his name was, a character I'd met before, shouted, 'Ya Calton bastarts!' And he made a lunge at me with a bread-knife, and took a piece from the lobe of my ear, but not before my weapon caught him on the chin. He fell.

I ducked as a half-empty stout-bottle passed over my head, to smash the gantry-mirror. Hood was clamping his arms around my legs trying to bring me down beside him. I kneed his face gently upwards till it was in full view, yet my eyes were everywhere but on the target as I again belted him with the razor. I was so sure that another adversary would literally catch me with my trousers down, with a pull of Hood's arm, that a temporary panic overcame me.

Fortunately, the grip on my legs was relaxed, and I found that no more blows were necessary, for Hood had 'chucked it'. Lying there, sprawled among the sawdust, he was crying, I think, and no one else had come near me.

Only then did I find time to see how Ben was faring. As I turned my head apprehensively I noticed one of our adversaries writhing on the floor, holding his guts and moaning like a stuck pig. There was no blood, so I correctly assumed it was the 'sub' that was applied. Ben would get the boot in sharp when he had two to cope with. I also noticed that the third hard-case was making a hurried exit through the door.

Ben had another kick at the bloke on the floor, nodded me out and left the shop. I glanced round at the few customers huddled at the far end of the horseshoe-shaped bar, and the waiter emerging from behind the counter, and following Ben out to the street, the night air refreshing me, cooling the sweat on my brow. I'm the squeamish type. Can't stand the sight of blood. But somehow, when it's you or the other fellow, you can forget, for a moment, such allergies. Yet I am invariably troubled afterwards by the inevitable nerve-attack. Must be reaction, or something.

I kept glancing over my shoulder for signs of the returning enemy. I couldn't see anything but a few kids playing 'kick-the-can' in the middle of the road, and three tousled-looking women yattering at a close-mouth. I turned once more to my silent companion. He had a small cut, high up on his cheek, which was bleeding profusely. He dabbed with his hanky, while I spoke:

31

'You shouldn't have screwed your nut, Ben.'

'Whit?' he cried. 'Dae ye want me tae staun' still tae the bastarts splits me wi' a measure? Ye seen 'im at it wi' the beer.' In his wrath he was stuttering.

'But ye didny need tae "claim" 'im. Who's worrying aboot a drap o' beer?' I argued, for the moment heedless of the possible consequences of my folly. 'If the coppers get a hau'd o' us your weddin'll be postponed.'

'Whit the hell are ye givin' us?' he shouted, and I knew it was time I closed my big mouth before I put my foot in it. 'Dae Ah havety have it oot wi' you tae?'

Silly question! But he looked as if he expected a sensible answer. Me! I answered not a word. You know the proverb. Well, valorously, I used my discretion.

'Did ye see whit happened tae Blaster?' I queried, realizing just then that he existed. 'He didny take ony part in the barney. Maybe he's still in the boozer.'

A voice at my side said:

'Naw – Ah've seen the day when Ah carried a chib wi' the best o' them, but Ah'm gettin' kinna aul' for that game noo. No' as quick on ma feet as Ah usety wiz. Ah'll leave the battlin' noo tae the younger fellas.'

Ben muttered, 'Yalla-bellied bastart,' and dabbed once more at his cheek with the blood-soaked hanky. Blaster looked at him quizzically and said nothing. I didn't agree with Ben but as usual refrained from telling him so.

By this time we'd reached Crown Street and the old fellow said: 'There's a caur comin'. If ye want tae get that stitched, Ben, Ah'll gie ye a butty up tae the Infirmary.' He looked at me and added, 'Bill's isny too bad.'

'Cheeses!' Ben muttered through clenched teeth. 'Ya sully aul' bastart.' Blaster looked blank. Too long since he'd been in a fight. 'Dae ye want tae finish the night in a "flowry". The quacks widny put a needle near ma face without lettin' the "grass" know. Dae ye think the polis are that stupit, that they couldny connect us wi' the turn-up in that boozer? For cheeses sake screw your bobbin.'

Blaster stood with a hurt look on his face and, contrariwise, Ben took a remorse of conscience. 'It's no' awfa deep onyway,' he told him. 'Ah'll manage tae get it patched up. Thanks onyway for the oaffer.'

All three of us stood looking at each other. Quite a few passers-by were staring at us. I thought, 'This is a helluva spot to be standing in. The police will be coming on the scene at any moment.' I suggested we hurry aboard the tram, since the member of the Hatchet who had escaped unscathed was liable to reappear, with reinforcements, pretty soon. The motion was carried unanimously, and we quickly made arrangements to see Blaster the following evening, then jumped on the tram, ignoring the stares of the other passengers. From the top of the car I could see Blaster hurry away. I sincerely hoped that he wouldn't run into any of the Hatchet while he was on his Tod, or better still, that they had no idea who had been speaking to us in the *Crow*. No respect for age, that mob.

The vehicle was gathering speed, and we had no sooner settled in a front seat than we found it necessary to duck. We had been spotted from the road, and, simultaneously, there was an angry roar from the pavement, and a resounding crash, as shattered remains of the nearest window showered over us, followed by an empty milk bottle, which missed my head by one of the hairs, to land at the feet of a prim middle-aged lady who seemed in the first stages of throwing a fit. This was something to startle her fellow-members at the weekly tea-meeting. Another missile flew past to fall in the passage, and the lady let out a shriek when she saw the raw potato, with razor-blades protruding from it, resting on the floor. She flaked out and a young couple came to her aid.

Ben was all for racing off the tram and getting to grips, but I managed to restrain him sufficiently, so that, when we scuttled along the passage, between the seats, to the rear staircase, we were a good three hundred yards from the yelling mob.

In the small compartment at the end of the car, two young fellows got to their feet as we stumbled in. For a moment I thought they were Hatchet members. Ben too. For he had his razor raised aloft before the light of recognition came into his eyes.

'Pat Carroll!' he ejaculated. 'Ah jist recognized ye in time.' He lowered his arm and breathed deeply. 'Ye nearly got yoursel' chibbed there.'

'Who's giein' ye the chase?' Pat asked.

'The Hatchet,' I answered laconically. 'An' they seem tae be "mob-handed".'

Pat drew a length of lead-piping from his trousers. He was a Calton boy we had known for years. He ran about the Schkipga Pass. 'Dae ye fancy gaun' back an' steamin' inty them?' he asked with an air of eagerness which I couldn't understand.

'Naw,' I said, without waiting for Ben's opinion. 'We'll wait tae we dig up a few handed an' then we'll have it oot wi' them.' Pat shrugged shoulders and pocketed piping.

'It's up tae youse,' he conceded.

The driver kept the tramcar going like the hammers of hell, straight up the Saltmarket, by-passing a couple of stops where groups of people stepped eagerly forward as we approached, and, as we rushed past, returned to the kerb with disgruntled mutterings, questioning the driver's parentage, and directing him to a terminus other than his indicator showed.

I had an idea that this particular Corporation employee had his eyes peeled all the while for coppers, so, at my suggestion, we raced downstairs, the four of us, and took a flying leap to the cobblestones, as he reduced his momentum to air-cruising speed approaching Glasgow Cross. We avoided any police who might have heard the driver's tale by negotiating a couple of back streets, then entered a house in Monteith Row. There dwelt a fellow who did a fair bit of patching up on Ben's cheek, and put a little bit of adhesive on the lobe of my ear. You should have seen Ben's antics when the bloke was applying some smart stuff which, he said, would draw the edges of the wound together. Ben braced himself like a Hollywood-version pioneer while a Daniel Boone type in a skunk-hat cuts away a bullet with a burnt-blade bowie-knife.

Back on the street, we found Pat and his 'mucker' waiting for us to accompany them along the London Road.

'Dae ye want tae have a buzz wi' that mob the night?' Pat asked again, as we neared the Schkipga. Persistent character. 'Ah can dig up a few handers right now if yese fancy it. Catch them on the stoat.' I was hedgy, but I couldn't let any of them see that. Definitely bad for my health.

Ben asked, 'How munny can ye get?'

'Whitever lads is at the coarner'll be alang wi' us.' Pat looked at his friend, who nodded in agreement. The silent man. 'You're no' gonny let they Soo' Side bastarts go aboot bummin' that they chased ony o' the Calton crowd, are ye?' Pat asked indignantly. 'C'mon an' we'll see who's a' at the coarner.'

There were about a dozen of them and they didn't require much coaxing. Especially the 'wined up' ones. Pat told them next to nothing. All he said was, 'That bloody Hatchet crowd gied us a chase the night an' we're lookin' for handers.'

Two or three of them said, 'We're along wi' yese,' or words to that effect, and the others nodded their heads.

'How are yese fixed for chibs?' Pat asked.

A few weapons of various kinds were flashed, and one bloke said, 'Mine's is up in the hoose. Ah'll go up an' get it. Ah'll no' be a minute.'

Another voice asked, 'Can ye get wan for me tae? Ah loast ma bicycle-chain in that barney the ither night.'

'Ah don't know – ,' the other hesitantly replied. 'But Ah'll see whit Ah can dae.' I saw him trot towards Charlotte Street.

'We'll meet ye at Kent Street,' Pat called after his retreating back, as we headed that way in a bunch. A few others joined us in ones and twos during our progress. They enquired as to the score and, when told, immediately affiliated themselves. I could sense a surge of excitement going through me that I wished to quell. The blood-pulsing sensations were being transmitted through the group, till I could picture us a lynch-mob in the Far West of fiction, or a Ku-Klux-Klan gathering in the deep southern states of the US. The bloke who reckoned that man sometimes reverts back to his dog-cat-dog, half-animal forebears knew what he was about. This was such an occasion. So, as we marched along London Road, the quiet mutterings of the crowd were louder in my ears than angry shouts could be. Nearing the corner of Kent Street we saw a bit of a scatter. Ben, who walked in front, tippled right off. 'It's a' right,' he shouted. 'It's no' a "claim".' Then, after a pause, 'It's me – McNulty.'

The Kent Street crowd who, under the impression that we were a rival gang on a raid, had deployed at sight of us, now gathered together again, while Ben and Pat explained things to some of the gang's most prominent personages. The remainder grouped round saying nothing.

I didn't want to walk into this battle but what could I do? Along with Ben it was my fight, and at any sign of ducking it my handers were likely to kick me up and down the London Road. Ever had a 'kicking'? Well don't judge me. Anyway while they confabbed I stood there, wishing only for peace and solitude, or alternatively, a penny for the Glasgow Cross public toilet.

Abstractedly I could hear Pat repeating himself. A one-track mind that fellow had. Esprit de corps and all that. 'Listen,' he was saying, 'are we gonny let they Soo' Side bampots think they can dae whit they like tae Calton fellas?' And all around rose an angry chorus of grunts and curses. 'They'll be thinking they can run Glesca a'thegither.' Another chorus, louder.

I saw the Charlotte Street bloke swagger across to us and hand a short bayonet to another fellow, who said, 'That's the gemme,' while he admired it. 'Have ye got wan for yoursel'?' Charlotte Street replied by producing from his jacket a large pair of engineer's calipers, which were in a folded position. He fondled them lovingly as he opened them out to show his interested audience the handy weapon he had. The calipers now resembled one of those scimitar things, and he stood there looking like a Turk who'd lost his baggy trousers.

Ben roused the engrossed watchers. 'Come on,' he cried. 'Let's get crackin'. We'll show this bloody lot whit's whit,' and, with a uniform grunt of approval, the group, which was by this time close on forty-handed, moved off across the car lines behind Ben's broad back, split in two, to allow through their midst a private car which was passing the telephone-booths, and rejoined once more, to march round Greendyke Street in a body. I hoped I wouldn't return just a body.

CHAPTER FOUR

As we passed the male and female 'models' in Greendyke Street, the meth-mopping men and women who sat around the grass verge of that particular part of the Glasgow Green directly opposite got up and edged away among the trees, while certain members of our group shouted ribald remarks at them. I could see that I wasn't the only one who was being bothered with his nerves.

We turned the corner into Saltmarket and strutted past the High Court buildings, seemingly without being reminded that it was just the place we could wind up, after this night's doings. Over the bridge to the other side of the Clyde we went, and into enemy territory.

We were approaching the junction of Crown Street and Ballater Street when someone cried out, 'There's some o' the bastarts at the coarner.' We were almost on top of them before they noticed us, and they scattered as they produced their weapons. But one fellow, game as hell, stood his ground, back to the wall, with a hatchet in his hand. We surrounded him, warily.

'Come an' get it, ya bloody shower,' he rasped, waving the weapon threateningly.

One of the crowd got too near and was felled to the ground. Two others dived at once. The first got the flat of the hatchet across the side of his head and the other stopped a boot, but not before he had wrapped a bicycle-chain round his opponent's face. There he stood, unflinchingly, as the blood seeped from all the little cuts and abrasions.

Ben took a hand. He ran forward and broke the force of a hatchet blow with an upraised arm, while he brought his other hand, with the razor, across the fellow's forehead.

It was all over. They kicked him senseless, while the others returned from chasing his friends. We stood looking around us. The place was deathly quiet. Not a soul in sight. Ben said, 'We'll go right up Croon Street,' and a general murmur of agreement could be heard. I looked again at the fellow lying on the ground. If we went up that street, I might finish the night in the same position. I couldn't let any of the others into my thoughts. They were too drunk with the victory I knew could only be temporary. So I trailed along with them, all the while glancing around me for the first signs of the massed attack that was bound to come. You couldn't make a raid on the Gorbals without being prepared for retaliation.

In consequence, I was the first to notice the dark figures lurking at the closemouths further on. Before I said anything to my companions, I glanced over my shoulder, to view my avenue of escape. I thought I would burst a blood-vessel with the effort I expended to control my quaking limbs. I'm a cowardly custard, but can you blame me? Behind us, the street was blocked by a dark hovering mass of moving figures. This had been planned like a military manoeuvre. I pulled my shaking nerves together a little.

'Well lads – it looks as if we've had it,' I said, with a nonchalant air I couldn't believe emanated from me. 'Hup, two, three – this is it.'

'Whyddye mean?' Ben grunted, turning angry eyes on me.

'Dae ye no' see them staunin' in a' the closes?' I asked, while he gave a visible start and peered towards the shadowy entries ahead of us. 'They're jist staunin' there, waitin' for us,' I told him, and, as he was about to make a confident retort, I added, 'An' have a look at your back. There's enough o' them there tae eat us an' crap us.'

With a curse, Ben halted and gazed backwards at the malignant throng. Glancing around I could see the tentacles of fear crawl over sundry faces, but, give them their due, not Ben or Pat. In fact, Ben looked as if he were enjoying the situation some. Yet I knew one matter was troubling him. The dubiety of the gameness of his handers. His next words confirmed this.

'Listen – we'll need tae stick thegither,' he said. He

stopped in his tracks and we did likewise, the better to hear him. 'If we split up – we've had it,' he warned us.

'We'll keep gaun' up the street,' he instructed quickly, his words running together in his haste. 'An' when that crowd make for us, we'll steam right inty them.' He gripped an arm on either side of him, and swung his head arcwise, to emphasise the remainder of his words. 'But for cheeses sake,' he stressed, 'don't stoap. Keep guan' nae maitter whit. An' naebuddy ran away fae the rest. Got it?'

The murmur of agreement was not now quite so audible, as the only one that could be heard clearly was the redoubtable Pat, who was saying, 'Ye heard 'im – mind noo – nae splittin' up – an' when it starts – we're right inty the bastarts.'

Some of our opponents must have doubled back through the back-courts, for there was a sudden surge from the closes on either side and slightly to our rear, and someone cried out, 'Come on the Slash,' which told me that there was more than one South Side mob in this barney. One or two of our handers yelled as they got to grips with the enemy, 'Aye, aye the Chinks!'

The other closes in front of us were spewing out their human contents, and the clatter of the antagonistic running feet could be heard in our rear, as we grappled with the figures that were blocking our escape. Panic-stricken, I slashed like a path-making Chindit at the malignant jungle. The fellow in front of me fell, only to be replaced by another. Regardless of the direction I faced I twisted and turned, dodging the clutching hands and swinging weapons. I kept running.

From the corner of my darting eye I saw Pat cop a right one on the coupon. The struggle with me was but a momentary thing. Fear won. I left Pat to his fate and hurried on. Here's where you learn the law of self-preservation and loyalty goes to hell.

A ᶜew yards farther on I halted dead in my tracks. It

dawned on me that I might be racing towards the other gang, who, by this time, must be almost on top of us. As I received a blow on the upper arm with a cosh, and dropped my chib from nerveless fingers, I glanced over the heads of the milling throng, and noted that we were almost in line with the corner of Cumberland Street. I took that corner like Split Waterman, the only difference between him and me being, he has a motor-cycle. But don't let anybody kid you – I was going every bit as fast as he ever would.

New adversaries were running from closes in Cumberland Street to obstruct us afresh. I felt like crying. Maybe I was. Nobody would have noticed anyway. Each one was far too engrossed in his own particular orbit. I had a helluva pain in my right arm but I didn't take time to think about it. I used it just as my friends alongside were using theirs. In a desperate effort to make an opening. When we at last found a path, fear lent us wings and we sped on our way.

We cut through a side street, took another turning and found ourselves in Caledonia Road – the dead centre of the South Side – where the cemetery lies. Here and there small groups of corner-boys blew themselves as we approached, but they needn't have worried. They were non-existent as far as we were concerned. We had outpaced our hunters, but we had no intention of stopping to chat.

The Ritz Cinema was emptying as we reached it. A few women and kids screamed. Some of them don't need much excuse. While one half of the patrons stood petrified, the remainder rushed back where they came from. I heard one little future delinquent voice pipe out, 'Come on oot an' see. It's a smashin' fight. Hurry up.'We didn't even stop to look at the stills. Pity. I'd like to have lectured that kid.

Across the tram-lines of the Rutherglen Road we ran, and down Waterside Street on the banks of the Clyde. Then we saw our first police observers that night. Two of them. The foolish fellows jumped into the middle of the street to try to stop us. How law-enforcing can you get? Like fence-posts in an all-action Western film, the stampede bowled the policemen buttocks over biceps. Their helmets went in one direction, they went another and the noise their drawn batons made as they hit the tarmacadammed surface of the street was like the crack of doom in my ears. Only mugs knock Glasgow policemen about. *Somehow* the city's bigwigs get you in the end.

Judging by the sound that wafted through the air as we turned on to James Street Bridge, the policemen were now doing their level best to blow the peas from their little whistles.

Just at that spot, the view can be reasonably pretty on a fine spring morning, for at that part of the city on both sides of you the river wends its way, bordered fully on one side by the Glasgow Green. The multi-coloured facade of the Templeton building and the glistening dome of the People's Palace and Winter Gardens are pleasant landmarks to look upon, and even the ash-covered football pitches with their wooden pavilions could not be called exactly ugly. But had it been daylight, we would still have seen none of this, as we raced past, cut round by the public pool, and up Templeton Street, and into the Calton. Only when we reached Stevenson Street did I, for one, breathe freely.

Most of us were showing sig.is of having been in a barney, and, after a check, we reckoned that seven of our number, including Pat, were missing in action. Like the War Office we dispatched word to the homes of the casualties. The word had gone round that we were away on a raid, and windows on all sides were raised, while the occupants of the houses placed pillows or cushions on the sills. The Glasgow window-hanger likes a bit of comfort, while he or she views the passing parade.

In no time large crowds had gathered around us and were plying us with questions as to the success, or otherwise, of our venture. We were all very brave about it now as we mentally licked our wounds and told the audience of our courageous stand in the face of heavy odds. The young women who watched and listened admiringly, as they clung to our arms, were promising just rewards with their eyes, but somehow I just wasn't interested. The other listeners were suitably impressed as they told each other, 'That was the stuff tae gie them,' 'The right way tae "tober up" that Soo' Side crowd,' and, 'Who the hell dae they think they are?'

In other words, 'Wha daur meddle wi' the Calton?' was the text for to-day.

As I stood pressing my arm, in an effort to halt the constant throb, the group around me parted, and I beheld Isa's bonny face, the perfect features somewhat marred by a worried frown.

'Are ye hurtit?' she anxiously asked.

'Naw,' I answered, bravely. 'It's only a scratch.' The same kind of talk as the film hero uses when his arm is hanging off.

My ears were festering, listening to the voices around us, especially the ones who were saying, 'You shoulda seen the way Ben took on that joker wi' the hatchet. He soon sortit him. Nae messin' aboot. An' if it hidny o' been for him an' Pat we might no' hae reddit them the way we did. Ben? He canny hauf shift. Ye shoulda seen 'im steamin' inty that mob. We soon showed them who we were.'

Somebody seconded that motion and there was another general murmur of agreement from the yes-men. So it was unanimously carried that Ben was about the hardest case in the Calton, the land where all the good fighters grow. The group agreed that Ben could shift, and their conversation made me want to shift, so I grabbed Isa's arm, and we left the army of

43

glorious gladiators for a cleaner clime.

Ben was standing on the outskirts of the crowd, happily, but silently, agreeing with all the nice things that were being said about him. Like an old-time Roman general, he had pitched his tent a short distance from the rabble of his army, and there he stood, one of his hands gripping the metal railing that surrounded the public convenience, while his girded loins rested on the brickwork base. He surveyed us with fiery eye and I got ready to be court-martialled for some minor misdemeanour.

'Where the hell are youse gaun'?' he asked, in his best Julius Caesar manner. Being treated thus in Isa's hearing, I felt like telling him to go and take a 'monkey's', but I controlled myself. I had better argument than that.

'The grass'll be makin' a redd onytime,' I told him. 'We're better gettin' aff the street. They're liable tae pick onybuddy they fund hinging aboot.' His expression changed slightly.

'That's a' right then,' he agreed grudgingly. 'Ah'll see ye the morra. Ah'll chase the rest o' them,' and he strutted towards the others.

As Isa and I strolled up her close I heard him bark, 'Ah wiz jist thinkin'. The grass'll be givin' us a turnover the night, so we better get aff the streets.' He had everything a real general had. Even to other people's ideas. I glanced at Isa, but her expression told me nothing, and we waited to hear the rest. 'There's nae sense in mixin' it wi' the coppers till we're ready,' he said.

Till we're ready. How did he get like that? If he thought I, for one, was, at any time, going to have a buzz with the police, he was a tattie short. He was 'not on'. In fact I didn't care if I never saw a fight of any kind. Believe me, I was very indignant.

I followed Isa round the back-court, and into a secluded corner we had reservations for, where I encircled her with my arms. I got a somewhat cold reception. I could not see her face, but I sensed that the anxious look which she wore earlier had been replaced by one of reproach. Instead of letting her warm body snuggle up to me as I expected, she stiffened, and pushed me away with the palm that she placed on my chest.

'Whit's the maitter, hen?' I asked in a hurt tone.

'The maitter?' she repeated, kind of snooty-like. 'Ah'll tell ye whit's the maitter.' I waited patiently while she swallowed something that lay in her throat. 'Ah'm no' gonny run aboot wi' ony chib-man,' she told me. 'An' ye can put that in your pipe an' smoke it.' Her head was turned away from me, although there was nothing to be seen but the overflowing dustbins in the communal midden. Surely I was more pleasant-looking than that.

'Honestly, hen, Ah didny want tae be in that battle,' I protested. 'Ye know whit Ben is like, when he gets started.'

'Naw, Ah don't,' she replied tartly. 'Whit like is he?'

It didn't do to run down a fellow, even a fellow like Ben, to his own sister. I said lamely, 'Och they startit it, onyway.'

'Ah've heard a hunn'er times the nigh how it a' startit, an' how it a' finished,' she argued, sounding really angry. 'Ma ears are beelin' listenin' tae it.' My sentiments exactly.

Without telling her I agreed, I asked wonderingly: 'Whit are ye worryin' aboot, onywey? It's a' by noo.'

'Aye,' she replied, and I thought I detected a hint of tears in her voice. 'For the night. Then whit? There'll be ither nights an' ither fights, an' Ah'll never know whether ye'll come hame needin' a new suit or a new heid – if ye come hame at a'.'

'No' for me, hen,' I assured her. 'Ah'll no' be in ony mair, honest.'

'Are ye sure?' she asked plaintively, turning her

lovely eyes to look into mine, as someone switched their electric-light on, and allowed me to behold her beauty. At that moment I'd have gone from here to hell and back for her. She only had to ask.

'Positively, darlin',' I reassured her gently, the unaccustomed word sounding oh so strange coming from my lips. She believed me. She threw herself back into my arms, with both hands pulled my head down and pressed her lips on mine.

I leaned back against the wall, holding her close, and, as my glance rose from the squalid surroundings at ground level, to the clear night sky, with its myriad twinkling stars, I wondered at the strange romantic aura that engulfed me. This was a new experience for me. But the mood was disturbed by the clump of heavy boots. We broke out of the clinch as a strong beam of light was directed on us.

'It's the polis,' Isa unnecessarily informed me.

'Whit are yese up tae there?' one of them asked, his voice coated with a thick layer of sarcasm.

Without thinking, I blurted out, 'Whit the hell dae ye think?'

Two of them marched over to us. 'Smart, eh?' the same voice said, 'A right hard-case – ye think.' He paused. 'Tell me,' he coaxed. '—Whaur were ye the night – earlier on?'

'We were away for a walk,' I answered warily.

'Zat right?' he darted the question at Isa, who silently nodded confirmation, then riveted his attention on my face. 'Ye didny, by ony chance, happen tae be walkin' ower by the Soo' Side, did ye?'

Isa gripped my sore arm and I almost yelled aloud. 'Naw – we were up Parkheid,' I replied. 'How?'

'Aw—,' he said, '—we just thought ye mighta been.' He suddenly stepped closer and ran his hands over me, before I could make a move.

'Here,' I cried, 'whit d'ye think you're on? Turn it up.'

The 'busy' addressed me confidently, 'Ye know fine whit Ah wiz after. McGhee's the name, isn't it? Never forget a face. Ah know ye've got "cons" an' Ah'm sure ye'd be inty that battle the night.' He stepped back in line with his mate, and said to him, 'Musta left ese chib in ese golf-trousers.' He turned his torch on us once more, saying, 'We've got some o' your chinas in bye.' He mentioned a few names, Pat Carroll's among them, and watched my face for the results of his disclosure. I said nothing till at last the 'busy' got fed up.

'Yese better be gettin' up tae your kips,' he said, 'or we'll be runnin' yese in.'

As Isa began to tug at my arm, I retorted angrily. 'That's whit you think. Ye canny run us in. We hivny done onythin'.' He raised his hand, as if to strike me, while Isa's tugs became more urgent.

'Gaun – jist try it,' I said, by this time so completely incensed as to be oblivious to any danger. 'Pit wan haun' on me an' Ah'll see that you're drummed oot the Brownies.'

Surprisingly, he didn't call my bluff, because of Isa's presence I think. He just opened his mouth and emitted an ignorant guffaw, as I finally allowed Isa to lead me away.

The police departed from the back-court by another close and I kissed Isa good night at the foot of the stairs. We couldn't recapture our previous enchantment, so I didn't waste much time. As I emerged from the entry, I could see the headlamp-rays of the squad car as it cruised towards Claythorn Street. Turning my back on them I headed for home through the now deserted streets, on my way bypassing another police 'drag' at the corner of Tobago Street, where the Eastern Police Office is situated. In Abercrombie Street I encountered yet another without mishap. They were certainly turning over the Calton tonight.

Only then did I remember the sticking-plaster

47

which adorned my ear, and wondered how the police had not noticed it. If they had, awkward questions would have been asked, and I would probably now be reclining on a foam-rubber mattress in a cold cell, I thought, as I fingered the dressing. I hurried all the faster to my own warm bed.

The old wife was sound asleep so, for the present, I found it unnecessary to fabricate complicated alibis. I tumbled into bed and fell asleep before my head hit the pillow, but it was the most restless night I'd ever spent. A gigantically proportioned Ben meandered through my dreams, chasing me all over the Gorbals, spitting flames at me, while a lot of Lilliputian policemen clambered over him, extracting numerous razors from his pockets. Isa too appeared wearing a policeman's uniform and sporting large size brogues. She was alternately haranguing me and crying and wringing her hands in despair.

The nightmarish characters agitated me so much as to waken me, to find I was lying in a pool of sweat. I tore off my damp singlet, and lit a smoke. Shortly afterwards I again dropped off, this time so completely exhausted that my subconscious didn't even have the energy to recall its earlier inhabitants.

CHAPTER FIVE

It was around midday when I awoke slowly, memories of the previous night gradually making themselves known. My mother wasn't around. Slipped out for 'cadgies' or something, without rousing me. I had a cup of tea, left a check in the door and went round to Stevenson Street. Mrs McNulty, too, was not at home, but her bonny daughter and hard-case son were there, he looking as if he'd fallen out of bed, and she looking as if she'd stepped from a dream.

While Isa pulled on her coat I told Ben I'd see him later. He wasn't very pleased, but I didn't give a damn. I wasn't going to let him, in any manner, come between his sister and me.

We took a stroll through the Green. It was a beautiful day and as we walked among the network of paths, the winter sun smiting my back and its pleasant penetrating warmth spreading over my shoulders, for a short time I forgot the trials and tribulations of a corner-boy's life. The gangs and police, either of them forever on your top, the hate and fear, which displaces friendship and respect, and what was apt to bother me most just now – the forthcoming job, and the penalty attached to failure.

On our way back to the house, I told Isa I had an important meet with someone that night. 'Nae mair gang-fights?' she asked, her brows arching quizzically.

'Naw, nothin' like that. Ah proamised ye,' I reassured her.

'Awright,' she said. 'Ah'll go tae the jiggin' wi' the lassies fae the street an' Ah'll see ye the morra.'

About half-past eight that night, I gave Ben a shout, and he and I went down to the pub at the corner. Blaster joined us later.

Ben had got the necessary information from the Divers girl, so, after a couple of drinks, the three of us left for Brown's house in the Gorbals. We pooled the last of our cash and carried with us a half-bottle of 'dragon's blood' and three screwtops.

After Mrs Brown had sent for fish-suppers and we had had our tea, we chatted over the drink. Ben told us, confidentially, that he was 'off the side', since his leave had expired the previous day. Neither Blaster nor I elected to voice an opinion on the wisdom or otherwise of what he had done. Until he answered his call-up, late, Jenny and he had been occupying a room in Parkhead, he told us, and she had remained there while he was away. When he had finished discussing his private affairs with us, the conversation drifted into other channels, while the time fast approached for our departure.

Shortly after midnight, Blaster got his kit out of the cupboard, and brought a 'barstick' from beneath the bed. It was one of the finest jemmies I have ever seen. He'd had it made in one of the shipyards. Only about a foot long, slightly bent at one end for leverage and fashioned from the finest steel, it looked strong enough to open a bank vault.

The little sweat factory we were about to enter illegally was situated in Scotland Street. We went there cautiously, keeping to the quiet back streets, and with a watchful eye out for grass. For the benefit of readers who are unacquainted with the law, there is a Powers Act in force in Scotland under which the police have the right to arrest any known thief who happens to be found loitering with intent, a charge which isn't very difficult to prove, especially when the arresting time is after midnight. The sentence can be up to three months. Short enough – but the screws-man hates to be caught thus.

The streets were practically deserted, and only one or two railway workers going off or coming on some ungodly shift passed us as we sidled along, hugging the tenement walls. My heart jumped in my mouth and nearly choked me when I stumbled among a group of tomcats who were lining up for inspection. As I cursed and kicked them aside, I was unable to distinguish which one was the tabby. But I knew it was there.

As soon as I saw the double doors, one step up from the street, that had to be busted, I knew how easy this part would be. Blaster used the barstick to prove that to me. He dealt with the bar and two locks in five or six minutes. Then two of us were ascending a flight of stairs, while Ben jambed the door tightly behind us, for the benefit of any passing policeman.

Just as we reached the office-door at the top of the stairs, Ben joined us and prepared to make an assault, when Blaster gripped his arm and said, 'Wait a minute. This looks too easy. If, as ye say, there's nae peter in there tae keep the cash in, they're bound tae take some precautions. Did the lassie no' say onythin' aboot burglar-alarms?'

'Naw! She didny. Come oan, let's get weavin',' Ben answered a trifle impatiently, but the old stager was taking no chances.

'Haud oan your shurt for a minute,' he protested. 'We've got bags o' time,' and produced a well-greased keyhole saw from one capacious pocket. While we sat on the stair-carpet having a smoke, he stood on the banister and attached the hardboard wall where it met the ceiling, close to the door.

In a little while Blaster broke the silence.

'Ah wiz a bitty lucky tae be at the right side o' the door,' he said. 'Here – have a look at this.'

He descended from his perch. Ben took the torch from his hand, clambered up and made an inspection. Then I had a go. I saw a horizontal slit at the top of the wall, measuring about six inches by two, through which could be observed a piece of insulated flex, stretched across on the inside.

'Ye can bet London tae a lump o' crap that's alarm-wire. Wirin' for lights an' sich are usually bedded in the wa', but in a wee place like this the alarm is oaften a recent addition.' So saying, Blaster took a slightly bigger saw, which had a sort of large-toothed, cross-cut look, and handed it to me, a bland smile lighting up his prematurely wrinkled face. He was obviously delighted with the fact that he had proven to Ben that he knew what he was about. At any rate, that should have been obvious to both of us, for he'd done more jobs than we had eaten hot dinners.

Ben scowled at Blaster and asked, 'Whit dae we dae noo?'

And I added, holding up the saw, 'Aye! Whit's this for? Don't tell me we're gonny cut a hole in that big wa' wi' this?' I laughed as if I had cracked a joke. The smile suddenly slipped from my face. I knew by the next remark I was no Bob Hope.

'That's jist whit we're gonny dae,' Blaster replied with an air of finality. 'Either that or we can chuck it an' go hame,' he added, with a questioning glance at Ben, who suggested:

'But Ah thoaght ye could cut the wire or somethin'?'

Blaster was shaking his head slowly, negatively.

'Ah've heard some o' them talkin' aboot it,' Ben persisted, and, 'Sure ye see them daein' it in the pictures.' I felt like telling him he'd been seeing too many comic pictures. As usual, I kept my mouth shut for fear I'd put my foot in it.

'Naw, naw,' Blaster argued confidently, sure of his subject. 'If ye cut that wire ye'll break the current an' it might be wan o' they new-fangled wans that don't ring here, but ring in the polis office. There's a way o' daein' it – but ye've got tae know the wirin' arrangements an' that.' He dismissed that method with an airy wave of the hand. 'If ye want tae get in there,' he asserted, pointing a grubby finger at the offending wall, 'Ah'm tellin' ye the best way.'

Ben and I looked at each other in silence, while Blaster nonchalantly lit up a Woodbine. He didn't offer us one but repocketed the pack. A bit bored with the argument, I watched him abstractedly, thinking, 'Miserable aul'—.' I had none of my own, and, as is usually the case, felt like another smoke. I reckoned I would chirp in on Ben's side for spite.

I asked, 'Dae ye mean tae tell us that they'd put a burglar-alarm inside a wee daft wa' that we can cut open wi' a saw?'

'There's nae accoontin' for some o' the things these people dae – thinkin' they're fly,' he replied. 'Mind ye – it'll no be easy – an' it'll take a wee bit time – but we can manage it a' right. The wey Ah said!' He hesitated for an instant. 'Well, whiddye say?' he asked, looking at each of us in turn.

'Come oan then,' Ben muttered bad-temperedly. 'For cheeses sake let's get startit.'

Our decision was made and we began the part-demolition.

Quite a while afterwards, we were clambering through a hole just large enough to take Blaster, who was by far the stoutest. Looking around, we found ourselves in a large main office, furnished with a half-dozen desks, and the accompanying paraphernalia. Apart from the main door, there were two others inscribed respectively: MANAGER and CASHIER. According to our information, our objective was the former, although one might normally associate the other word with cash. This may have been a weak attempt at subterfuge which would be doomed to failure, since the place would be thoroughly searched in any case.

Inside the manager's office we found a large cashbox, secreted in a hidden compartment under the huge old-fashioned mahogany desk. It took a bit of finding and we had begun to doubt our informant, when we finally made the discovery. The Divers girl, who was not a secretary or anything of that sort, must have been 'well-quoted' with the Jew-boy, to learn of such a hiding-place. I used to wonder where she got all the money for clothes. I wonder no longer. This was where they were earned.

Watched impatiently by Ben and myself, Blaster spent five minutes with the jemmy before he had the strong-box open. It appeared, at first glance, to contain a great number of notes, not neatly bundled, as one might expect them to be.

Anyway, my guess was that we were a bit short of

the two hundred that Ben had prophesied. Still, it was cash. And cash, in large or small bulk, is always a delight to behold, especially when it is conspicuously absent from your pocket at the time.

Now I found that I was the most trustworthy member of the company, for Blaster put up a squeal when Ben attempted to pocket the money, saying he, Blaster, would rather see me holding the kitty. Ben didn't look pleased but agreed to this, adding that he wouldn't trust the aul' yin as far as he could throw him. I stuffed the notes in my pockets, and we gave the cashier's and outer offices a quick turnover, picking up a few quid more before we left.

Ben, for some unknown reason, wanted to set fire to the place. It may have been just that he was an ardent anti-Semitic, or, what was more likely, an ardent lunatic. Anyway, I managed to restrain him and we trundled downstairs and through the broken door.

As we strolled along Scotland Street, I felt my mouth twitch and my hands tremble. My usual attack for after-job nerves. I thought, 'Hell! It's high time I chucked this game. Must be gettin' old or somethin'.' I mentioned my need of a drink to my companions and advocated going along to Maggie Murphy's 'cane', an all-night shebeen in the Rutherglen Road. They were in agreement, and I immediately felt better, as I mentally slaked my thirst.

I needn't point out that we made the return journey at a much faster pace, with a seeming disregard for any stout minions of the law who might be lurking in the shadowy shop-doors or closemouths. Even a night-shift beat-walloper is entitled to his cup of tea. We were lucky. It must have been the 'grass' NAAFI-break just then.

Maggie opened the door to us herself, clad in a voluminous nightgown that looked as if it was made from a whole parachute. It had a frilly plunging-neckline that was doing a belly-flop, and, large and fat as she was, allowing half of her body to ooze out. Without knowing anything about fashion, I knew Dior hadn't modelled that creation. In the first place, he would have to visit a circus to find a model. In the second place, his warehouse would hae run short of material, and, in the third place, he would have been jailed immediately for selling it, under some Indecency Act. It was the most negligent negligée ever built.

Maggie herself was a striking figure. If you were the type to hit women. Her hair was luxuriant in a sort of gypsy way. You know. Straw hanging from a midden. The only features of her face that could be discerned under the folds of flesh were the beads that were her eyes, darting about in tiny slits, and, when she opened her mouth, a row of broken teeth that lacked but one colour – white – for a snooker-set.

Her hands were like pigs' feet, covered in cheap bracelets and rings of coloured glass in elaborate tin settings.

She always appeared to be smiling, till one took a closer look, if the stomach would stand it. Then you found it was a permanent sneer she wore on her face. She sneered at the world in general, and probably herself in particular. Nobody knew her better than she did.

She was certainly a 'leery' customer. Knew more ways of making money than the fellow who wrote that book. She had tried them all. Starting as a shoplifter and 'brass-nail' on the beat, and, when her charms became so jaded that even the 'modellers' wouldn't entertain her, passing through the contraceptive-peddling, and other stages, and winding-up selling doctored booze, illegally, at any hour of the day or night, with an occasional few bob for allowing some of her clients to use one of her two rooms for demitasse purposes. She had run the whole gamut.

She lived alone, her best friend being a pickle of coin

with which to purchase her worst enemy, alcohol, in any form.

I knew she was glad to see us, although it was hard to tell from the semi-vacant expression, result of too many drinks, too often, that dwelt on her haphazard features. Maggie's mercenary machinations were far too powerful to be sidetracked by a small matter like lost, or disturbed, sleep.

She ushered us into a room, and was back in a jiffy with a half-bottle of whisky and *four* glasses, which was a broad enough hint. When I tendered the fifty bob, she went over to the far wall, lit the electric-fire and moved it into a better position with a shabby-slippered foot, singeing a ragged pom-pom in the process.

I filled the glasses and handed her one, which she grabbed with a massive paw, making the glass look like a thimble. Ben and Blaster were too busy disposing of their whisky quota to pay any attention to her just then. They were leaving me to deal with her.

She said, 'Och, ye shouldny o' bothered,' threw the whisky against her tonsils, gulped it down and passed the empty glass back to me. I laid it on the table, turning my back on her as I did so. I wasn't heeding any more of her hints.

Glancing from the corner of my eye while I took a drink myself, I observed the manner in which she was hanging around. I knew she was under the impression that the bottle would be split with her as usual. Ben was on tenterhooks to get her out of the room and get down to brass-tacks, for, although Maggie had a good reputation for keeping her mouth shut, there was no sense in taking unnecessary risks. You never knew what would happen when a seldom-sober heard too much, and that was Maggie over the back.

Ben blurted out, 'For cheeses sake get tae hell oota

here, ya bloody aul' sneeveler. We want tae talk bizness.'

Her face fell. About three storeys. And she stood silent, searching her hooch-hazed mind for a suitable retort.

'Aw right, aw right – keep the bloody heid,' she mumbled. 'Ye can stick your drink in your jacksy for a' Ah care.'

Ben was incensed. His hand went to his pocket, and I grabbed his arm, saying, 'For God's sake, Ben.'

He shoved my hand away, but withdrew his own without the weapon. Maggie shrugged her gigantic shoulders and left the room, but not before she had clocked the electric-fire back off. Apparently, we no longer rated all the comforts of home. While the beads of perspiration dried on my pores, I placed a chair against the handle of the door, and returned to the table where the other two were resting their elbows in expectancy. We started counting the take.

Our haul, including the petty cash we had found, amounted to one hundred and sixty pounds, five shillings, plus the fifty bob I'd given Maggie. It wasn't two hundred, but it was near enough to be close. While I was coming, I mentally spent half my whack. Maybe it was just as well I did.

Something happened now that I never thought my one-time best friend capable of. It completely took the feet from me, and from this time my attitude towards Ben gradually altered. The rot was setting in, and I wondered, at the time, if the Blairgowrie girl was helping to effect the change. Although he had always been a bit of a rat, a decent girl might have made an attempt to hide his long tail. Ben had reversed this process. His tail was growing more visible day by day, so, to my way of thinking, Jenny didn't come under the said category.

Spread out on the table were seven piles, each

57

consisting of twenty single-pound notes, and a little heap of ten-shilling notes, silver and coppers. Ben reached out with two large hands, grabbed four of the neat piles, pocketed them, and said, 'You can take the ither eighty, Bill, an' you Blaster, can take your whack oota here.' With a forefinger he touched the tip of his nose.

It was a lousebag's trick. He knew the old fellow could never stand up to him.

The ominous silence made me feel extremely uncomfortable, but I much preferred that to the sound of Ben's voice as he again spoke.

'Ye heard me,' he said to us both, although neither of us had spoken, then turned his eyes to the bottle that stood on the middle of the table.

Blaster sat watching him pour another drink and swallow it with an exaggerated smack of the lips, then a long drawn-out 'A-a-a-ah'. The old fellow turned to me with a trace of tears in his eyes, whether of rage or self-pity, I was unable to judge. He made no attempt to lift any of the eighty pounds that were still on the table. I think he saw the pity in my eyes, for he put up a sudden show of courage.

'Ya lousy bastart,' he shouted at Ben, who jumped up, reaching for his pocket.

'Ah'll cut the—,' he shouted in rage, while Blaster, who was also on his feet, tried to bawl him down.

'Gaun—,' he shouted, '– go ahead – chib me. If ye think that'll dae ye ony good. Dae ye think Ah've nae handers? Ah can get ye sortit, nae bother. It's only an aul' man like me ye could fight, ya balloon.'

Ben raised the hand bearing the weapon. 'Ya bloody aul'—.'

I halted both his razor and his words, as gently as I could. I'm afraid I was very much of a coward at that moment. Often though I've tried, I can never properly analyse my attitude towards Ben in moments such as these. As you might have gathered, I was always a bit windy when a battle of any kind threatened. Yet, when it comes to a showdown, I can usually produce a bit of courage, of sorts, from my make-up. But in any situation where Ben was involved, it was different. The gumption just wasn't there. He seemed to kind of hypnotise me, just as a poised snake does with the smaller of animals. Anyway, the malevolent depths of Ben's dark eyes always had the power to start my knees on an uncontrollable shaking. Maybe it's just that this will was stronger than mine, but that's the way it was.

'Ben,' I hesitated, '—you don't want tae chib 'im. How wad you feel if ye got knocked for your whack?'

He let his arm relax and his hand dropped slowly to his side, saying, with a derisive snigger, 'There's no' much danger o' that.'

I relaxed the grip I had on his arm and breathed a sigh of relief. For a moment I had thought he was about to turn on me. The minute I let his hand go, he belted the old fellow across the 'coupon' with the razor. Blaster fell back on his chair, clapping hands to his bloody face. 'Oh Gawd,' he moaned.

Tears of mortification were blinding me. I should have been able to prevent this. Why hadn't I? The words of reprimand were bubbling in my mouth, and I was afraid they would spew out. So afraid.

'Come on, Bill,' Ben said, cold-bloodedly wiping the razor on Blaster's waistcoat. 'Are ye comin' up the road?'

He was positively glowing. 'The head's definitely away,' I thought, but answered 'Okay!' Anything to keep him from doing more damage.

He opened the door and left, but, before I followed, I slipped half of my whack into Blaster's pocket, while he remained seated there, silent, unmoving. I still had forty quid which was, after all, twice as much as I had expected to collect from the tobacconist's.

CHAPTER SIX

Not wishing to awaken my mother in the middle of the night, I had intended to finish the hours of darkness in Blaster's house, but the 'ball was up on the dyke', as far as that was concerned. It seemed there was nothing else for it but to knock the old wife up, when Ben suggested I bed down with him at his mother's house, where he was staying, presumably for the sake of appearances, until the day of his wedding. The way I felt about tonight's happenings made bed-mating with Ben an unpleasant prospect, but I grudgingly agreed.

Taking the shortest route between two points, at an hour when no transport could be had, we crossed the Clyde by the McNeil Street suspension bridge and cut through the Green to the Calton and Stevenson Street.

Up the stairs we went, I treading as quietly as possible, in an effort to make our objective without disturbing his family. I was hoping to get out of the house in the early morning, without Isa being aware that I had been there. My stealthy efforts, I might add, were futile, since Ben was clumping upwards like a tattie-howker at a clog-wallop.

The house was on the second storey of a tenement, and, as Ben stood fumbling for his key, we heard the sound of flushing in the communal lavatory at the top of the next flight of stairs.

Ben glanced upwards as the door was flung open, and a scowl appeared on his handsome face. I followed his gaze and saw the object of his displeasure was the Divers girl. I couldn't imagine what he had against her, since thanks to her we were, between us, some one hundred and twenty pounds better of.

I said, 'Hullo, Susie,' and the bitch ignored me. She shuffled her feet halfway down the flight of stairs, holding a shabby blue coat around her well-formed body. Her pretty blue eyes, only partly losing their gleam because of sleepiness, were resting intently on my friend's scowling countenance. She knew that, for some reason or other, Ben was displeased with her, but seemed understandably puzzled as to the reason.

'How did yese get oan?' she asked in a quiet tone that was almost a whisper, with just the faintest trace of anxiety evident. Without giving either of us time to reply, she hurried on. 'Ah wiz hopin' Ah'd get ma "bung". Ah need money tae pey ma aul' man's fine oan Monday mornin'. He wiz drunk last night and got luftit for anither "breach",' she said with a resigned air. Her father could have papered the house with fine-receipts and it was breach-of-the-peace every time.

A thoughtful look appeared on the girl's face. 'Maybe Ah could git 'im oot oan bail the morra?' she mused. She was now standing between us, and I sincerely wished she would turn up her coat-collar and close it, for the view I was getting of lush white flesh, with a suggestion of the mounds which were just out of sight, was very disconcerting to say the least.

Suddenly the scowl left Ben's face, to be replaced by a calculating smile, which may have looked engaging to the girl, but not to me. I wondered what he was at. Ben wasn't in the habit of bestowing smiles on anyone.

'Is that you in the house yoursel'?' he asked ingratiatingly, and I wondered no more at his plans.

She nodded her head and replied in one word, 'Aye!' Ben knew better than I did that her mother had run off with the head-waiter from the corner-bar, less than a year before. A good move. Any stocktaking he might do would prove infinitely more profitable than

61

her husband's methods had achieved. Her new bloke was better at filling his pockets than her husband had been with his gut, and that's saying something. In any case Ben's question had been unnecessary, and it surprised me that the girl had deigned to answer at all.

Ben stood looking at Susan for a moment. He grasped her hand just as an infatuated young lover would. Who was he trying to kid? Or is that another silly question?

'We'll come up tae the hoose the noo and tell ye aboot it, an' Ah can gie ye your "bung",' he said, putting his foot on the first step.

'Oh naw! Ah couldny let yese in,' she said, but not very convincingly. I wasn't a bit surprised when Ben continued on his way upstairs, taking her arm, and, as I took up the rear, I decided maybe it was just as well for Susie that she hadn't made a fuss. Surveying Susan's nether regions as she retreated, dressed in her bulky coat, there was the slightest resemblance to Sophie Loren, and it was interesting to imagine her swaying her kipper-hips draped in a Paris creation. She was on the small side, but what she had was stacked up in the right places.

Susie hung the lavatory-key on a nail behind the door, and hurried over to the fire which was burning cheerily on the far side of the single-end. The time was now around quarter-to-four and the grate was full of coal, so she must have been doing a bit of stoking in the early hours. Thoughtfully I pondered the probable time when she had returned from wherever she had been. I was getting more and more ideas about Susan, and none of them were very nice things to think about any girl.

I commandeered a straight-backed wooden chair with a split seat, and a piece of egg-box nailed across beneath, while Ben stood in the middle of the floor, behind the girl, feet apart, rubbing the knuckles of one hand in the palm of the other. I think he'd seen James Cagney or Humphrey Bogart do that in a film. He opened his mouth, sidewise. Just as the convicts do in these Yankee prison films.

'How the hell did ye no' tell us there wiz a burlgar-alarm?' he asked. The threatening scowl had returned to his face and a fleck of saliva had appeared on his pendulous lower lip.

Susie turned round quickly, startled, her face registering consternation.

'Ah didny know there wiz wan,' she answered. 'Whit happened? Did yese get a chase?' She was trembling visibly, knowing full well how badly she had slipped up with the information she had supplied.

'Naw, we didny get a chase,' he answered, mocking for a moment her high strident tone. 'An' it's nae thanks tae you, ya stupit bitch.'

As he finished mouthing the insult, he drew the back of his hand across her face. Another Cagney trick. I told you he had been seeing too many pictures. Susie cried out more in surprise than pain, since the blow had been principally a gesture, and fell back on a shakedown-bed that was spread on the floor. As she dropped, her coat fell open, disclosing the fact that she was in the habit of sleeping in nothing but a pair of the briefest of panties imaginable, and the naked top half of her body, with its firm pointed breasts, was exposed to the lustful eyes of Ben and myself.

She lay there like something from an illustrated Yankee calendar, while I was able to enlarge on the thoughts I already had had as we came upstairs. The girl was really out of this world. And any other. She started to speak, and I found it very difficult to hear her, for a couple of drums were thudding in my ears.

'Ah'm sorry, Ben,' she was saying. 'Ah didny – honestly!'

She had made no move to cover her nakedness, and

I could see by this time that Ben was positively drooling. I won't comment further on my own reactions.

'That's a' right then,' Ben said. 'But maybe that'll be a lesson tae ye. We mighta got "done" ower the heid o' ye. Don't let it happen again.' He fumbled in the cash-pocket at the waistband of his trousers. 'There's a "County Down" the noo, an' Ah'll gie ye some mair mibbe the morra,' he said, grudgingly handing her a note. 'But you're no' tae bail your aul' man oot, mind ye! The lie-in'll dae the aul' bastart good,' he continued, with his hands pulling back his jacket, inserting his thumbs between shirt and trousers and pulling up the latter, although there was no evidence that they were falling down. Watching Ben was like viewing a rehearsal of mannerisms being enacted.

He stressed his point with a rigid forefinger as he said, 'If ye got 'im oot oan a Sunday, he'd be runnin' aboot daft, lookin' for a drink. He canny afford Maggie Murphy's prices.'

Susan accepted the pound he was offering her, regarded it as she would a tuppenny stamp, then asked in a quiet coaxing voice, 'How much did yese get?'

Ben lifted his right hand above his head in a threatening gesture. 'If ye ask me ony mair cheeky questions, Ah'll gie ye anither slap oan the mooth!' he shouted.

She cowered back, saying, 'Awright, Ben. Ah'm sorry. Ah'll no' ask ye for ony mair.' It struck me, though, that she might have other methods of increasing her whack.

As we both stood there, looking at her in silence for a moment a coquettish smile began to replace the frightened look and I congratulated myself on my correct estimate of the score. It was quite easy really, for a fellow with my intellect. A girl that could get money from a Jew-boy must be fly to the game.

Ben started to remove his jacket.

'There's no' much use in wakin' the aul' wife when there's an empty kip lyin' here,' he said, nodding towards the set-in bed. He was showing consideration for his mother all of a sudden.

They tell me his old wife had a difficult time of it when he was born, and I knew Ben had kept things much the same ever since. Now it seemed the much-revered woman was not to have her sleep disturbed, although it was common knowledge that she had suffered from chronic insomnia for many years.

Susie, like myself, knew all this, but she said nothing, so I also began to undress. As she clambered under the old coats and pieces of blanket on the floor, she said, 'Mind an' put the light oot.'

It was only natural that, when Ben switched the room to semi-darkness, he didn't get in beside me in the set-in, but joined the girl on the floor. And, let me tell you, I wished to hell it was me. Ben, as far as I was concerned, never had much at any time that he could be envied for, but just then I wished myself into his shoes, which wouldn't have been much good, because he'd removed them before ducking in beside the girl.

I heard her say quietly, 'Naw, Ben!' when he drew aside the bedclothes. And his answer.

'Whit the hell are ye givin' us?' he muttered as he forcibly made room.

The illuminating flames leapt from the coals that burnt fiercely in the grate, and I had a final glimpse of the girl's shapely body, so meagrely covered by the flimsy piece of pink material. And those 'trams'. That was one pair of legs that needed no stiletto-heeled shoes, like the pin-ups wear, to set them off. They were just right the way they were.

'Ben,' Susie said, when Ben had settled down beside her, 'could ye no' gie me anither ten bob?' I never heard coaxing tones so expertly put over. 'Ah seen a smashin' wee coat doon the barras last Sunday. The man was sellin' it for thirty bob. He might still have it.'

As she continued in that strain, I knew Ben was fighting a losing battle for the protection of his pocket.

After a bit of humming and hawing, the still flickering fire showed me Ben's hand, as it reached out for his trousers, and a moment later my ears caught the rustle of paper. Susie definitely knew her stuff.

The talking ceased abruptly, and I turned my face towards the wall.

The sound of regular heavy breathing is sleep-inducing, and I must have dozed off, for I woke with a start, to feel someone lift the ragged bedclothes from me. I turned my head and opened my eyes. I could still see absolutely nothing. The fire had gone out and the utter darkness seemed like solid matter that one could touch, filling the house from wall to wall and ceiling to floor. But I knew instinctively that it was Susie's voice that shushed me to silence, before she crept in beside me, by which time I was in no mood for arguing. She threw her arms around my neck, and I felt the heat of her naked body scar my skin like a branding-iron.

'D'ye like me, Bill?' she whispered in my ear, as she fiddled with my hair on the nape of my neck.

My hands ran over her curves and the blood pounded in my temples. I had to swallow, before I could answer. 'Sure Ah like ye, hen,' I gasped. 'Ah think you're a smashin' burd.'

'Wad ye take me away fae here?' she whispered, and suddenly she was all agitated. 'It's terrible when ma Da's here,' she hurried on, in her excitement running her words together and allowing her voice to rise in a mounting pitch, until I was forced to clap my hands over her mouth and admonish her.

'For cheeses sake, Susie. No' sae loud,' I told her.

When I considered her sufficiently subdued I removed my hand and she continued in a quieter tone.

'He drinks a' wur money,' she said, 'an' comes hame

every night miroculous an' he'll no go tae ese ain bed but always wants tae sleep wi' me, an' when ese in the bed he'll no' lay me alane.'

I've got certain views on this subject. Some people should be locked up and the key thrown away. Under that category, I would place Susie's old man. But I found it impossible to concentrate on such things at the moment.

As she rambled on, I tried to control my sexual feelings that I might understand fully what she was suggesting, but it was so difficult to produce a coherent thought.

At last she repeated her original question. 'Could ye no' take me away fae here?' she persisted.

I recovered sufficiently to answer angrily. 'Could Ah, hell!' At which point her shoulders began to shake with what I imagined to be sobs.

'It's a' right, hen,' I continued a little embarrassedly. 'Some nice fella'll come soon an' take ye oot it.' I patted her shoulders in an effort to calm her, and it wasn't my fault that my hands, inadvertently, kept moving further down her arm with each pat. I pressed her closer to me and added, 'Don't worry about it, Susie.'

She moved away from me slightly. I tried to restrain her, but she placed her hands on my chest and pushed. I couldn't make her out.

Suddenly, I got an idea. My money was under the make-shift. I groped around till I finally got hold of it, withdrew a note and handed it to her, saying, 'Here! Get yoursel' a hat wi' that coat the morra.'

Then the penny dropped. It wasn't sobs that were shaking her body. It was silent laughter. But I lost all sense of thought as she snuggled up close to me again . . .

I woke with a start, probably because of the strange bed, and as my mind recollected the situation when I'd fallen asleep, I glanced through half-closed lids at the empty space beside me. Through the uncovered window came the first traces of the sun's light to show me clearly all that remained – the indentation on the pillow where her head had lain, and my nostrils caught the faintest trace of the aroma that most cosmetics leave, lingering in the air.

Another look disclosed the fact that two recumbent forms again reposed beneath the coats. Susie had returned to the bed on the floor. Idly, I wondered if she had managed to extract any more money from my friend. It wouldn't have surprised me in the least. As I've already said, Susan knew her onions, and various other vegetables.

The old fashioned bell-alarm told me it was half-past nine. I removed it from the mantelpiece and had a closer look. These winter mornings it was hard to tell the time by the amount of daylight that could be seen. Because of that and the fact that the Glasgow streets are more or less deserted on a Sunday morning, I had imagined the time was nearer seven than ten.

A further glance at the makeshift bed with the completely covered, unrecognizable heap that was Ben, and the white shoulder and softly rounded arm of the girl, served to remind me that it could cost me more money if I stayed, so I hurriedly dressed and left the house without waking either of them.

Just as I was closing the door, Susan tossed restlessly in her sleep, the blankets were thrown aside, then returned to their original position, and I all but re-entered the house. But I took a hold of myself – and threw myself downstairs – sharpish. Susan needed her sleep. She'd had a busy night.

CHAPTER SEVEN

I stepped out on the street and a fresh breeze hit me like a Joe Louis wallop. I literally staggered on my feet.

I braced my legs and breathed deeply. Sunday, in Glasgow, is the only day when the air smells a little clean, and you can take a chance on breathing deep.

I contemplated the deserted streets and didn't feel like going home to bed. I felt like a drink. Short of kicking in the nearest boozer-door, there was only one other way of getting it – Maggie's! I ambled down to the London Road, pondering on whether I wanted a drink badly enough to trot over to the South Side. I decided I did. I took the usual short-cut through the Green, swallowing as much as I could of that factory-free atmosphere, and, by the time I got to Ballater Street, I felt fit enough to mix it with Louis and a couple of his seconds.

Maggie welcomed me with the usual heartiness, accepted the notes I handed her, and produced a bottle of her rot-gut and two glasses. We had a pair of liberal measures apiece before we started to converse.

'Whit happened last night?' she asked, glancing shrewdly at me from the corner of her slit-eyes.

'How dae ye mean?' I parried.

'We-e-el-ll—, Ah heard a wee bit o' a schemozzle while yese were in the room. But ye know me. Ah always mind ma ain bizness,' she said as if she thought it were true.

'There wizny ony schemozzle that Ah know o',' I told her with the same air. Two could play that game.

'Aw, don't give us that,' she persisted. 'You an' Ben left first: then, a wee while after that, the ither fella went tae.' She turned and looked squarely at me. 'How did yese no' leave thegither?' she asked.

I felt like opening my heart to her on the matter, but you never could tell. Ben might get to her about it. After a moment's hesitation, 'Blaster want it tae finish the boattle,' I invented, 'an' we were in a hurry.'

'Well – he didny finish the boattle,' and with an air of having caught me out, she added, 'An' since when have youse fellas startit tae leave the hauf o' a boattle, efter peyin'?' That was a slight exaggeration, but nevertheless it was an approximately true observation. Maggie's prices were too high to make a habit of leaving so much as the dregs in the bottle. I gave up the idea of trying to deceive her, deciding instead to come the silent man.

'Look, Maggie,' I told her, 'if ye were meant tae know everythin' that happened, ye'd be telt. So whit aboot jist drappin' it?' I knew how Ben would have handled the situation, and that certainly wasn't the approach he would have used. But I wasn't Ben, thank the Lord.

Anyway, I achieved the necessary results, for she said, 'Okay, son, okay. It's jist that Ah don't want the place tae get a bad name, that's aw. An' ye should always wipe up the blood.' Although taken aback by her last observation, that wasn't my main emotion. I turned away my head, pretending to look at the clock on the wall. I didn't want to laugh in her face. She patted my hand, adding, 'Ye'll have tae excuse a wumman's natural curiosity.' Funny – I never thought of Maggie as a woman. Most of the city's queers looked more like one than she did. But I didn't tell her that. It doesn't do.

We had another belt at the so-called whisky and Maggie jumped to her feet, saying, 'Hing oan a minute, son. Ah've a wee treat for ye.' She imparted the news in such a manner that I thought she was about to produce Lana Turner from the next room. When she reappeared it was only a minor disappointment.

In her large arms she held three McEwan's screw-tops. Just the job. The way she stood in the doorway cradling them, made me think of a large jovial midwife, producing triplets for a father's inspection, but no woman ever gave birth to such a lovely trio.

'Ye've saved my life, Maggie,' I sighed.

She came across the room and leaned over me till I

70

thought her enormous chest was going to smother me, and I was ready for puking.

'Dae Ah get a wee kiss for that?' she asked, wearing an expression that was meant to portray coyness.

Words jumped into my mouth: 'Away an' kiss ma cookie!'

Maggie sat down, with a laugh that sounded like Paul Robeson tuning up, and the nauseating moment was over.

By the time we had seen off most of the contents of the McEwan bottles, and had opened another bottle of swill, I had drifted partways into another world, on the magic carpet of drunkenness. Maggie, too, was half-seas-over, and she had a capacity like a kitchen-sink. The reason for her condition at present was obvious. She had been at it, most likely, since the first crack of dawn and, probably, half of the hours of darkness. I imagine she kept a constant supply by her bedside, for she never, at any time, looked completely sober.

'Bill,' she said, while replenishing our glasses for the umpteenth time, 'whit about givin' us a song?'

'A song?' I ejaculated. 'Are ye kiddin'? Ah canny sing nane. Gie's wan yoursel'.' I didn't really want her to sing, although I'd have bet that she was a first class basso profundo, but I couldn't think of anything else to say.

'C'mon – give us a love-song, an' get me in a good mood,' she laughed, edging nearer to me. If I had known a number entitled 'Serenade to a Sot', I might have rendered it, but as far as I know it hasn't been written.

My drink-fuddled brain was trying to devise a diplomatic let-out for me when the bell saved me. The door-bell. Maggie cursed loudly, rose clumsily and lurched drunkenly across the room and into the lobby.

I heard voices at the door, then Maggie returned with a fellow about thirty-five years old, hair slicked

71

down, a nose like a parrot and lips like a duck. He planted those lips right on top of Maggie's. He must have been short for a drink – or something.

My stomach retched some and I decided I needed some more of that clean Sunday air, so I lifted the part-full bottle from the table, and left. Maggie wouldn't be needing it, and if her boyfriend wanted a drink later, she could provide it.

Down on the streets, I wandered aimlessly while the fresh breeze chased the alcohol fumes up to the top of my head. I turned corners, stepped off pavements and on to others, seemingly without rhyme or reason, till suddenly I found myself at Blaster's close. I peered up at the little black enamel plate with the white numbers and wondered what the hell I was doing here. The effort was too much for me, and, without thinking more about it, I negotiated the stairs by holding the walls on either side of me with both hands.

I knocked on the door with one hand while clinging to the lintel with the other. Two women opened the door. Dead spit of one another, too, they were. Like twins, I shook my head and had another look. They were still there. I wasn't imagining them. They both spoke and I could only hear one of them. Must be something wrong with one of my ears, I thought, while the voice, as if speaking from a distance said, 'Whit are you daein' here? Get doon that stair quick, afore Ah gets the polis.'

The two faces in front of me were drifting away so I leaned over to get a closer look. A ton of bricks hit me on the chin, and I opened my eyes and examined the flowers and squares and leaves and diamonds that someone had pushed against my face. Someone else got hold of both my arms and lifted me off the linoleum, while a voice said, 'It wizny him that done it. He's a' right. Bring 'im in.'

I didn't understand a word at the time, but I allowed

the guiding hands to lead me into a room and hang me over a sink. Somebody's finger – I think it was my own – poked down my throat, and the voice said, 'That's right, son. Bring it up. Ye'll feel better efter that.'

Without much help from me, my stomach complied, and my head slowly descended from the ceiling, where it had been floating like a kid's balloon, on to my shoulders. Finally, the heaving in my stomach ceased, only to be replaced by a banging in my head, till I wished it was back up on the ceiling again.

Now the voice, which I recognized as Blaster's, said, 'Come ower here an' have a seat, son.'

My legs felt like two pieces of soft toffee as they carried me over to a chair and dropped me in it.

I sank my throbbing head in my hands and listened to Blaster tell his wife, 'Put oot some o' that stew an' totties, Bella.'

Without raising my head, I saw a plate banged down on the table by my side, and I glanced up as Bella grudgingly spooned some of the steaming food from the pot. It smelled good, and served to remind me that I had eaten nothing since the previous night, when it had been fish and chips, at the same table. I tried a spoonful and it tasted even better than it smelled.

Blaster said, 'That's the stuff tae settle your stomach. Some people say tea or coaffee. Ithers believe in a carter's curer – a beer wi' a glass o' whisky in it. Masel' – Ah like tae get a tight'ner in me when Ah'm feelin' bad.'

I continued to eat hungrily, while Mrs Brown stood glowering at me, and her husband urged, 'Take a bit o' breed wi' it.' I did as he said.

When I wiped the last drop of gravy with the last piece of bread, and swallowed it, I felt a hundred per cent. I relaxed back on the chair, produced cigarettes and offered them. Blaster extracted one and put it to his lips, but the woman made no move. Yet I knew she smoked. 'What the hell's up with her?' I thought, as I returned the pack to my pocket and struck a match.

I let the thought become oral and asked Blaster, 'Whit's up wi' the wife. She's lookin' at me as if Ah'd stole her scone.' Blaster grinned lop-sidedly as the adhesive and wadding held taut the one side of his face.

'It's because o' ma coupon,' he answered.

'But ye know that had nothin' tae dae wi' me,' I pointed out.

'Ah know that,' he replied, nodding his head forgetfully and grimacing with the resultant pain, 'an' Ah've telt her that. But ye know whit weemin are.'

Mrs Brown was tossing venom-tipped darts at me with her eyes. 'Ye were alang wi' that liberty-taker last night,' she accused, through stiff lips. 'Birds o' a feather!'

'But Ah didny want tae see Blaster gettin' chibbed,' I persisted indignantly.

'Then how did ye no' stoap it?'

She had me there. How do you tell someone, particularly a person whose attitude is antagonistic, that you are mortally afraid of a certain party. It's hard enough to admit a thing like that to oneself. Blaster, with his insight into human nature, knew. He came to my rescue.

'Ah told ye,' he said exasperatedly. 'He tried tae, but the ither fella wiz too fly.' Then he added what to me seemed a good argument: 'Sure the lad gied me forty quid.'

But the woman wasn't in a receptive mood. 'The forty pounds'll no' make up for the scar ye'll have when that plaster comes aff,' she finished, and proceeded about her household duties. Blaster and I had a couple of drinks from my bottle, and when his wife started to clean out the fireplace, I glanced at the clock which showed half-past five, got to my feet and bade both of them a toper's farewell. The usual kind, interspersed with burps. I excused myself by admitting it might be the stew.

Incongruously, I hadn't walked five hundred yards along the streets, when I felt like another drink, so I nipped up a close and saw off the remainder of the bottle. Talk about the lost week-end! If Ray Milland had seen me just then, he would have been put to shame. I don't know what Maggie's main booze ingredient was, but it certainly made one crave for more.

I went into a café for cigarettes, and two young fellows who were standing conversing with a lovely Latin-looking lassie from behind the counter, started to take the rise out of me, which was their way of wooing women. I stood there, in two minds whether to steam into them, while the dark limpid eyes of the girl rested on me anxiously. One of the blokes swaggered over to a seat where three others were eating hot pies. He leaned over and said something to them. They raised their heads and looked in my direction. I decided I'd better blow.

Further along the street I passed another crowd of youths who were kicking a ball around. People don't have much reaction on a Glasgow Sunday. A police-man came round a corner and the young fellows scattered, abandoning the ball, which the copper picked up and slit with a pocket-knife.

Gorbals was reckoned to be just about the most densely populated district in the city, and the evidence of that was there before my eyes. There were kids everywhere. Running from a closemouth, in front of you, so that if you weren't careful you stumbled over them. Chasing about the streets on bikes, on home-made carts, on foot after balls. Some of them whipping 'peeries' all over the place, and others just having a friendly fight, while their parents shouted encourage-ment or dire threats at them from upstairs windows, the actual words depending upon the temperaments of said parents. The women who weren't resting

75

elbows on a cushioned window-sill were standing around the closes, some of them going through the bouncing motions that a woman uses when she has a baby wrapped up in her shawl. Other weans were being pushed backwards and forwards in decrepit-looking prams, showing no signs of enjoying it, judging by the sounds they made, while their mothers did a sort of soft-shoe shuffle behind them, all the time engaging in ceaseless jaw-exercise with their neighbours, which kept in rhythm with their feet. A dry Sunday in the Gorbals. Nothing quite like it. Other people can be thankful.

Inevitably, I found myself back at Maggie's cane. The Ru'glen Road had more to offer me than my own district. The way I was feeling, the Calton held nothing for me whatever. There was a burning sensation deep in the pit of my stomach that could only be eased with more of the firewater, and the heat Isa could generate within me wasn't a suitable antidote. Besides, I had one helluva urge to get drunk. The main cause of this being, of course, that I had quite a bit of money in my pocket. There were other reasons too.

Up the stairs again I went, following the groove I was beginning to wear away in each step. I was battering away at the door for a full minute before I got an answer. Then I found out why I had been unheard. The character who opened the door to me wandered away into the darkness of the lobby, before I got a proper look at him. I closed the door and followed. The only room I had ever been in in the house was filled to overflowing. The kitchen door stood open and I walked in there.

Maggie was sitting on the bed with her arm around Duck-Lips. They were singing an Ink-Spot number and I wanted to laugh, for the bloke was using a high falsetto tone, while Maggie boom-boomed the bass harmony. I wouldn't want to insult the late Eddy-McDonald team. Maggie and the muscle-bound canary

76

were nearly as good as Abbott and Costello.

She drew a half bottle of stuff from beneath the bedclothes, and split two 'booms' with the words, 'Fifty bob.' I took the bottle from her and watched her insert the money where film-actresses sometimes do. I wondered how far it would fall before it stopped.

I poured myself out a large drink and, with bottle and glass, strolled over to the fireplace, an unnecessary journey, since there was no fire burning in the grate. The 'Sunday Mail' lay on a chair. I lifted it and took its place, then settled down with the whisky and the newspaper, to see how long I could ignore the noise that emanated from the next room, and the actions that might take place in this.

Don't ask me to explain my actions. Can any of us explain any move we made in our cups? For a while I even hoped Ben might appear on the scene, though why I should want to be with him, I can't, for the life of me, explain. Anyway he didn't materialize, which maybe was just as well. Possibly there was just something in the past that I wanted to forget, or maybe it was premonition of the future that was worrying me, and alcohol was a temporary curtain. Anyway, I sat there and got as drunk as a monkey, worked my way through most of the paper, and dozed off as the noises around me became fainter and fainter, and the couple on the bed lapsed into a drunken stupor.

To-morrow would bring home none of the dreary dismalness that the working-class Glasgow Sunday engenders. Then there was Isa. I had a fairly ambitious outlook towards her. In fact she was the dominant factor in my last clear thoughts.

It was going on for eleven on Maggie's wristlet-watch when I awoke next morning. I lifted it from the dresser to have a closer look. It was a good watch. I had probably bought it for her many times over, at the price she charged me for drink. I dropped the watch in my pocket. I can't control my sticky fingers, and anyway, Maggie wouldn't know who, of her many visitors, had taken it. More than likely half of the movable contents of the house had, by this time, taken feet and walked, and she could always find money for more.

I felt terrible. Apart from the depredation that Maggie's hooch was perpetrating on my innards and head, I had a crick in my neck and an indeterminate pain somewhere in my lumbar region through lying on her chair.

As I left I glanced over at the bed but could see no signs of Duck-Lips, which is understandable, when you think of his paramour's enormous proportions. By this time the fellow was either halfway through the green-painted brickwork at the back of the bed, or he had twisted some of the blankets into a rope, and climbed up and over. I closed the door behind me and with it the smell of sweat, sour beer and spewings, and tottered unsteadily downstairs.

Thoughts of Blaster's wounded face and Ben's maniacal expression when wielding the razor kept running through my head, till it seemed I was watching it all on a cinema-screen, and the show was even accompanied by theme-music of a kind, for there was a throbbing like giant percussion instruments in my temples, and every sound the passing traffic made in the busy streets mingled together in a crescendo of weird unheard-of instruments.

Blaster's sore face was one of the things I had, subconsciously, been trying to forget. Just shows you. Whatever one tries to drown in alcohol only comes back refreshed after its swim, when the effects wear off.

My tongue tasted like, and resembled in shape and size, a worn-out shoe which had been coated with a mixture of whitewash and cream of tartar. God, but I needed a drink! A decent drink. Not a glass of belly-corrosion such as Maggie had been serving me all week-end. No wonder I felt bad.

I had now reached Bridgeton Cross and the clock showed eleven o'clock. Directly in front of me a public-house door was being opened by some good Samaritan on the inside. That was for me. I nearly knocked over a tramcar, crossing that road.

A couple of whiskies later, I was again ready to face my fellow humans, particularly my mother, who would question me as to my whereabouts on the last two nights. I'd have a good excuse ready for her. I'm glad to say that some of the hard men would consider me a bit of a 'steamer' as far as the old wife was concerned. Ben and his kind can't help but play the hard-case with their parents. At that time we were both fatherless: Ben, for four years, since McNulty senior, during a drinking bout, had fallen downstairs and broken his silly neck. In my own case the situation was slightly, but not much different. My father had emigrated to Australia when I was six years old. Every five years or so, we get a letter saying that it won't be long now till he sends for us. Funny thing is – the old wife always acts as if she believes it, even though she has told me many times that he bends his elbow too much ever to have any money.

Most of that Monday I spent with Isa, still without, I'm glad to say, encountering Ben. I didn't particularly want to see him, and wasn't in the least interested in his movements. Isa quizzed me about my own where-abouts, Saturday and Sunday, and I told her about the job we'd screwed. I omitted to mention our sojourn in Susie's shack. She wouldn't have understood. I also omitted to relate the tale of the remainder of my lost week-end. I told her I had been away on a necessary visit to relatives all day Sunday. Strange though, she didn't ask why I hadn't taken her with me. I only hoped that she wasn't keeping her thoughts to herself until a later date, when she could compare stories with

79

the old wife. You know how these women carry on when they get together.

CHAPTER EIGHT

When I called at the McNulty menage, late afternoon on the Tuesday, wedding preparations were in progress. Because of financial difficulties, the renting of a hall was out of the question, so the celebrations were to take place in the house.

The kitchen (living-room) was cluttered with cutlery and crockery (some of it borrowed for the occasion), and half-open parcels of bedspreads, curtains and tablecloths. The hob was rendered invisible by a conglomeration of utensils, and the house itself was as industrious as a beehive. The honey was there too. Isa – with Jenny a near second. They had both been to the hairdresser's earlier in the day, and he had surpassed himself. The attire they were to wear at the ceremony, in the nearby church, hung in the wardrobe, and they wore cross-over overalls, and nothing more.

What with the excessive bending and hurrying around, it was obvious they had forgotten that the garments were never meant to be worn as solitary coverings. Consequently, now and again I could see a shapely knee emerge from the cloth followed by the thigh to which it was attached, and, just as I lost all track of any conversation directed at me, the folds would fall back into place. The plunging necklines that were being paraded were as startling as any that Monroe or Mansfield might use to offend the censor. Isa's breasts, in particular, fascinated me. The tips were clearly showing through the thin material, and when she bent over . . .

I had not yet got at my games with her, but who would not wish to see a film when the trailer was so interesting. I was in need of some air, so, after Ben had shown me the booze he had in the room, I removed myself from the hive.

When I got to my own, I found the old wife busy, pressing my best suit, extracting from the Cellophane paper and laying out my brand-new shirt, ironing my most sedate looking tie, and hunting through all the drawers in the house for a pair of socks with no holes. The flap she was in, trying to do everything at once, you'd have thought *she* was about to be married. I managed to calm her down and we finally got organized.

At six o'clock sharp the taxi pulled up at my close, and, as I had been pacing up and down since five, I wasted no time in starting. I picked up the other three, and in less than an hour the formalities all had been seen to, without a hitch, and we were back in the McNulty house, with the two love-birds welded into one.

I brought the taxi driver up to the house, and included him in the first toast to the new bride. I thought he did so over-eagerly with eyes for no one else, which wasn't surprising, considering the manner in which she was ogling him. What did I tell you about her and the men? But there are limits. On her wedding night? Still – no one made any comment, so why should I?

After the driver had left, with I thought, a last lingering, longing look, and while the women made final preparations for the arrival of the first guests, we adjourned to the boozer at the corner, there to have a small refreshment, and to enable me to purchase my 'carry out'. I bought three cases of screwtops which, in return for a small remuneration, were carried up to the house by two of the corner boys, and three bottles of whisky, which I preferred to deliver myself. One in each side pocket and one in my hand. You should have seen the neighbours' tongues lolling as we passed. After this it was to be a money-short week. Some of them stood about the closes – others were to be seen at their windows. Susie was at hers . . . She waved to us, but we pretended we were like coal deliverers – short-sighted when it comes to houses above one storey . . . We pushed past the gaping faces that blocked our way and marched upstairs.

Now the guests were filling the house. Some I knew by sight, and there were others who looked as if they hated the sight of me. These were mostly relatives of Jenny, who seemed to have attended for traditional reasons only, as they would a funeral, and probably looked at marriage to a McNulty as a similar fate.

Proper 'pan-loaf' crowd, they were. You know, hoity-toity. That is, all except Uncle Joe, the white sheep of the family, his wife, and Jenny's mother, a small kindly body, so completely different from her offspring.

For some reason or other, which to me seemed obvious, Mr. Forrester was absent on the auspicious occasion of his daughter's nuptials. I believe he had forbidden his daughter to marry a Glasgow hooligan, but it was a case of one word from him and she did as she pleased. Anyway, everyone discreetly refrained from mentioning the self-righteous man's name.

Despite the cold war which threatened to develop between the vastly different families, Isa, Jenny, Uncle Joe and myself, with the aid of a continuous stream of refreshments, managed to keep the company in a more or less festive mood.

Uncle Joe had a head like a billiard ball, and a nose which bore a striking resemblance to Mr. Durante's meal-ticket. This tended to make his appearance laughter-provoking, particularly when he utilised the nasal organ in some very good impressions of the great Schnozzola himself. In between times Isa and Jenny did a bit of hip-wiggling and shoulder-shaking, at the same time vocalizing with some jazz. Now and again I led a round of community singing.

Someone had borrowed a radiogram and a pile of the latest records, and, when we settled down in relays to consume the large platefuls of steak pie, peas and potatoes, we had music while we ate. Joe removed his teeth and champed his gums exaggeratedly to the rhythm of a rumba. That raised a snigger. Someone, because of Joe's antics, choked over a sip of tea, and that caused more laughter all round. If the company wasn't cheery it wasn't because Joe didn't try to keep them that way.

When we had all dined, the table and most of the chairs were piled 'ben-the-room', and the festivities again began.

On occasions, Jenny, while doing a number, would extend her arms towards me in an invitation to dance, and on each occasion I obliged. The way she wriggled about, rubbing her body against mine like a cat, God knows what would have happened if Ben hadn't been my china. As it was, although the others were by this time slightly under the influence, I couldn't prevent myself from suffering a certain amount of embarrassment, imagining as I did that we were being stared at. One thing I was pretty sure of, and that was that Isa, for one, was watching us closely. I didn't want her to think I would, under any circumstances, get at it with Jenny, of all people. I wanted my girl to know that, in my eyes, Jenny couldn't lace her boots, and I resolved to make her aware of the fact as soon as possible.

We arrived at the culminating point when Jenny and I were waltzing round the far side of the kitchen. She propelled me through the open door into the lobby, encircled my neck with her arms, and gently bit my tongue. With her breasts pressed hard against my chest, and the heady fragrance of some rather seductive perfume mingling with the slightest tang of perspiration drifting into my nostrils, I was on the verge of succumbing, but the good fellow in me took over. I pushed her from me, and put everything I had into a disgusted glare.

'You're nothin' but a cow,' I told her, and strutted indignantly back into the kitchen. I think she went downstairs to the toilet, to cover her embarrassment – or something.

Thankfully, I found that Ben hadn't noticed anything. By the look of things he had been drinking 'talking whisky', and was yattering away engrossedly to one of his cousins, who himself appeared completely unaware of his whereabouts, or that anyone was with him. He might have been in another world for all the attention he was paying, but Ben didn't seem to mind.

I watched Isa's face as I rejoined her. Her expression told me that she had a fair idea of what had transpired in the lobby. There was an infinitesimal trace of the green-eyed monster in her glance, but I like to think it was tempered by some emotion more tender. Love perhaps, or faith. I thought it was one of these. We didn't discuss it.

For the remainder of the evening I kept close by Isa, but for me, however, the party was spoilt every time I looked in Jenny's direction and saw the glares she was throwing at me. The others of the company who were sober enough to be aware were finding it dull too, for Joe had now been left to keep the fun going by himself. Paradoxically, the more noise that is being made on these occasions, the less alcohol is being disposed of; so, around one o'clock, the party had become so quiet that Mrs McNulty had succumbed, with a number of others, to a quantity of spirits that far exceeded her normal consumption, and lay atop the bed fully dressed. Uncle Joe, his wife and two others, stood by the door, engaged in animated conversation. Ben was muttering incoherently on the couch, with his eyes closed against the light and his head on Jenny's shapely bosom. Various others sat or stood around the walls.

A large number of the guests had departed by now, and, as I sat with my arm around my girl, and felt the warmth of her body through the thin material of her dress, I decided I would like to be alone with her for a little while.

'Wad ye like tae go for a wee stagger, hen?' I suggested hopefully, with a furtive glance around in search of snoopers.

'Sure Ah wad, darlin', C'moan,' she replied, looking and sounding as keen as I was. We rose from our seats with Jenny's malevolent eyes on us.

I followed Isa into the lobby, where her coat was hanging, and she closed the kitchen-door behind us, but made no attempt to remove the garment from its hanger. Instead she took my hand in hers and led me into a room which was in darkness.

'There's naebuddy in here, an it'll be mair private than the back coort,' she said, as we manoeuvred our way between the furniture which had been brought from the kitchen.

I wasn't so sure about that, with a kitchen full of people who could, and might, enter the room at any moment. By this time however, Isa, after moving some of the guests' coats, hats and scarves, had me seated on the bed and was practising jiu-jitsu on me. I might say I was a fairly willing participant, but still a wee bit hedgy.

Her lips drained the last drop of hesitation from my system and I abandoned myself to the project, throwing my arms around her and crushing her to me.

The mumble of voices that filtered through the closed doors was fading into a far distant drone, as the hands I had placed on her shoulder-blades felt the outline of her bra-straps through the soft material of her outer garments, and I knew that said garment had vanished, and my fingers now rested on her lovely

85

velvet skin. I was still reluctant about going further, wishing to marry her as I did, and not wanting her to think that I would take advantage of the fact that she was slightly drunk.

Surprise! Surprise! *She* began to take advantage of me. By taking my hand from her waist where it now rested, and cupping one firm breast with it, I could feel the soft flesh pulsing with passion, as she once more slid her arms around my neck, and slowly lay back on the bed, pulling me on top of her. The blood was hammering in my ear-drums and my knees were shaking like a fiddler's elbows, as she encouraged my hands to explore her body in the darkness, and I finally touched the filmy material of her panties with my fingers. She arched her back that I might remove them. I did so, automatically, without a single qualm about interruptions. I had forgotten there was anyone else in the world, other than we two.

Now we were both breathing heavily, our hearts beating as one, and I, realizing that nothing could ever be like this, had lost myself in that moment. No girl would ever compare with my Isa and I loved her with all my being . . .

Suddenly the door was flung open and, simultaneously, the light was switched on. There stood Ben, his face horribly twisted in rage, his eyes bloodshot with drink and drowsiness. My limbs stiffened of their own volition and an unholy terror seized me. At the back of my mind I had been dreading such a moment as this since that very first night when I had taken Isa to the pictures. I had always had a powerful feeling that something like this would happen, and here it was. But it was too late to do anything about it.

'Take a liberty wi' ma sister, wad ye?' he mouthed through slobbering lips. 'Ya bloody hoormaister.' I gazed at him hypnotised, as I slowly sat up on the bed. But, right or wrong, in front of my girl, I had to defend myself against the verbal onslaught.

'You don't gie a damn aboot Isa,' I retaliated. 'It's only the booze bringin' oot the "nutter" in ye that's makin' ye talk.'

When the words had left my mouth I felt like cutting out my tongue. Clumsily pushing his way past the obstructive furniture, he flew at me, pulling the razor from his pocket. Then I saw the blade swinging at my cheek. I saw it coming and couldn't duck. That was the way Ben chibbed. Drunk or sober, he was quick. Strange to say, I hardly felt a thing, but I knew by the blood that spurted all over the place and gushed into my eye that I had got it right. My hands, of their own accord, jumped up and covered my face, as I sank back on the bed. I could feel the gaping wound, beginning at my hair-line, and running down across my eye, to my mouth. Then, in an uncontrollable surge of panic, I wondered if I would lose my eye altogether.

All I said was, 'Oh, ya bastart.'

He lifted his weapon to strike me again, but Isa, with tears streaming down her face, jumped between us, crying in a half-hysterical key, 'Leave 'im alane, you. We're gonny be mairrit. You keep your durty haun's aff 'im, ya rat.'

I removed one hand from my undamaged eye, saw him threaten to slap her with his open hand, and his words, 'Shut up, ya wee cow. You're as bad as him. Tryin' tae make a kip shop o' the hoose,' and I reached for my pocket furtively. I knew if he touched Isa, I'd kill him. I didn't realize just how mad Isa was, but she swore to me later that, if she'd had a gun in her hand when he struck me, she would have shot him. That was the way it was with us, and yet he had the audacity to criticize our conduct. And, as I'd told him, it certainly wasn't on account of any brotherly love. He didn't know the meaning of the words.

Just at that moment there was an intervention from

an unexpected source. From nowhere a hand appeared above Ben's head, and gripped in that hand was an empty beer-bottle. Down it came, and, a surprised look on his face, Ben went out like a light. Good for Jenny's Uncle Joe. He knew how to wield a screwtop scientifically.

He turned to Jenny and said, 'Ah'm sorry Ah had tae dae that, hen, but he was askin' for it.' He looked down at Ben. 'Your man's a bit o' a head-case, eh?' he mused whimsically, a woebegone smile quirking his lips.

I looked at Jenny standing in the doorway and realized that she hadn't heard a word Uncle Joe had said, nor was she bothering about her husband, who lay unconscious on the floor. She was otherwise occupied. She stood there like Hitler in a synagogue, with the hatred pouring from her eyes, and it was all directed at me. I've seen a lot of people in a temper. I've seen blokes in such a rage they looked ready for the strait-jacket. But I never saw anything like this that I could remember. Not a muscle twitched. A deadly stillness held her rigid. And yet you knew that untold currents were charging along those beautiful limbs to short-circuit somewhere in her head – resulting in those dangerous sparks that were thrown from her eyes. If my upbringing hadn't taught me that man was the masterful sex, I think I would have been a bit frightened. In fact I wouldn't like to lay the odds that I wasn't.

Although my mind was in a turmoil, due, I suppose, to shock, a couple of things became clear to me, and it all added up.

Ben had burst into the room with the express purpose of surprising Isa and me. Not because he had been sufficiently sober to notice our absence, or to detect our presence in the room rather than the back-court. No! Not because of that at all. Simply because Jenny had informed him, and while she was at it, she had stressed the fact that I should be 'sorted'. Ben didn't need much encouragement for assault at any time, and less when he was in his cups, but what little he did need on this occasion had been supplied by her. If I hadn't opened my mouth I'd still have got it. I was glad I had tried to be a man about it.

Looking at Jenny, who was still standing there, I knew that when I had added two and two and made four, my mental arithmetic had been correct. I knew it as sure as I knew my own name. And the reason for it all was so obvious too. I had refused to avail myself of Jenny's charms. On her wedding night. Jenny was a nymphomaniac. What an unholy partnership in holy wedlock. A nymphomaniac and a psychopath. I couldn't wish them worse than each other.

I hadn't noticed that Ben's mother was in the room, and that Isa was now relating the sorry tale to her, omitting nothing. Mrs Mac came over to the bed, put her hands on my shoulders, and, in a kindly voice, said, 'Come inty the kitchen, son. We'll wash it an' see how bad it is.'

As I rose, unsteadily, to my feet, she turned to the others in the lobby. 'Somebuddy run doon for the polis,' she said. 'Ah'll put Ben the whole road for this night's work.'

'But, Ma!' Jenny exclaimed, sufficiently startled from her preoccupation to turn from me to her mother-in-law. 'Ye wadny jail your ain son?' I was glad she had removed her eyes from my person. Mrs McNulty turned on her angrily.

'Son?' she cried. 'Son, did ye say? He's nae son o' mine. Look at the mess this lad's face is in.' She took hold of my chin, firmly but gently, and turned the offending object full in Jenny's direction. She didn't turn a hair. Not surprising, since that was the way she'd wanted it to look. But Mrs Mac didn't know this or she would have been more harsh with her. As it was, her anger was really directed against Ben.

'It's a godsend the boy's still alive,' Mrs Mac added, screwing up her eyes bad-temperedly. 'An' it's nae fau't o' Ben's that he is.' She stopped her tirade for a moment, and gazed round at the sea of faces as if seeking the answer to some inner question, then continued, 'Ah'll leave it up tae Bill here, tae jail 'im.' Again facing Jenny, she waved her forefinger at the crumpled heap on the floor. 'Anywey,' she shouted, 'ye can take this man o' yours oot o' here this minute, an' tell 'im, when he wakes up, no' tae show ese face back here – ever.'

'But where can we go at this time o' night?' Jenny protested.

'Ah don't care where yese go,' was the answer, 'as long as ye take 'im oot this hoose.' So saying, Mrs Mac, aided by Isa, herded me into the kitchen, pushing Jenny aside during the process.

Over at the sink they sat me in a chair while they washed the blood from my face, and made a vain attempt to stop the flow. I knew by their expressions that I was in a bad state. Isa still had a few tears in the corners of her eyes, relics of the crying bout in the room. They were now being washed out by a fresh flow. It almost made me forget my predicament, in an ardent wish to comfort her.

Ma was saying, 'Bill – it's – like this.' She hesitated, choosing her words while her kindly efficient hands made the best of a bad job with my face. 'Ah knew by the wey ye kept lookin' at Isa, ye thoaght a loat o' 'er, so Ah hivny been worryin' owermuch aboot whit yese got up tae.' Her homely features adopted a frown which she didn't seem particularly keen to confront me with. She turned her head slightly as she finished, 'But ye shouldny have done a thing like that in the hoose.' Her voice sounded apologetic, but firm.

I tried to express the guilt I felt, but couldn't find the words.

'Ah – Ah'm daft aboot Isa,' I stammered shamefacedly, remembering how I had been found in the room, and glad that Mrs Mac had not been there to see. 'Ah – Ah suppose Ah had too much tae drink.'

She was about to demolish my puny excuse when Isa took over the role of counsel for the defence.

'But it wiz mair ma fau't than his, maw,' she said in the best QC manner, and I thought to myself, 'And that's the truth,' while she continued, 'Ah encouraged him an awfa loat. Ah've been hopin' he wad hurry up an' ask me tae mairry 'im.'

Ma looked at me directly.

'Well – it's no' a very good time tae ask,' she said, 'but Ah'd like tae know. Are ye gonny mairry 'er, Bill?'

'Gie me hauf a chance,' I answered eagerly.

'That's fine, son,' Mrs Mac said, smiling. 'Ye know it wizny a shotgun case. It's jist that Ah think Ah'd like ye for a son-in-law.'

A thought struck me and became oral. 'Mibbe Isa'll no' want me noo wi' a face like a pun' o' mince.'

They were both trying to convince me that my face would be all right, when a voice interrupted. 'But it'll need stitchin'.'

It was Uncle Joe, who had just returned after putting his niece and her husband in a taxi, bound for Parkhead and their room. They hadn't intended to go back there as newly-weds, since the landlady was under the impression that they had got over that stage months ago.

Joe offered to accompany Isa and me to the Infirmary, and we accepted. We left Joe's wife with Mrs Mac. Fortunately, Jenny's mother had found it necessary to leave earlier in the evening, for the purpose of catching a bus. In so doing she had missed the practical example of her son-in-law's viciousness. If she had witnessed the barney, she might have worried unnecessarily on her daughter's behalf. But I couldn't see Jenny coming off second-best with Ben. She had him taped.

When the fight was over and Ben had been shipped off to other parts, the few remaining guests had left when they saw there was to be no more excitement, so we left the two elderly ladies alone, and travelled luxuriously, in a taxi, since the trams and buses had stopped running for the night.

The people at the Infirmary put twelve stitches in my face. Five above and seven below the eye. They told me I was very fortunate in so far as the optic itself was undamaged. While they were doing the job they also called the police. When they interrogated me, I spun them a yarn about being attacked by unknown assailants, and, although they were obviously dubious about my statement, there wasn't much they could do about it. Especially when my tale was backed up by Joe and Isa, bless their hearts.

The police finally got fed up and left just before we did.

When we got back to the house Mrs McNulty suggested I should lie on the couch for the remainder of the dark hours, saying with a chuckle, 'It wadny dae tae waken your maw in the middle o' the night wi' your face rowed up like a bun'le for the pawn.'

I'm sorry to say the wan smile I assumed was not in the least spontaneous, since I thought it was no laughing matter. But I knew she was only trying to cheer me up. Just the same, she gave me another worry. I was picturing the state the old wife would get in when she saw me. I hoped that the news of my engagement would help soften the blow.

My head was aching something terrible and the wound was by now really making itself felt, so, after we had had a much-needed drink, I managed forty winks on the couch, with my head resting on Isa's lap – a pillow fit for a king. While the cool slender fingers of her right hand moved ever so gently through my hair, her left hand was clenched in mine, and, once or twice, she planted a soothing kiss on my burning lips, one of the few parts of my face left uncovered.

But a few hours of the year 1942 had elapsed. Such a short time since the bells had rung and the factory hooters had sounded, welcoming a new year. The old customs had gone on as usual. The 'first-footers' had walked about the streets, the neighbours had knocked on each other's doors, and goodwill and friendship had spread over the city. But not in this house. Bad blood had been mounting just about that time, and look at the results. During that short period, my face had been badly marked for life; I had lost so much blood that the quack had given me tablets to supplement the small amount I had left, and my views on friendship had been drastically changed. I couldn't see myself trusting a pal again.

But it's an ill-wind that's sickening to everyone. There was one factor that was, to me, wonderful. I was engaged to be married. And with Isa the prospective bride, this particular breeze couldn't have blown me more good.

CHAPTER NINE

I didn't see anything of Ben for the next four months, but I got quite a few reports about him from various sources. There exists in the city a sort of street-corner telegraph, such as they have in prisons up and down the country.

After the New Year he had been on the run for a few weeks, till the Army caught up with him and sentenced him to fifty-six days' detention. He had again been on the trot, since he came out.

Jenny and he were staying up the High Road somewhere. Somebody told me they had a room in Garngad, and that's the district he was running around. He'd been in a couple of fights of course, and was making a bit of a name for himself. Nutty Deane, one of the 'head-bummers' there, had copped it right, and my information was that Ben had given him it. Then there was a wee bit of a turn-up with the High Road people and a crowd from Anderson district, and Ben had taken a prominent part. He 'gied it' to someone else on that occasion too. His name was becoming a household word – in the 'housey'.

I fixed a date in September for my marriage to Isa. If I didn't get a leave at the proper time I could take one.

During a furlough I got in April, Isa and I spent almost every night together, mainly hunting for secluded spots, where we could go through the blessed routine of young lovers. Late at night, we strolled over the Green, but each time we found a likely place to kiss and cuddle, you could bet your life for some of the 'knee-creepers' to appear on the scene. Sometimes, I chased after one, but fleetness of foot seems to go hand-in-glove with that obnoxious kind of amusement. If I could have got hold of one of them, he'd have been separated from his breath, I can tell you.

After all the time I'd spent in Isa's company, it came as no great surprise to me when she elected to stay home one evening, while I went on my own to Barrowland.

In the middle of the always crowded floor, I was trying to execute some intricate steps I had devised, to the tune of a quick-step, when I bumped full-tilt into someone. I turned round. It was Ben. When I saw he had a drink in him, I was dead scared, and I think he knew it. He seemed pleased about that.

'How's it gaun', Bill?' he greeted me with a forced heartiness, as he patted my shoulder. 'If you're no' a sight for sore eyes.'

I shrugged my shoulder-pad back into place, and slipped a sickly grin across my face.

'No' bad,' I answered, hoping that the hatred I felt

towards him wasn't showing.

With a perfectly normal show of bad manners, he left his partner stranded on the spot, took my arm and dragged me across the floor. She must have known him pretty well, for the shrewd girl didn't crack a light.

'Could ye go a jag?' he asked as we reached the outskirts of the milling throng. 'C'mon inty the lavvy. Ah've a boattle of "scud" here,' patting his jacket pocket. Although I suspected his motives for luring me from the crowd, I knew perfectly well he couldn't produce a bottle in full view of the bouncers. If one has managed to smuggle a drink into the dance hall it is normal procedure to sneak into the toilet. And I could see that the outline of the bottle was plainly showing. 'Hell,' I thought, 'Napoleon took a chance,' and with some misgivings, I nodded acquiescence, doged round a pair of jitterbugs and followed him.

There were three blokes in the toilet, but they didn't give us a second glance, as they left together. Why should they? How were they to know that I both hated and feared my companion, and that I expected, at any moment, to feel the caress of a razor on my cheek?

Ben handed me the bottle and, while I took a slug, warily, without removing my eyes from him, he began asking how his mother and Isa were keeping. But I knew my answers were of no interest to him. I wondered what was really going on in his twisted mind. The idea came that he might be playing a cat-and-mouse game with me, but I dismissed the notion as improbable. If he had intentions of wiring into me, he would have carried them out by now.

We continued our commonplace conversation for a few minutes more, washed it down with more booze and returned to the dance floor.

I was congratulating myself on having escaped unhurt from the toilet, when I felt his hand grip my arm tightly. I turned my head in his direction and he nodded, wordlessly, to the other side of the hall. I looked that way, and there was Jenny with a gang of blokes around her, like flies round a dry latrine. I suppose she looked beautiful to most men. Even more so since her marriage.

Her youthful figure now had about it the full roundness that only matrimony, or the equivalent, can bring, and she carried herself with the sort of sophisticated self-assurance that the male animal likes in his women. Trouble with me was, I had seen what those others hadn't. The vileness that lay just beneath the skin, and clear through. Jenny would never be beautiful in my eyes. In fact, to put it crudely, I wouldn't touch her with a ten-foot pole, with crap on the end of it.

As we stood watching, one fellow, known as Flash O'Hara, seemingly oblivious to our rapt attention, had his arms around her waist, and was squeezing her for all he was worth. She had her hands against his chest and was pushing. I've seen a blow-football pushed harder. In other words, she was loving it. She hadn't changed a bit. Just her same sweet self.

'Are ye handin' me?' Ben asked me, slipping his malky from his pocket and palming it. Now I knew why he had acted so friendly. There had to be a reason in the first place, and this was it. I felt like telling him to go to hell, but I didn't.

Instead I said, 'Ah don't want tae get involved in ony battles, Ben.'

His brows dropped till they rested on his cheeks, and I continued, 'Ah'm livin' it quiet noo. It's better that wey.'

'Feart the bird'll give ye a row?' he taunted. 'We'll no' tell 'er, then she'll no' know, an' she'll no' hit ye.'

'Isa?' I reiterated. 'Naw – but Ah think it's your wumman ye should wire inty onywey. Knoack hell oota her when ye git 'er hame.'

96

'Ach,' he scowled. 'She's nae mair sense. She's only a kid.'

All the time he kept his grip on my arm, and his eyes on the group facing us.

Just at that moment, Jenny, who had been crossing the floor close to the orchestra-dais, laughing and swinging those kipper-hips of hers like the Finnieston ferry, was escorted through the door by her convoy. Obviously, Ben had not been boozing by himself, for Jenny too appeared to be carrying quite a cargo of hooch.

'Well? Are ye comin' wi' me or no'?' Ben asked. And before I could gather enough courage to refuse, 'Your card'll be marked onywey, noo that ye've been seen alang wi' me.' Now he wore a grin that said, 'You have a choice. Get in a fight – or – get in a later fight.' Then he added another nail in the coffin.

'Ah've already had a needle wi' them the night, an' ye'll no' get leavin' here wi'oot gettin' tackled.' I had been trying to shrug his hand from my arm, but I'm afraid my attempts were becoming weaker with each word. 'We'll be better gaun' oot two-handed, than wan at a time,' was his final argument. He had a point there. I didn't want to help him, but neither did I wish to step out alone to a street-fight, and it was on the cards that, if I let him leave, they would wait until I also appeared, and deal with me. That was the way things often went.

'Well, a' right,' I told him. 'As long as you don't start onythin' if they don't,' and we started along the hall to the door. Ben pushing people aside in the process.

'It's okay,' he replied over his shoulder, 'Ah'll no' start it.'

But I couldn't blame him when he did.

Outside the dance hall door, at the end of the foyer, Jenny stood against the wall, her coat over one arm and her hands at her back. Her shoulders, too, were pushed back, so that her breasts stood out sharply, invitingly. She was asking for trouble, and yet everybody, but her, was going to get it.

Flash O'Hara was kissing her, some of the others were pawing her, and she was giggling and tee-heeing away like a silly-schoolgirl. This was the scene that met our eyes as a passing tram illuminated that part of the Gallowgate. Not a pretty sight for a conscientious husband.

Ben 'done his nut'. Swinging his malky and cursing at the top of his voice, he made a lunge for the group, while they drew various weapons as they scattered.

In less time than it takes to tell I was in a quandary. If I wasn't going to take part in the barney, I would have to blow myself – and sharp, in which case some of the gang would probably light after me. Then I would have to defend myself. Attack seemed better than defence, so I drew my chib, just as a big baw-faced character with a turn in his eye had a go at me.

He swung a bicycle-chain at my head, but, luckily enough, he was so busy watching my razor, that his aim wasn't so good, and ducking, I sunk my boot in his groin as he got close, upon which he lost all interest in the proceedings. Another fellow was at my side, but I managed to lay the razor across his head. His skull must have been solid bone right through, for the blade broke clean in two as it made contact. But he dropped.

I didn't have time to congratulate myself, for someone landed heavily on my back, at the same time dealing me a glancing blow on the head with the proverbial blunt instrument. Partially stunned, I fell to the ground, my adversary with me. I managed to roll on top of him, but, from some other source, I received a kick on the shoulder, which sent waves of pain shooting through my body. Luckily enough, I had sufficient presence of mind left to roll away from the follow-up blow that was aimed at my head. I kept on rolling, miraculously avoiding the booted feet that stamped around on all sides, till I could roll no further.

There I lay, next to the wall, my eyes dimmed by the tears that intense pain brings, and I was barely able to see the large number of people who were now involved in the mêlée. Some other mob had taken the opportunity to wire into Flash's crowd, which, by now, had been reinforced. Dim shapes struggled around me, weapons of all sorts were swung, now and again the throat of some person would emit a grunt, moan, yell or curse, depending on how he was faring, and I concentrated on keeping as close to the wall as possible to avoid the scuffling boots.

Nausea was taking hold of me, and I fought hard to control it. Each time I was about to retch, I tightened my stomach-muscles in anticipation, but the strain was terrific, and with the pain I was suffering I wasn't surprised to feel the trickle of sweat start at the roots of my hair, and continue to trickle down my face. Then I heard the police whistles; and while the crowd around me scattered, I made an effort to get to my feet, using the arm on my uninjured side as a lever. Now, in addition to the sickness, unconsciousness was like small waves, lapping over, and receding from my brain. I was in a helluva state.

I had no sooner straightened my knees and pressed the small of my back tightly against the brickwork, when someone grabbed at the arm that hung limply at my side, and everything went black as the awful pain again wracked my body, bringing with it the final tremendous breaker to engulf my conscious mind. Mercifully the cloak of darkness was dropped over me, and I succumbed – gladly.

I recovered in the Royal Infirmary, my shoulder and arm encased in plaster. The collar-bone and a bone in my upper arm were broken, they told me. They also said a lot of other things to me. Mainly that razor-slashers couldn't be hurt enough, and so on, and so on. Theme-song of the uninitiated. That's what living a good, clean life can do to you. Makes you hard-hearted.

They kept me in the Royal for ten uncomfortable days, after which time the case came up for trial at the Sheriff's Court in Brunswick Street.

Still wearing the plaster, but my legs being strong enough to carry me a few paces, I was transported there along with O'Hara, to be joined in a waiting cell by our fighting partners.

The five of us were charged with mobbing and rioting, which is really only a breach of the peace, with complications. There were no witnesses to press assault charges against any of us.

You should have heard the Prosecutor Fiscal talk. He could have talked a gramophone into scrap-iron. On and on he went, hardly stopping to draw breath: 'I must draw the attention of your honour to the fact that in recent weeks a great number of gang-fights have been taking place. These young hooligans are running wild around the streets, and are a constant danger to the life and limb of the law-abiding public. I must stress your honour, blah – blah – blah.' I thought he was never going to finish.

But he met his match in our mouthpiece. He must have been vaccinated with a gramophone-needle for he talked continuously for even longer, and I thought everyone would burst into tears. Anyway, he had such good patter, he managed to get us off with light sentences.

Ben, myself and the fellow I had kicked, all had previous convictions, so we were sentenced to three months apiece.

Did you ever study a sheriff's (or a judge's) face, while he is sentencing you to imprisonment. That's right. You're not seeing things. 'Sheriff,' I said, but don't let me hear you make that crack about stage coaches. They don't wear six-guns, and they don't ride any wonder horses. Very dignified gentlemen, they are. I suppose you could call him a glorified magistrate, since he has a mighty heavy sentencing power, in his court.

Anyway, when he is saying, 'William McGhee – I sentence you to three month's imprisonment in Her Majesty's Prison,' his piercing eyes (they all have them) and his stern mouth are the only parts of his face to show any signs of life. Inscrutable, they call it.

Well, I wasn't really cribbing about my sentence. I was quite happy with a 'carpet'. At a Summary Court, such as this was, we could have got a 'sixer'.

Flash and the other bloke, being first offenders, got sixty days. But, in addition to the 'deuce' sentence, Flash had come out of it with a bit of a sore face. Plus the dislocated knee which had rested him in the Royal. You could say he 'backed a deuce' all round.

My time was dragging, constantly thinking of Isa as I was.

After tea, when we had been locked up for the night in our single cells, I'd open my library book and try to become immersed in it. Hopeless! Before I had completed a chapter, my mind was wandering.

'Ah wonder whit Isa is daein' the noo?' and, 'Surely she'll no' far' for somebody else?' were questions I would ask myself and be unable to answer. It was self-created hell. Jail can be like that, for a normal, jealous man.

Moving my chair over to the open window, I'd stand on it. And through the small space between the opaque glass and the window frame, I'd watch the progress of the number seven car, as it trundled past, on its return journey from the Millerston terminus to the city. How I wished I were on it.

'There – we've missed anither caur,' came a voice from the window of the adjoining cell, and we carried on a desultory conversation in this manner, till the patrol screw came along the gallery and battered the cell door crying:

101

'Aw right! Aw right! Quieten doon in there.'

Then I'd crawl between my cold, canvas sheets with my book. When the screw came round again, and flicked each cell to darkness, sleep overcame me slowly, grudgingly, but didn't bring the complete oblivion it should have. Fitful dreams chased each other through my subconscious, and, when my mind became absolutely vacant, damned if the screw didn't throw open the door and shout, 'C'moan – Get the blankets aff ye. Whiddye think you're on?'

The normal daily routine wasn't too bad, as a few hours were spent working in the sheds, but the weekends were murder. From noon Saturday till Monday morning, apart from one hour's exercise on a Sunday, and a visit to church, you were hardly outside your 'flowery'.

Ben and I were both employed in the mat shed making doormats, at first, so I saw quite a lot of him for part of the two months we spent in Barlinnie. But as usual Ben couldn't help but 'screw his nut'. He'd start a fight in an empty house. He and another prisoner had a duel with mat-knives, and although he came off best in the fight, he finished his time in an observation cell, in another block. He was lucky. They didn't charge him, but I was glad they moved him, for I still hated his guts.

There were occasions when I became involved in furtive conversation with Flash and his confederates. I got on fairly well with them, but it was obvious they didn't fancy Ben, and that there would be more trouble between them at a later date. No skin off my nose.

At that time, the prison reform people were still battling for better conditions. Any convicted prisoner doing six months or over, received, in return for a stipulated amount of work, sufficient money to buy one-eighth of an ounce of shag and a packet of cigarette-papers per week. The first two months were served minus this, among other privileges.

Of course, we didn't qualify for 'snout' allowance, but Flash got me 'quoted' with some of his snout-king friends. These are prisoners who, by various means, acquire stocks of illicit tobacco, and use it for business purposes. In English prisons they prefer to call them Barons.

I had a little over a fortnight to do when Flash was released, but his friends kept me well supplied with a few 'spider's-legs' a day. As the name implies, these are very thin roll-ups, made from strong shag. But, to a smoke-hungry con, they're sweeter tasting than Corona-Coronas. If every slice of 'tommy' I've seen exchanged for spider's-legs were laid end to end, that would be some bread-line.

At last the day of my release arrived, and I was awake and dressed, waiting for the unlocking of my cell door. For the last time, I heard the welcome rattle of the key in the lock, and I joined the jostling throng who were headed for the 'arches' in the middle of the landings, there to empty their pots, tipping buckets in the toilets, and some of them indulging in a hurried wash at the sink.

I heard the screw downstairs bawling, just as I had so many times, 'All men for release, down here at the double. Bring your door-cards and bedding.' Only this morning it sounded different. He meant me.

After I'd emptied my pot I hurried back to my cell and grabbed my gear. Out on the landing, I bade a couple of friendly neighbours farewell, hurried downstairs, dumped my bedding and joined the other six who were leaving the block. The screw who opened hall door for us said something like, 'Mind an' no' let us see ye back.'

One of the others, who fancied himself as a bit of a hard-case, retorted, 'You mind an' keep ma ain cell for me, or Ah'll no' visit ye again.'

There was a general snigger from the other prisoners who were in a mood to laugh at just about anything, but the door-screw turned on the would-be hard-case angrily. 'Any mair o' your lip,' he blazed, 'an' Ah'll have ye back in the cell, quicker than that. Ye haveny earned your remission yet tae ye get oot that big door.'

With a sickly embarrassed grin at the rest of us, the con shut his mouth.

In the receptions, before we were installed in the 'dog-boxes', I managed to exchange a very few words with Ben.

The 'dog-boxes'. Now there's an apt description if you like.

These little compartments are about three feet square, with a wooden seat embedded in one wall, facing the door, which has a bolt on the outside. Here, incoming and outgoing prisoners strip for bathing and medical inspection, and change from civvies to prison garb, and vice versa.

Outgoing prisoners, while discarding the antiquated, tied-at-the-knee, *that*-length trousers, and button-single-breasted-if-you're-lucky jacket, the mid-thigh length, finger-breadth-shrunken woollen stockings, and the two left boots with square, upturned toes that are normally issued, are handed a cog of cold porridge you can stand on, and a mug of muddy tea that looks as if it's been stood in, plus two slices of 'tommy'. One is supposed to eat, and dress, simultaneously, in the darkness of the dog-box. If you leave the tea, it gets colder, and if you let the clothes wait your body suffers.

Sometimes, particularly on admission to the prison, one is apt to be abandoned here for a rather overlong period, which is doubly appreciated by the occupant.

This morning we were lucky. By seven o'clock, they had us out of the main gate, and, you know, I could swear the air smells totally different on either side of that wall.

I filled my lungs with it, jauntily ran down the hill

past some of my erstwhile fellow-boarders, who were being effusively greeted by their women-folk, and jumped aboard one of the tramcars I had been viewing from my lofty perch during the past two months.

As in the case of most releases, the cog of porridge and mug of tea lay untouched in the dog-box I had just vacated, so naturally my first thoughts were concerned with the bacon and eggs (my favourite breakfast) that would be laid for me on my mother's table. Despite the rationing restrictions, she usually managed to cater for my tastes.

Since my sleepless nights had been caused by a kind of starvation, different from the type described in hot night-cap adverts, most of my other thoughts were centred around my pending meeting with Isa. But I spared a thought for Ben, who had left Barlinnie with a Marine escort, to face a desertion charge, hell slap it into him.

CHAPTER TEN

Because I had not been AWOL when arrested, and having been held up for reasons outwith my control, the Army authorities were allowing me to rejoin my unit under my own steam. I decided to catch a train late that evening.

At home, I made a proper pig of myself at my mother's table, and afterwards lay back on an armchair with a Capstan between my fingers that felt and looked like a Churchillian cigar. An eloquent illustration of the girth of the aforementioned spider's-legs.

The old wife was yattering away about jail, and the people who go into such places. I knew all her words, added together, only meant that she didn't ever think any son of hers would be a jailbird, and she hoped it wouldn't happen again. I'd heard it all before. I closed my eyes and relaxed.

At eleven o'clock I was startled from my sleep by a

knock on the door. The old wife was doing a washing in the sink. While I drew myself erect in the chair and wiped a saliva dribble from the corner of my mouth, she dried her hands on her apron, crossed the floor and flung the door wide. The way she always did it. Not like some of those people who act like the butler in a mystery film.

'Hello, Isa, hen,' mother said, waving her arm expansively. 'Come right in.'

I was getting to my feet quickly, the drowsy feeling fleeing at the sound of her name, when Isa hurried over and grabbed me, planting lips firmly on mine, and squeezing me like a toothpaste-tube. I made no effort to hold her. It suited me the way it was. Holding a woman in your arms is not half as much fun as letting her hold you. Ask any baby.

At last she released me and we stood there, silently gazing at each other, while we got our breath back. I liked what I saw in her eyes.

In her usual hospitable way, the old wife immediately poured a cup of tea for Isa. I told her to give me one when she was at it. She did so and we sat for a while sipping, smoking and not saying a great deal. I'm as fond of my mother as the next bloke, but I was impatient to get the girl by herself.

At noon the old wife gave us some dinner. That's what we Glaswegians call the mid-day meal. When we had eaten our fill, Isa and I left. We did the matinée at the Argyle Cinema. Don't ask me what films were on. I haven't a clue. I was far too interested in my companion to pay much attention. By the time we left I was all het up.

We strolled arm in arm along Argyle Street till we got to Kent Street, then cut down into the Green and wandered aimlessly around, till we found ourselves over by the open-air theatre, where the concert-parties used to hold summer shows. We got down on the grass there and had a heavy necking session. Just as well it was broad daylight or I might have been tempted. As it was, every time Isa pressed her lips on mine and pushed her voluptuous body nearer, I just about 'lost the place'. But I, too, am a glutton for punishment. Much later, we got to our feet and headed back for civilisation.

Through Morris Place we went, to London Road, and only when we got to Green Street did I realise it was the old lady's usual night for the pictures. Never missed them. I dragged Isa along to my house, feeling like taking the stairs three at a time, in my eagerness.

To make sure that mother had not changed her routine on account of the fact that I was to leave that night, I knocked on the door. When I got no answer, I borrowed a check-key from Isa.

I closed the door behind us and, without waiting to enter the kitchen proper, I grabbed Isa. She responded in kind, and we lost ourselves in a wild surge of animal passion that could only be experienced by a couple one of whom has been, for a period of time, away from the sight of a member of the opposite sex. We made up for lost time.

Quarter-to-nine, the old wife came in, and we adopted a Sunday-school look. My train was due to leave at half-past the hour and Isa was going with me to the station. We left at nine o'clock.

On the tram I don't believe either of us spoke a word, and on the station-platform it was much the same. The only remarks that were made were the banal ones of everyday conversation. Nothing that mattered. While on the large station-clock the minute hand drew nearer to the time when the guard would blow his whistle to separate us for God knows how long. Maybe for ever.

Carriage-doors were banging shut before I grabbed Isa to me and, as we embraced, I didn't give two hoots in hell whether we were scandalizing everyone. When I think back, I don't suppose any of the onlookers had any such ideas about our conduct; they probably felt sympathetic towards us. Many kindred spirits were there, and not only there, but in railway-stations all over the country, where such scenes were being enacted till they had become commonplace. But I didn't think so then. I forced myself to be brave while Isa sobbed on my shoulder, only breaking off now and then to kiss me fiercely.

A station porter behind me was saying, 'Hey, so'djer. Ye better get oan or ye'll miss the train.' Isa was pushing my arm away with the palm of her hand, but her fingers were still gripping tightly the sleeve of my Number One battledress-tunic.

I managed to bundle some of my thoughts into a few disjointed sentences which I won't attempt to chronicle, before the flag finally fell and the train began to move. With tears flooding her eyes, Isa gave me one last possessive kiss and a little push, and I ran for the open carriage-door. Helping hands stretched out and pulled me aboard.

Hanging from the window, I saw her run alongside the train, right to the end of the platform, all the time waving a tiny hand, and I felt like disembarking immediately. But common sense took a grip. I found myself a vacant seat and drifted into an idyllic coma, where Isa and I were cast away on a wonderous desert island paradise, where there were no army, MPs, police, razor-slashing gangsters, or, in fact, other men and women. Only she and I, communing with nature. I am aware I was not the first to have such daydreams, and I don't suppose I'll be the last. Especially in times of stress, and nothing could have been more distressing than that parting.

For close on a year, I had been bothered intermittently with my stomach. At first it had seemed the direct result of heavy drinking, but at later stage, when I had been completely teetotal, I still had been troubled a lot.

I had only been a fortnight back at camp when it started to play me up. I really thought I was for the 'brothpot'. Most of what I ate was immediately returned, and, even when it didn't rise to the occasion, it gave me hell during the passage through my body. Some of the other lads thought I was working my ticket, swallowing carbon copy paper or some such stunt. But I wouldn't have gone through that caper for my 'brief', even if they had devised a diamond-studded one with a solid gold back especially for me. No! It was straight up. My guts had sold me out.

By devious means – X-rays and such – they discovered I was suffering from gastric ulcers, and slung me out, Grade Four.

That was in August, and, as I once more travelled up the line to Glasgow and Isa, I wondered why the railways always put slow obsolete engines on north-bound trains and arrange that fast expresses pull any that are heading south.

From August for a couple of weeks, I became as tight as a drum with my money. The few quid I got to cover my discharge leave I sank, and then looked around for some means of earning a few bob, rather than lie around idle. A friend of mine, whose identity is not important, put a wee turn my way, when he started taking me with him on his business trips. He owned a handy little fifteen-hundredweight lorry, and, when he wasn't hawking the Ayrshire or Lanark-shire districts, he was doing a bit locally, with fish, or fruit, or anything he could lay his hands on.

Rationing restrictions naturally curtailed our activi-ties considerably, but most days found us out on some scheme or other, and there were occasional removal jobs and such, of a night. He paid me well, and by the time September, and my wedding day, came around, I had saved a few quid. In addition, Isa had managed to keep a bit by from her wages.

You'd have thought it was Lent or something, the

way we 'renegued' the pictures every night, and cut the cigarettes down to a minimum. We either sat in the house or wore the shoe-leather off our feet, walking.

The wedding was a quiet affair, though the guests didn't come up the stairs on tiptoe.

A cousin of mine was best man, and the best maid was a girl who worked beside Isa. The four of us were at the first house of the Empire, and, when we came back, our mothers, and a few friends and neighbours, held a nice orderly do in Mrs Mac's house. Mrs Mac and the old wife had a right good 'greet' together, and everyone enjoyed themselves tremendously, including yours truly. I got mildly drunk and sang for half the night.

In the morning, when I awoke and surveyed my domain – Mrs Mac's at present somewhat disorderly room – and my lovely wife lying beside me – all this, mind you, in spite of my facial disfiguration – I felt that all was right with the world. The future looked exceedingly rosy to me.

Later, I thought of Ben's wedding, and, with that, of Ben himself, and I fervently prayed that none of us would clap eyes on him again.

Actually, I was out of luck, for it was only two months later when I met him. And, of course, that meant trouble as usual.

November it was when I saw him, and he gave me a résumé of his story. I'll omit Ben's over-flowery language, and tell you that part in my own way.

CHAPTER ELEVEN

For absenting himself while awaiting overseas posting, Ben was sentenced, by court-martial, to fifteen months' detention in the original glasshouse at Aldershot. The sentence might have been lighter, considering his short period of absence, and Ben reckoned it would have been, if his defending officer hadn't been such a 'bampot'. (His own words.)

Most probably, Ben's arrogant, insolent manner had been a strong contributing factor in determining the length of sentence.

Anyway, the Detention Barracks received him with, if not exactly open arms, open mouths, at least. They shouted and bawled at him doubling him all over the place, till his shirt felt like a piece of damp wallpaper clinging to his back and he didn't have enough air left in his lungs to blow out the candles on a first birthday cake. And all the days afterwards were just the same. They opened your cell in the morning, and 'sherricked' you till they closed the door at tea-time.

As one would expect, Ben hadn't been in the barracks a month before he was 'doing his nut' regularly. Smashing up his cell, reading the riot act on parade, refusing to do this, that and the other, and generally making a nuisance of himself. The other prisoners wondered if he was trying to work his 'brief', or if it was a genuine case of stir-happiness. As I have already stated, I have my own doubts about Ben's sanity.

Albeit, he spent most of his time consuming bread and water, or gruel and potatoes (the secondary punishment diet), and losing the appropriate remission of sentence.

One of the other prisoners was a small stocky hard-case from Govan, Bandy Johnson, who was just finishing a two-year sentence. His job was to keep the gallery and arches on Ben's landing clean, so he saw quite a lot of Ben. He and Ben had a great deal in common, and they struck up an acquaintanceship, which was as near friendship as such people get. The other prisoners Ben completely ignored, and the Staff Corps warders got nothing but abuse from him, which was sometimes rewarded with a clout on the lug. Unofficially, of course.

Ben finally 'lost the head', and wired into one of the screws, after which the commandant sent him to consult with a couple of psychiatrists, pending a further GCM.

During his sessions with the 'trick-cyclists' he became convinced that they were the 'potty-cases' rather than he. Maybe association with weak minds was the cause, he decided. Maybe mental deficiency was contagious. One of them kept plucking at Ben's cheek and calling him his little man, till Ben felt like spitting right in his eye. But he calmed down with the thought that the medico might OK his IQ on the QT just for spite. So he decided to watch his Ps and Qs.

They brought out their books with the silly little puzzles, told him to fit sillier shapes in their own receptacles, and asked him the silliest questions. And all this only made him think. 'Well if I wasn't barmy before this, these fellows are liable to drive me that way.' Maybe they did. For he had only completed four months of his sentence, when he was 'papped' out of the Armed Services – 'grade sausage'. A psychopathic personality, they called him.

Shortly afterwards, Johnson, on completion of his sentence, got his dishonourable discharge.

Ben was suspicious about Jenny's movements during his absence, and you couldn't blame him for that. He omitted to inform her of his impending arrival, and arranged his journey so that he would reach Glasgow around nine o'clock on the evening of October twenty-eighth.

Jenny wasn't home when he got there, and the landlady imparted some very disturbing information. He didn't have to twist her arm. She volunteered the fact that she seldom, if ever, saw Jenny of a night. In fact, quite often, she (Jenny) failed to show her face

112

until morning, and then she would lie in bed all day, waiting for cups of tea to be brought to her, and she (the landlady) wasn't fit to be running after people all day, and she (Jenny) should have enough sense to know that, and she (the landlady) didn't know what the young women nowadays were coming to.

Ben had an idea that the landlady had been well paid for the additional services, but where would the money come from? It was oh so obvious. And now that he was home, the landlady knew that the hobbies would be put on the goose that laid the golden eggs, so it was no skin off her nose when she gave Ben the wire.

Just when he thought the garrulous woman was going to have him climbing the walls, she suddenly remembered something she had to see a neighbour about, and left, while Ben closed the door behind her and lay, fully-clothed, on top of the bed, his eyes closed.

He felt like crying, and probably did. That was the way Jenny had him, although he would never admit it to anyone, least of all her. 'I married a "brass",' he kept telling himself, and it sounded like the title of a book. Only it wasn't fiction. It was all too true. And what to do?

He woke with a start but didn't get up immediately. For a moment he thought he was back in the Glasshouse, then reality returned to him. He lay awake, listening for sounds of activity in any part of the building or out on the streets, wondering what time it was, since he had no clock.

You could have cut the silence with a knife. He pulled a packet of Players from his pocket and lit one, then shivered as the chill night air crept through his bones. He drew the heavy patchwork quilt around him, and continued to smoke.

He was halfway through the cigarette and leaning across the bed, discarding ash, when the old-fashioned clock in the kitchen began chiming. One! He waited. That was all. One o'clock in the morning and Jenny still absent. Seemed it was one of her stay-away nights.

Suddenly a decision came to him. Any kind of activity was better than lying here. He would have a look around the city. He was through the door before both arms were in his jacket sleeves.

He checked the coffee-stall at St Vincent Street. There were lots of street-women, pimps, queers and others, but no Jenny. He accepted a couple of swigs of whisky from a Yank, and bought him a cup of coffee in return. The Yank had plenty to say about that coffee, and what Yank hadn't. But Ben didn't pay much attention. He was impatient to be off. The Yank turned his head to speak to a young woman with an old face, and Ben seized his opportunity.

As he hurried away a group of troublesome words were hammering at his frantic mind. 'Some other Yank might be talking to Jenny at this minute,' he was thinking. 'Talking – aye – or even worse.'

He had a look at the Broomielaw and St Enoch Square stalls with the same negative result, and, finally, after an unsuccessful inspection of the crowd at the Charing Cross stall, he made his despondent way home, his mind in a turmoil, and his stomach in a mess, with a series of sausage-rolls, pies and coffees, which were all having three rounds there. The whisky, which was the first he'd touched in months, was making a poor job of referee, and his nerves, which were sitting on ringside seats, were jumping about something awful, just as excited fight fans do.

In his room he spent half an hour trying to fill a pail with vomit, then fell back on the bed to doze fitfully.

When Jenny ambled in at nine a.m., he was wide awake and in a murderous mood. Grabbing her arm, he shouted, 'Where the hell have you been a' night?'

Wincing at the painful grip on her arm, she faced

114

him squarely.

'Where the hell dae ye think?' she replied, not yet realizing her danger.

He lifted his free hand in a threatening gesture and repeated his question, only louder, 'Where have ye been?'

Fear now showed in her eyes.

'Leave me alane. Ah wiz only up on a lassie's hoose,' she answered, breathing whisky-fumes all over him. That was all he needed. His stomach retched with a memory, and a wave of anger and feverish blood rolled over his head, to break with a roar at his temples.

'An' did the lassie wear troosers? Ya durty cow!' he yelled, slapping her across the face with the back of his hand. The fight might have ended then, physically, and continued as a verbal battle, if Jenny had 'screwed her bobbin'. Instead she was either foolish enough, or more likely, drunk enough, to attempt retaliation, and suffered the consequences. He got steamed right into her, and how, I must admit, I would have loved to see that.

After he'd beaten her black and blue, ignoring her screams, he threw her on the bed, saying, 'Ah should throw you oot on the street. That's whit you're due.' She lay on the bed sobbing her heart out, while he continued, as he stamped about the room. 'You're a "no-user" an' yet Ah'm stuck oan ye. Ah need ma heid examined.' He smothered the pity that he felt for her. He hated to see her cry, but she'd deserved all she'd got and more, for he knew, deep in his heart, that she'd been 'playing a hard game'. That was an irrevocable fact, but there was nothing more he could do about it. He wondered if he could ever forget. He doubted it.

'Listen,' he shouted, in an effort to drown the sound of her sobs. 'There's wan thing sure. Ye've been "at it". Ah know that as sure as Ah know ma ain name.

115

But get this straight, if Ah catch ye lookin' at anither man again – Ah'll kill ye. Sure as chrise Ah wull.'

On the bed her body trembled, but her mouth still wasn't under control.

She stopped crying for a moment and said, 'Ah'm gaunny jail ye for this.'

Ben nearly 'done his nut' again.

'Squeal on me, ya bastart?' he roared. 'You'll only bring the "grass" tae me wance, an' ye'll never live tae talk aboot it.'

The conversation continued in much similar vein for a while, without Ben again lifting his hands, till finally, during a lull, Jenny fell asleep. Ben left her to it, and had some breakfast at a nearby restaurant, by which time the pubs were open, and what more did a bloke need to forget his troubles?

During the next few days they spoke not a word.

In the room, they had an old-fashioned, one-armed couch. Ben slept on that, using the arm as the basis for a pillow.

Sometimes in the forenoons, Ben got up and sat around the house reading the war news in the daily papers, or studying the 'Noon Record' for likely jumpers at the hurdle meetings. Before each mealtime he laid two or three shillings on the table, without saying a word. In the same manner, his wife removed the coins, went out for some 'cadgies', was back in a quarter of an hour, and laid his meal for him. It became a routine.

Any time after noon, he would leave the house to stand at the bookie's 'tishy-board' in the back-court, and his evenings were spent in the pub at the corner. But it was all getting him down, for Jenny, sporting a black eye and covered in bruises, went about her household duties with a face as long as a fiddle. He was yearning for her embraces, but wouldn't even admit it to himself. He thought a change of scenery might do him some good, so he wandered out of the district one day, and that's when I ran into him.

It was about eleven o'clock on a Saturday morning, which to me, and I guess most people, is the best day of the week. Best day, that is, if you have a few bob in your pocket. As it happened, I had left the house with over a pound that morning. Not a lot, but, if you've ever been on the floor on a Saturday, you will know what I mean. The crave for lots of drink was less demanding on me now, and I knew Isa had sufficient money to squeeze by with the week's victual supplies.

It was one of those winter days that make you wonder why we in Scotland look forward to the kind of summer we usually have. A cloudless sky, a sun, which was doing its best to make up for the time it had lost in July, a crisp, fresh feeling in the air, the fact that my ulcers hadn't been bothering me much for a fortnight, and I felt that all was right with my world. It wasn't.

I was enjoying a quiet pint in Danny's bar in Abercrombie Street when Ben walked in and spoiled it. He joined me at the bar, and the ray of sunshine that shone through the window quickly became cooler on my neck.

He was the last person I wanted to be with, but short of snubbing and thus antagonizing him, I could see no way of getting away from him.

We yattered away for about half an hour, Ben doing most of the talking, giving me the crude material for the beginning of this chapter. Then, when I had almost given up hope of escaping his company, I hit on what I thought was a good idea. I might have known.

'Ah don't know whit you're daein' in the afternin, but Ah wiz thinkin' o' gaun' ower tae the tossin',' I told him. I wanted to go up to the house for my dinner, but, if he tagged along, Isa was liable to start the

117

trouble all over again. Ben had never liked tossing-schools, so I might ditch him.

'Is the Shawfield school started up again?' he queried.

'It's been oan for the past two or three weeks,' I said. 'Ah could dae a wi' a wee turn. Things are a bit tight.'

'Ah could dae wi' a wee turn masel',' he said, and my spirits fell. 'Ah think Ah'll take a run ower wi'ye.' Then he asked, 'Who's inty it, noo?'

'The Main Street crowd as usual. Ah hear they're daein' no' tae bad.'

'Ah'll gie ye a walk ower then, an' we'll see whit we can dae.'

Well – there was nothing else for it. My brainwave had taken the usual course and come unstuck. I just had to make the best of a bad job.

'How much gelt have ye got?' I asked him, and added, 'Dae ye fancy hau'fin' it?' He was already counting.

'Whit aboot a half a quid apiece?' he asked.

I took the four half-crowns from him, extracted a ten-shilling note from my trouser-pocket, added it to his money and placed it in my jacket-pocket.

'That'll dae fine,' I said, and we left Danny's.

I saw Isa emerge from the door of a shop on the other side of the street. I couldn't tell whether she saw us or not, but I knew if she had there'd be a quiz programme in the Calton tonight with second prizes for the right answers.

On our way to the dog track we had a couple of drinks in Main Street pubs, for the school wasn't due to start until a bit after one.

For the uninitiated, I had best explain here the workings of the tossing school movement, which is something of an institution in working-class Glasgow.

The school is formed by a small group of men known as 'tollers'. The tollers find a likely site. A back court, or a piece of waste ground, with convenient

118

escape routes, in the event of a police raid. The tossing addicts are then informed by word of mouth that a school is about to start in such and such a place at a certain time. When a number have gathered there, someone is induced to take the first toss and the school starts. Tossing-man is given two pennies, his purpose being to throw them in the air so that they fall to the ground showing two heads. A head and tail showing means a re-toss, and if two tails, tossing-man loses and someone else takes the pennies.

Before tossing-man starts his effort he hands to the tollers his stake-money, which varies according to his own pocket. By-standers are allowed to add to his stake money, and after three successful tosses, the stake money, which is now multiplied by the others to eight times the original amount, is divided in the following way – five parts to tossing-man and his backers, one part to the tollers and the remaining two parts are staked on the fourth pair of heads.

After the sixth pair, tossing-man and his backers can withdraw with fourteen parts, leaving the tollers with two. The tollers have everything to gain, and nothing to lose.

Did I hear you say, 'Very profitable for the tollers?' That's the idea. That's what they're there for.

The tollers handle all the money, while one of their number picks up the pennies, and restores them to tossing-man. With shrewd side-betting a considerable take can be made by the tollers.

But don't get the idea that the customers get nothing. In a reasonably straight school, with the necessary luck, an addict can pick up a packet. That's why they come back. Even after being fined at a police court.

The Shawfield school blew hot and cold, depending on how straight it was being run, and how often the local police force were making a raid. At times, business had become so bad that the site had been abandoned, only to be restarted at a later date.

At this particular time the dog meeting was held during daylight on Saturdays. The present two week-night meetings were not in force because of black-out restrictions. When the Clyde football team, who use the same stadium, were at home, the racing started in the forenoon, and, when the team was playing away, the dogs were brought out later in the day, so the tossing school, also, was later, since it was run for the benefit of the gambling fraternity who followed the greyhounds.

The day we went over the football team was at home.

As we turned the corner of Main Street and our eyes looked along the Rutherglen Bridge, I could see that it was a fairly big school. Anything up to forty men were standing around in a large circle, and, judging by the cash that was lying around at the punters' feet, the tollers should have been quite pleased with themselves. Apparently they weren't. They were walking around the inside of the ring with their faces 'tripping them', half-heartedly calling out, 'Heads up tae two poun',' 'Heads half a croon or a dollar,' or, 'Heads money.'

Here and there, someone would shout in reply, 'Tails a dollar,' or, 'Gie me half a quid ower here.'

No one paid particular attention to us as we found a not too crowded spot, at the edge of the ring. A couple of fellows did condescend to give us a nod of recognition, and immediately turned away to conduct what they considered to be shrewd bets.

Wee Max Baxter, one of our corners boys who had moved down to Bridgeton just before the War, halted in front of us and dropped two florins and a shilling at the foot of a respectable-looking fellow who stood next to us. When the dog meeting finished you got all types at the Shawfield school. Baxter spotted us and nodded acknowledgement.

'How's it gaun', Max?' I asked him, more by way of a greeting than an enquiry as to how the tollers were faring. Max took me literally.

'Dead loss, Bill,' he groaned. 'Wan three pair for fifteen bob, an' that sody-heided mug Tam-the-Bam loast it on the next toss.'

Tam was the kitty holder and side better of the group. It was unusual for the tollers to be doing so bad. There were methods of correcting that.

I leaned over to Max and whispered. 'Whit aboot the two-heider?'

He hesitated, glanced around him and muttered almost inaudibly, 'Aye – Ah think they'll be stickin' it in directly. 'I looked at him hopefully. 'Ah'll gie ye the wire,' he said, and moved on as the cry went up.

'Two tails' came, interspersed with curses and indescribable remarks from all parts of the ring. The side betters didn't like a bloke to show two tails on his first throw.

While the tollers shouted, 'Who wants tae toss them?' I whispered to Ben that the two-headed penny was soon to be used. Charlie Cross, who habitually retrieved the fallen pennies and handed them to tossing-man, could do a neat bit of sleight-of-hand, and, when things were going bad, he made it a cert that tossing-man (and the tollers) wouldn't lose, by means of a simple substitution.

He didn't do it often, mind you. Not enough to make the mugs suspicious, but just sufficient to keep the tollers on the right side if things weren't working out that way.

I watched Max closely. When he gave me the slightest of nods, I turned to the insurance-man type beside me.

'Bet ye a poun' he heads them?' I asked, in just the right tone. I hadn't made a mistake. He was the type of fellow who doesn't try to have hunches, but just opposes everyone's heads on principle. Without saying

121

a word, he handed me a note.

The ring money was on. The pennies were tossed. No messing about. Two heads!

'Is it a bet?' I asked my neighbour, knowing full well that it was, since he was already separating his money.

'You're on,' he answered, handing me two pounds.

The money in the ring was again soon covered, most of the fellows who had bet on the first pair doubling up.

'You're on,' Tam-the-Bam told tossing-man, who threw the coins, from a small piece of wood, spinning crazily in the air to a height of about fifteen feet. A good toss, but as they reached their zenith and began their descent, they collided and, before they hit the ground, one of the punters kicked out at them, and shouted, 'Bar them!'

Only customers betting against tossing-man, in the ring, are allowed this privilege.

The toss was retaken showing first a head, and a tail (on the genuine penny), then two heads. The fellow next to me didn't wait for my offer, but said quickly, "Sa bet,' and handed me another four crisp notes. By this time he was becoming a bit worried-looking.

The pennies inevitably turned up heads again, and the tollers began to pay out tossing-man while my neighbour dug into his pocket.

'How much?' he asked, since I could quite legitimately stop betting after the third pair.

Ben was tugging at my sleeve, saying, 'Come on. We'll get crackin'.' The other fellow interrupted him.

'What? Aren't ye gaunny gie me a chance tae get ma money back?'

I noticed, abstractedly, that, in his excitement, he spoke with a curious mixture of accents. About fifty per cent Kelvingrove 'pan-loaf', and the remainder Calton back court.

I wasn't paying much attention either to Ben's persistent grip on my arm, although I heard him say to the fellow, 'Whit the hell dae ye think we took it aff ye for? Tae gie ye it back?'

I was too busy watching the tollers. I saw Tam slip the tollers' share (three pounds) into Maxy's hand, and my eyes followed him intently as he strolled round the ring, while the others bawled, 'Heads up tae six quid.'

Max was now talking to a tall, thin Lord Derby coat with an Anthony Eden hat on top. There didn't seem to be anything inside these clothes except a coat-hanger with shoulders like a milk bottle. The invisible man held out a hand like a claw, and took the three pounds from Max. A side-bet. The two-header was being retained for one more pair, and the tollers were still Swindle, Robb and Co., so my decision was made for me.

Ben had my neighbour by the lapel now, but I held out a restraining arm. 'Ye can have a bet,' I said, and Ben looked at me like he was ready to throw a fit. As I told you, he wasn't much of a tossing-school hand. He wasn't fly to the game. But he didn't say anything. He was content to wait and see the result of my decision.

'How much?' the insurance man asked, without taking his eyes from the money he held in his hand.

'Eight quid,' I answered, trying to hide my eagerness.

'Eight quid?' he ejaculated incredulously.

'That's the way Ah gam'le,' I told him. 'Bet the lot.'

He peered at me, and the crafty look that came to his eyes would have told me, under normal circumstances, that I was a sucker. A fourth pair of heads is always a bad gamble, even with a good tosser.

The poker face I was striving for must have been achieved.

'You're on,' my neighbour cried jubilantly.

'Last bet, mind,' I told him, and he nodded agreement.

The pennies were tossed with the usual result, and we walked away, but the fly mug alternately gazed

123

after us, and contemplated the two-pounds odd he still held in his hand.

I handed Ben eight pounds, saying, 'If we gie wee Maxy a drink when we see 'im, we'll be fixed up for the wire anither time.'

Ben said, 'Sure – but ye'd ma heart in ma mooth there.' I laughed at the folly of the ignorant. I could afford to.

As we crossed the tramlines at the Main Street end of the bridge, we had to leap for the pavement, to avoid a taxi which came careering round the bend at breakneck speed. Ben made some remark about the driver's parentage, but further along the road he soon cheered up. He was flush.

We were too late to get a drink, since the pubs shut at half-past two, but it wouldn't be too long till five o'clock.

CHAPTER TWELVE

We spent about an hour in the Workmen's Club at Bridgeton Cross, playing snooker, and when Danny's bar opened, we were there on the dot. We were the only customers, so we challenged Danny and his head waiter to a game of dominoes. Then, who walks in but Max.

I thought to myself, 'He's not long in coming in for the drink we owe him,' and ordered a half and a beer for him.

He said, 'Cheers,' and knocked back the half. Ben bought him another.

He stood, watching us play, while we all spoke of nothing in particular. But when Ben played the two-five and knocked the table to signify he was 'away' and I went 'domino' with the last five, he said, 'Ah wantit tae speak tae yese aboot somethin'.'

I lifted the half-pints Ben and I had won, Ben ordered another three whiskies and we moved over to the domino-table by the fire. When we were settled in our seats comfortably, Max spoke.

'We had a visit fae Gunn efter yese left,' he told us, watching our expressions as he did.

Speaking for myself, I haven't a doubt that the emotion of fear was plain on my face. I had a feeling that we were going to finish up mixing it with Shooter Gunn, and that would be no party. I didn't like it a bit. Shooter Gunn was a top-class 'nutter', and, as both his surname and nickname implied, he was in the habit of appearing on the scene with a pistol, usually a Luger, which was easily acquired from some of the visiting servicemen at the coffee-stalls. All you needed was a few quid and the nerve to carry one.

I extracted a Woodbine butt from my ticket pocket, tore the edge off a newspaper that was lying on the seat, folded it and lit my dog end, singeing my 'tash' in the process, while Ben made complicated circular designs on the table top with the wet bottom of his beer glass. We both sat in silence, waiting patiently for Maxy to speak. Danny stood watching us with the barman's inherent curiosity, as he served a newly arrived customer. His waiter had gone downstairs to water up the whisky, or whatever publicans' assistants do down in their cellars.

As Max started a lengthy, detailed description of the afternoon's happenings, following our departure from the tossing, I searched Ben's face for sentiments similar to my own. Searched in vain. There was not a vestige of fear there. Ben was probably as much of a nut-case as Shooter, only he didn't take kindly to firearms. Confidentially, I don't think he could make a bullet hit a cow's crapper if he was holding it by the tail.

The gist of Maxy's tale was as follows.

A taxi, probably the one which had all but bowled us

over, drew up at the car-stop next to the dog-track gate. A trilbied figure hopped out of it, but no one paid any attention till he got nearer, when some of them noticed the gun in his fist. Then they all stood around like the audience in a mass-hypnotism show.

The intruder pushed some of the punters aside and walked round the ring, picking the money from the ground. Occasionally he pulled a few pounds from some unsuspecting fellow's clutch, and some of them even who had been fly enough to sink their money were unlucky, when he stopped here and there to dip his hand in a jacket-pocket. He seemed to be able to tell by an expression when this would be worthwhile.

Most of those present, especially the tollers, knew him by reputation, if not by sight, and didn't dare to move. But one stranger protested and attempted to retrieve five single pound notes that lay at his feet. A shot rang out, and the soil beside the stranger's foot was scattered as the bullet hit the ashes.

'The next yin'll be in your belly,' Shooter grunted, as he gathered the remainder of the money, and, with a contemptuous backward glance, ran across the open ground, into the taxi and away.

The punters put up a squeal. A big squeal. The tollers had a job trying to pacify them. Some of them thought that the tollers should return the stolen money, which was, of course, impossible. While others even hinted that, in their opinion, it was all a cut-up between Shooter and the tollers. In other words, they said that the whole thing had been arranged. The upshot of it all was that a lot of the punters swore that they'd never come back. Maxy looked quite perturbed at the end of his tale.

It wasn't a very unusual story to hear. Such things do happen at the various schools. An occupational hazard. But the raids are seldom carried out by a single individual, and the use of a gun is a rare factor.

Next, Max got to the crux of his conversation,

126

which Ben, for one, seemed to be expecting.

'We've a proposition tae put tae yese,' he said. 'We want yese tae come ower an' staun' by, in case Shooter turns up again.'

I didn't like the way my heart jumped and clogged my windpipe, leaving me with two Adam's apples. I stood up and walked over to the bar.

'Anither three haufs,' I told Danny. I could have drunk them all myself.

He poured them out expertly and without looking at his hands. His eyes were too busy; watching me closely, trying to figure our conversation from my worried look. I felt as if my slip were showing. I shrugged the feeling off, braced myself, and walked back to the domino-table, the drinks in my hand.

'We were gaunny get some o' the hard men fae Brighton,' Maxy was saying, as I placed a small glass beside his elbow, 'but they're a' kinn' a hedgy aboot Shooter.' I didn't blame them. As the Red Indians always say, 'He heap bad medicine.' 'Big Mick Muharg wad've entertained him,' Maxy mused, talking more to himself than us, 'but he got a laggin' at the last High Coort.'

'We heard aboot that,' Ben interrupted, but Max continued as if he hadn't noticed.

'Dagger Dixon mighta had a buzz, but he went doon tae the "Smoke" three weeks ago. He's gettin' rung in wi' a London "grovet-team".' Maxy kept scrutinizing our faces while he spoke, and my innermost thoughts were making me feel uncomfortable. I was in an awkward position. As Ben's side-kick I had a certain reputation, and with that name I wasn't supposed to hedge. The only trouble was I was scared. Dead scared!

'If we don't get somebody,' Maxy pointed out. 'Gunn'll likely keep comin' back, an' the ba'll be oan the slates as faur as the school's concerned,' and, after a pause, 'Ah thoaght o' youse through seein' yese ower there the day.'

I was putting light to another butt, a feat which, in my nervousness, I found extremely difficult. The charred end of the cigarette kept moving away from the flame. Maxy gulped down some beer and replaced his glass.

'It wizny a bad wee school, tae,' he sighed, fatalistically, as if referring to someone who had just been interred. 'We were just beginnin' tae get it built up.' He looked at Ben intently. 'But yese don't fancy it – dae yese?' he finished.

I, too, was looking at Ben. I could see what his reply was going to be and I didn't like it one bit. If I had been really game, I'd have got up and walked out. But I didn't. I was probably more scared of Ben than of Shooter, or anyone else. I had already tasted the grapes of his wrath.

'How much is in it for us?' Ben asked, but I knew that the money involved was only a secondary consideration. Ben would take on the task for an opportunity to 'do' the Shooter fellow, and thus enhance his own reputation.

'We-e-e-ell. We could gie yese an even cut wi' the rest o' us,' Maxy answered. 'Whit could be fairer than that?'

'Whit could be fairer?' Ben repeated. 'Who's talkin' aboot bein' fair? Whit are ye tryin' tae gie us? You're bang in trouble an' yese know it. An' it'll cost yese money tae get oot of it. Noo is that no' fair enough?' He laughed, then quoted his terms. 'Oor whack'll be hauf o' whit yese draw, an' if it's gaun' bad, ye'll need tae guarantee us three quid apiece.' He hadn't completely forgotten the financial side of the affair after all.

Maxy looked flabbergasted, sitting there with gaping mouth and stark incredulity appearing in his eyes. Ben's demands had surprised him somewhat. Silly billy. He might have had the sense to expect something like that. Then again, maybe he had imagined, like me that the lure of a barney with Shooter would be sufficient incentive.

'Aw, wait a minute, Ben,' he mumbled, slowly getting to his feet. 'Ye know the rest o' them'll no' have that.'

Ben looked at him and sniggered, and you've no idea of the feeling that sound evoked in me. Ben was pioneering Widmark's gimmick.

'Well, it's up tae them,' he said, with an air of finality that brooked no argument, but with the self-satisfied grin still evident on his countenance. 'They can have hauf o' whit's gaun' between them, or they can have "sweet" if the Shooter fella sickens the school.' While Ben laid down the law he was smirking like a soldier-daft bloke with a new stripe.

Max finished the drop of beer, and I had an idea that it wasn't only the liquid that made his Adam's apple bob up and down like a monkey on a stick.

'Ah'll see whit the rest o' them say, onywey, an' Ah'll let ye know,' he said, pulling the back of his jacket down and shooting out his neck nervously. The fly-man gestures become automatic and one uses them without thinking. With Danny's eyes on him he walked away from us, but before he passed through the door, Ben couldn't refrain from firing a parting shot at his rear.

'There's nothin' tae stoap us fae comin' ower,' he laughed, 'if Gunn dizny.'

Max glanced back with a deadpan expression, but hurriedly continued on his way. Sensible fellow.

I looked across at Danny. He had overheard at least that last remark, and his curiosity was killing him. I thought that it might if he tried to satisfy it. Ben didn't like questionnaires. Fortunately Danny didn't give him one.

While we sat over another couple of drinks, I tried to transmit my views of the coming stramash to Ben, but he wasn't in a receptive mood. For that matter, when was he, ever? He had a bit of a dictator complex. On the spur of the moment he made decisions, then he took the spur if everyone concerned was not in complete agreement with him. You just had to string along, or have a battle with him, and I wasn't up to it.

I knew that the Brighton division would accept his terms for the present. Better to get 'a leaf oot the orange than nane at a'.'

I also knew that the orange was likely to be proved a blood one before very long, yet I finally agreed to accompany him on his guard duties. If I had failed to appear he would have hunted me down, which I knew all too well.

For a couple of weeks nothing much happened. We attended the tossing during each session, and received quite a bit of money in return. We were due it, I thought, and more.

I was drinking all I could get my hands on, even more greedily than usual. Menuhin could have played Hungarian dances on my nerve-fibres, and, although the booze doesn't help things much, under such circumstances putting a glass to one's mouth can become a completely involuntary action.

Isa noticed the state I was geting into and was worried. I could see it in her eyes, and was able to understand that. I was a bit worried too.

I saw very little of her during that time. Apart from any twinges of my guilty conscience the sight of her might set in action, she was nagging me continuously about the drink, and I avoided her as much as possible. At any moment I expected her to be told about my renewed companionship with Ben, then there would be hell to pay. But surprisingly enough the wagging tongues kept still on my account.

One afternoon the school was nearing its final stages, and I stood among the crowd on the opposite side of the ring from Ben, my thoughts fighting clear of the mists of uncertainty that had enveloped them since we had first joined the group at one o'clock.

'Well,' I told myself, 'this is another day nearly past and no signs of Gunn.' The usual talk was going on around me but I heard none of it. 'Maybe he won't come back,' I added in an effort to comfort myself. My thoughts might have been a prayer, considering the state of nervous tension I was in, but I chased them into other channels. 'Anyway, it's not a bad wee turn we're getting here.'

My eyes were glued to the Rutherglen Bridge directly facing me, and one part of my mind was calculating that there must be about twenty quid in the kitty – a 'flim' each for Ben and me – when I heard the engine of an approaching motor-car.

Oh no! Plenty of traffic passed that particular spot all the time, but I had an evil premonition about this vehicle before I clapped eyes on it, and my pregnant mother hadn't been frightened by a gypsy fortune-teller. It was just one of those things, and it certainly gave me the shakes. I suddenly realized that the cab was coming towards us via Shawfield Drive, a short houseless street with a public park on one side, that forms one part of the triangle which is the dog track.

I turned my head as the taxi drew up at the kerb, and Shooter hopped out, gun in hand.

All eyes were turned in his direction, except for a couple of fellows who stooped to collect the cash at their feet. Gunn's eyesight must have been pheno-menal, for the semi-darkness that comes with a late winter afternoon, and the crowded pitch, deterred him none.

'Drap it!' he called out gruffly, waving the wicked-looking black muzzle in the shortest of arcs. 'If onybuddy touches ony o' that gelt Ah'll blaw his brains oot – if he's got ony.' He strode over with watchful eyes and, as before, pushed some of the punters aside to get to the centre of the ring, where he

131

stood feet apart, and surveyed the gathering. 'The furst wan tae move'll no' move faur,' he warned.

I had my malky, unopened, in my hand, where it had rested since the car-engine brought on the hunch, but I couldn't grip the weapon properly for the sweat that was oozing from the pores of my palms. With one corner of my eye, I glanced across the ring, but could see no sign of Ben.

'Gawd a'mighty!' I thought with one half of my brain, 'he's beaten it!' while the other half continued to sweat. What was I to do now? I hadn't expected the game fellow to run away. I wished I had thought of that a few moments ago – and acted on it.

Tam-the-Bam interrupted my thoughts.

'Well – whit are yese waitin' for?' he asked from my side.

Shooter's hearing was every bit as reliable as his sight for, although Tam had spoken in the merest undertone, and Gunn was a bit away, he strode over, all the time wagging a reproving gun-muzzle at us.

'So this is him?' he said as he faced me. 'Ah heard yese had got a "sticker" in case Ah came back.' He laughed: a hard rattling croak that chilled the marrow in my bones, while his red-rimmed eyes raked me up and down, till I felt the clothing, skin and all, were being torn from my body. Finally, with his glance resting on my scar, he said in a ridiculing tone, 'Yese mighta got a right hard case when yese were at it, instead o' a bampot like this. Have a pipe at the "second prize" he's cairryin'.'

All the time he was speaking, the gun was pointing directly in line with the pit of my stomach, and it was as if I was paralysed as I waited for his finger to tighten on the trigger and send a bullet in among my dinner. He was crazy enough to do just that, but a faint ray of hope glimmered somewhere at the back of my head. His contempt might save me. The only thing that moved about me, at that moment, was a trickle of perspiration that ran from my forehead down the side of my nose, the salt making my eyes smart in passing. I didn't even blink.

Now, without moving the gun, Shooter turned his head towards Tam, to let him see just how dangerous he thought he was. Or maybe he wanted me to try something. He wasn't the only one.

I still had my hand down by my side, but it was no longer rigid. Seemingly without a word of command from my brain the fingers were now, slowly, easing out from its handle the blade of my razor, and all the time I kept telling myself, 'This fellow's really barmy enough to pull that trigger right now. Remember the stories you've heard about him.' But the words that were being scrawled on my grey matter had no effect on the movement of my delinquent right hand.

Again he faced in my direction. 'Well – ah'm waitin',' he muttered aggressively, while he kept the gun concentrated on my midriff with a fist that was as steady as a rock. 'Whit are ye gaunny dae?'

That was, as the Yankees say, the sixty-four dollar question. If Al Capone and Jack 'Legs' Diamond had been friends of mine, and, if they had been with me right then, I would have soon given him an answer to that. As it was, here I stood, a sweating craven, with a gun in my gut, and a razor in my hand that could have been a toothpick for all the chance I was likely to get of using it. He repeated the question angrily, urging me to start something.

'Ye heard me. Whit the hell dae ye think you're gaunny dae?' All around us people held their breath in anticipation, while I tried to control my panicking reflexes.

I had my chib completely ready. I was wondering how I could possibly give him it, and, at the same time, avoid a bullet, when I perceived behind Gunn, the slightest of movements in the crowd. They were parted and Ben was sliding through.

133

Shooter must have noted the slight directional change in my eyes, for he quickly swivelled his head in an over-the-shoulder glance. It was just like one of those poses that the screen's glamour-queens have been doing on publicity stills for years. But I didn't stop to admire it. This was my chance. It was now or never.

If I stayed put, I looked a cert to stop a bullet when Ben went at the tackle, so I moved. Towards Gunn, but obliquely, so that the muzzle was no longer in line with my guts. I sprang to his right side, in the same movement bringing my razor up and then down on his wrist. I felt a shock run up my arm as the weapon bit deeply into the bone. His finger jerked on the trigger, the deafening report of a single shot at close quarters smote my ears. I felt the wind of the passing slug as it tore through my open jacket, and a bloke at my back fell to the ground, clutching his knee. The sobbing screeching yell his throat emitted bore down on my ears like some new form of torture.

While I was making my move, Ben had been dealing in his own expert manner with Gunn's face, and, when the pistol dropped to the ground, its owner's left hand seemed undecided whether to clutch his injured arm or protect the remainder of his face. Ben helped him decide when he gave him another blow on the face, and I, for the moment seized with an all-powerful rage, since a split second before this character had contemplated killing me, aimed a blow at his belly with my shoe. It connected with his thigh. His left hand changed its mind again and gripped the leg, as he curled up like a concertina. On his way to the ground I noticed two or three other boots land on various parts of his anatomy, and I felt sick.

I had to get away from there. Away, from Ben and his razor and his happy, crazy grin when he used it. Away from the flashback to another night, when I had been at the receiving end. Away from the sight of a man being kicked senseless, near to death, while he lay steeped in his own blood and spewings – kicked senseless by a more-or-less disinterested crowd, who had turned into animals when a fellow they were afraid of no longer was in a standing position. They all kept kicking just to show how happy they were that their miserable few bob was safe.

But, above all, I had to get away from the hands that patted my back serving as a reminder that I was part and parcel of all this.

Fortunately, just at that moment, someone on the outskirts of the crowd shouted, 'Coppers!' and I ran with the rest. Across the bridge I sped, down the steps and along the banks of the Clyde towards the Green. All roads, around that quarter, seem to lead to the Green.

On my way, I threw the bloody razor from me, far into the muddy waters of the Clyde, but I couldn't do that with a memory that will stay with me all the days of my life.

I went home to Isa with my mind made up to forget this stage of my life, and, since I didn't see Ben till a lot of water had passed through the mill, the remainder of his story will be more or less second-hand, but authentic.

Isa and I found comparative peace together, without the ominous shadow that was Ben. Razors, gangsters, police and prisons became things of the past in our lives, while Ben stayed on the bandwagon, or should I say Black Maria, till it was too late to jump off.

About the tossing-school incident. Suffice to say that no arrests were made for the assault on Gunn. He himself was charged with discharging a firearm at someone's leg, but was found unfit to plead. That was understandable enough. After the doing he had got, it surprised me altogether that he was alive to face any charges. I might add that his remaining years have been spent in hospitals, sanatoriums, model-lodging houses and mental institutions.

He was lucky. There were still worse endings for a hard-case, as Ben was destined to find out.

CHAPTER THIRTEEN

Ben had not yet spoken to Jenny. In fact, he had spent very little time in the house, and she, wisely enough, had more or less confined herself to its precincts. She sensed that that was the way he wanted it.

That afternoon, when he sped away from the tossing-school, his twisted mind was glorying in his vicious encounter with Gunn. He knew the word would travel round the city, penetrating even the walls of Barlinnie. And it was nearly a cert that the news would be carried up to the penal prison at Peterhead. He was a big shot now. He had 'sorted' Shooter Gunn. He was happy. Small wonder that, as he made his way home, he had the urge to make up his quarrel with his wife. But the lure of the public-house was too strong while he had money in his pocket, and that's where he went. Then slightly mellowed by a liberal amount of whisky, he trudged up the turnpike stair as a wireless in a house across the landing pipped out ten o'clock.

Still without breaking the marathon silence, they had a cup of tea together while he wondered how to start the reconciliation, without taking himself down a peg. The bloke who had sorted Shooter Gunn couldn't go snivelling to his wife. What he should do, he told himself, was give her another tanking, beating her into submission. That was the way a hard-case's woman expected to live. But you never knew. She might get off her mark first chance she got. Maybe he'd hit her enough.

While he sat musing thus, Jenny began preparing for bed in a manner designed to break down the last barrier of resistance. Then Ben realized that he hadn't held her in his arms for nigh on six months.

He took a large sip of tea and sat back in the chair, pretending to be engrossed in the 'Evening Times', while his brain considered various methods of approach, rejecting each one in turn, for one reason or another. But the stubborn streak in him began to waver as his eyes were drawn to her.

She sat in a low easy-chair facing him, with her frock halfway up her thighs, and, when her fingers reached for the top of the sheer silk stockings, he caught a glimpse of black lace panties, which were, as far as he knew, a recent addition to Jenny's wardrobe. It didn't dawn on him that he had never given her enough money to buy such frills. He was too interested in the garment itself and the anatomy it encased to think about whys and wherefores.

As she removed the stocking at a snail's gallop, he tried to withdraw his eyes or, at least, re-socket the pupils. But after all he was only human.

The frock was up around her waist and he had an unobstructed view of the panties. Funny how such filmy material could radiate heat. The stuff concealed very little, revealed plenty, and as her white flesh gleamed through the semi-transparency, his imagination did the rest.

Jenny went through the same ritual with the other stocking and by this time Ben had broken sweat. He raised the newspapers so that she might not see the result of her manoeuvres, but the temptation was too great, and once more he slowly lowered the obstruction to give himself an uninterrupted view.

She got to her feet and drew the dress up over her head, and Ben noticed that she wore a matching bra that was even more heat-inducing than the other

137

garments. His memory told him that her breasts needed no uplift to mould them into shape, but all the same, the gossamer material, like silkworm product woven by spiders, was a fascinating accessory.

Somehow or other, she got her hair tangled in the zipper of her dress, and stood there struggling, her breasts heaving and swaying with exertion. A real-life pin-up girl if ever there was one.

She ceased her efforts and stood stock-still. 'Gaunny gie me a haun' wi' this, Ben?' she pleaded, and he couldn't resist any longer.

'C'mere ower here,' he gasped, saliva clogging his wind-pipe. She complied, still with the dress covering her head, but he had an idea that her eyes, beneath the cloth, were studying his reactions.

Before he got time to inhale a whiff of her perfume that wafted towards him, she was sitting on the couch, next to his chair, her body turned slightly away, and, as he glanced over her shoulder, he could see the inviting hollow between her breasts.

With trembling hands he freed the strands of hair and removed the frock from her head. But before she could move he encircled her with his arms, cupping his hands and cooing longingly, 'Aw Jenny darlin', Ah've no' hauf missed ye.'

'Me tae,' she sighed, ignorant of the humorous aspect of her words, and, turning towards him, allowed her lips to meet his.

They both uttered the things that are usually said while his hands slid down her back and over her hips, removing their wispy covering. There she lay, flat out on the couch, her eyes brimful of passion, her white teeth biting deeply into her lower lip till flecks of blood showed at the corners of her mouth. This was one of the occasions when Jenny's animal instincts were thoroughly roused; the nearest she could get to love, and Ben was one of the few fellows who could really get her desires stirred. But he, the fool, thought this was a great all-conquering love she felt for him, and he gazed at her adoringly as he uncovered her breasts and lifted her into bed . . .

They were like a couple of newlyweds on waking late next morning. He kissed and cuddled her, she responding eagerly, and both of them reluctant to rise from the bed.

When finally they arose, they did so together, and stood on the carpet in front of the hearth, naked, in passionate embrace, till their goose-pimpled flesh protested, and, with an embarrassed snigger, they hurriedly dressed. Ben was already thinking about tonight and a return to bed.

Over breakfast he told her about the barney the previous day, and she, shrewdlike, inflated his ego a bit, if that were possible.

'You could have a go wi' onybuddy noo, Ben,' she told him. 'You're wan o' the hardest cases in Glesca.'

'Wan o' them?' he queried, partly pretending and nearly wholly in earnest. 'Who's better?' What he meant was 'Who's worse?' and Jenny answered correctly.

'Naebuddy,' she asserted. 'You're the best. Naebuddy could beat ye.'

'That's better,' he laughed, and, placing one hand on the back of her neck, he pulled her lips to his, while his other hand caressed her.

Such conversations became a regular thing with them during the next few weeks. He would report his progress, and she would smile up at him and give him the patter. For the word 'idyllic', substitute 'idiotic'.

Other people, too, helped build up his own opinion of himself. When he visited any of the pubs up the High Road, most of the 'Tims' were rushing to buy him a drink. Some of them asked him to 'hand' them in one fracas or another. He thought it was a compliment to be asked and agreed forthwith.

The little shopkeepers were getting the squeeze.

'Are ye shoart o' gelt?' he would ask whichever of the corner-boys happened to be handy, and, when he got the only possible answer, he would tell them, 'Ah'm a bit shoart masel'. C'mon an' we'll see Santy Claus. We'll no' be long withoot the price o' a drink.'

Then the other fellow would tail along, not because of the monetary consideration only, but also activated by the desire to be an associate of the big-shot. A china of the well-known Ben McNulty. He would swallow his misgivings and follow Ben into the little café or newsagent's shop, or over to the fruit-hawker's barrow, and Ben would open the one-sided conversation thus.

'We're collectin' for the orphans' fund. Ah'll be an orphan in aboot twenty years time.' That was his favourite overture. If the man or woman just stood and looked at him, or showed signs of protesting, Ben showed his teeth. Flashing the razor, he'd say, 'Gie us some cash or Ah'll cut ye fae earhole tae—.' When the shopkeeper took in the razor in Ben's hand, he usually complied. If he still wasn't convinced, he was out of luck. He got a 'sore-face'. Then he was asked again.

Most of them agreed to the first request.

The publicans were also very charitable. They had to be, or a tidy bar and gantry were liable to be slightly smashed up. There's one for you. A paradox if ever there was one where the publicans were Samaritans. This was exceptionally handy at the New Year when everyone was trying to beat the whisky shortage. The 'demand-merchants' didn't have to worry. They just asked, and received, without even paying.

Of course Ben's Hogmanay celebrations ended in a bit of a fight as usual. Three brothers, who were his neighbours, tried to take him apart, and, while everybody was holding everyone else back, the police appeared on the scene. The four of them banded together and had an unsuccessful go at the coppers. Ben got an egg-lump on his skull from a baton. He also had a week-end 'lie-in', but managed to get away with a five-pounds fine, since the charge was left at a simple breach, and the date had been the thirty-first of December.

This encounter with the police only served to build up his reputation more, for his hangers-on spread the word around that Ben had 'had a go wi' the polis'.

Funny thing though – Ben was certainly carrying the luck. All his chibbing, squeezing and other depredations were going unpunished, since nobody saw fit to shop him. Usually there is someone game enough to go to the coppers and give them an opening. In Ben's case nobody did.

Jenny, who was looked on with awe by most of the neighbours, was basking in her husband's glory, and was thoroughly enjoying the passionate love-making that he nightly indulged in. She wanted it to last – but knew it wouldn't. There was that part of her that felt the urge for other men, and it was a hard fight to keep it from taking over. There were moments too, when she wondered how she would take it if Ben backed a deuce one of these days. If someone gave him a right doing. One of the qualities that endeared him most to her was his fighting record. Like the society women who grace the up-and-coming punchers with their favours, her emotions were tied up in a legend. How would it be if the legend was suddenly smashed? And besides, day after day Ben was flirting with danger, in so far as the law was concerned. At any moment, he could be arrested and put out of harm's way for a long period. She knew she wouldn't go a fortnight without male companionship. That was the way she was made.

But most of the time she pushed these thoughts from her, and lived for the present.

However, one thing was rankling in her mind. But she was afraid to broach the subject. Ben was always too busy to take her out, and Jenny was essentially a gallivanter. Contrary to her environment, no country

141

bumpkin she, who would content herself with waiting around her husband's domain for his return. She was glad when that problem was solved, the reason being that her husband met a distant cousin of his, who was, due to some strange twist, liked by Ben. Nowadays, you couldn't expect much sentiment from Ben, but seemingly this was the exception.

One Friday night in February, when they were preparing for bed, he spoke to her about it.

'Wad ye like tae go oot for a wee drink the moarra night?'

She looked at him, surprised, but hesitated not at all with her answer.

'Oh aye, Ben,' she replied eagerly. 'Ah'd like that an awfa loat. Ah get fed up messin' aboot the hoose.'

She laid her hand on his cheeks, kissed her thanks and asked, 'Where'll we go?'

He smiled and patted the part she used for sitting. 'Ower the Soo' side,' he told her. 'Ah telt that cousin o' mine Ah'd bring ye ower. Him an' ese wife run aboot a boozer wi' a sing-song in it.'

Jenny nodded her head. She wasn't fussy where she went as long as she had a convivial evening.

'We'll have a nice quiet night,' Ben continued as she clambered into bed beside him. 'Two or three haufs an' nane o' the "dadlum".' Jenny thought it strange that her husband was going to leave the cheap wine alone for once, since it was meat and drink to him, but she made no comment.

'How much cash have ye goat?' he asked.

'Ah'll pawn a coupla things in the moarnin', an' Ah'll get wan or two messages tae put us ower tae Monday.' She paused. 'Ah should have aboot thurty-bob left,' she mused.

'That'll dae fine,' Ben murmured as he snuggled up to her and sleep overcame him. But Jenny lay awake for a time, contemplating the next evening's excursion. South Side!

On the Saturday, Ben had a few drinks during the 'first-house', spent the afternoon watching the Rangers football team play at Ibrox, then went home for tea, and to collect Jenny, who had, after attending to monetary considerations, nipped into the boozer for a couple of drinks, before half-past two. Just to put her in the mood. Ben wouldn't have minded, she kidded herself, but neglected to mention it.

Ben's cousin, Jackie Sinclair, and his wife were already in the pub when the McNulty's arrived. But the sing-song hadn't yet started, and a few of the seats in the room were still vacant. The clock at the bar said a little after seven when they filled two of the vacancies, and the usual introductions were made.

Ben was meeting Mrs Sinclair for the first time. He found here a complete contrast to her husband – the living proof of the existing attraction between opposites. Whereas she was built like the gable-end of a house, he hadn't as much fat on him as would fry an egg. Add the fact that her five-foot-nothing looked utterly ridiculous alongside his lanky six-foot-plus frame, and viewed together they were like a couple of freaks from a circus. The clothes Mrs Sinclair wore did nothing to correct this illusion. Still, she was a cheery soul, and, when Ben's eyes had become accustomed to the dazzle of this feminine humpty-dumpty with the paint-daubed face, bedecked in multi-coloured frock, hat, coat and shoes, lacking only the neck and cuff ruffles of a clown, the whole of which so obviously, and pathetically, constituted her festive finery, she proved to be good company.

Her husband, too, looked as if he had put on clothes to entertain the public. He was dressed in what can only be described as a suit of potato-bag tweed, which we might say fitted him like a glove. But we won't. Anyway, it was shaped like one. The cuffs of the jacket-sleeves were running up his arms in an effort to get under his armpits, and the lapels were outward-bent to such an extent that a strong breeze might have started a take-off. The seat of his trousers gave one the impression that he'd dropped something, and, from the front, he appeared to be wearing charladies' kneepads beneath his trouser-legs. In short, a scare-crow wouldn't have been seen dead in such attire.

Jenny glanced from Jackie to Ben's faultlessly dressed self, and her already substantial bust mea-surement increased by an inch.

About eight o'clock, when the pub had become rather crowded, and the singing had been in progress for half an hour, someone requested a song from Ben, but he wasn't having any. Not that he wasn't a 'sweet' singer. Everybody always knew he could sing 'sweet'. Anyway, he renegued, and a young fellow in his early twenties elected to perform on his behalf, with the general approval of those present. He got to his feet, inserted one hand in a trouser-pocket and treated them to his arrangement of 'Begin the Beguine', in a manner befitting a corner-boy Caruso. He acknow-ledged the applause with a self-conscious nod and eased himself back to his seat.

Various other entertainers took their turn, with the permission of the resident MC, an old bloke who spoke, and looked, like an ex-sergeant-major, waxed moustaches and all.

Ben and his spouse were content to sit and listen, and sometimes join in, when the company in general was asked to help out with a second chorus. This didn't happen often, since the whole thing was illegal and the police would have been unwelcome guests.

Seated in the far corner, over by the window which had a Guinness advert adhering to it, was a big luscious blonde, who was knocking back halfs like pouring water down a sink, the drinks being provided by two fellows who sat on either side of her. One of them, a fair-haired, quiet-looking chap, who wore spectacles, seemed to be all set for repayment, later in the evening. For a moment Ben wished himself in another's shoes. He glanced from the woman's low-necked frock to the advert above her head. Looking downwards with popping eyes, was a funny little man with a black moustache. Coming from his mouth were the words, 'MY GOODNESS!' Very appropriate.

As Ben again studied the group, for no apparent reason, he found he was taking a keen dislike to the third member. It may have been due to over-indulgence on Ben's part or even the condescending smirk that dwelt on the fellow's face. Ben didn't think anyone, besides himself, should wear an expression like that. The point was, he didn't seem to have anything to be pleased about. His china had evidently won the blonde's affections, for the moment at least, and he himself had made an unsuccessful attempt at singing 'Ah, Sweet Mystery of Life'. In the middle he had made a right mess of it, and left it for someone else to finish. Since then he had been sitting across the room, glowing with self-satisfaction, and acting as if Moss's Empires had just signed him to a contract.

Ben felt a distinct urge to alter the bloke's expression, a task which shouldn't prove too difficult, considering the fellow wasn't the height for toasting bread at the fire. Remembering the company he was in, Ben managed to control the feeling, and kept his gaze, as much as possible, away from the trio for the rest of the evening.

Nine-fifteen, and a quarter of an hour to closing time. Ben and Jackie left their wives in the room, while they moved to the bar to purchase a 'carry-out'. The beer and stout were lined up on the counter, and Jackie was counting out the coins, when Ben glanced in the direction of the room they had just vacated, and realized that his dislike for the wee 'nadger' hadn't been misplaced, for the said nadger was, at the moment, leaning over Jenny, engaged in animated conversation with her. Ben didn't like strange men or half-men talking to his wife during his absence.

With Ben's eyes boring through him, the little fellow suddenly clamped his mouth shut, straightened his back and pulled down the rear of his jacket. Gripping his cuffs with his fingers, he pushed open the glass-panelled door and swaggered over to the 'Gents' at the end of the L-shaped bar. Ben's eyes were still focused on him when the door swung to.

Ben turned to Sinclair, saying, 'Hing oan a minute tae Ah go tae the "Houses o' Parliament",' and followed the wee nadger.

'Whit were ye talkin' tae the weemin aboot, Shorty?' he asked. 'Or wiz it private?'

The wee fellow's lack of stature was accompanied by an understandable nervousness. He turned as white as a detergent advertisement, licked his lips and stammered, 'Ah – eh – Ah wiz – eh – wiz jist – eh – sayin' that it was – eh – a good – sing-song in here, an' – Ah – eh – always enjoy it.' He gulped down a goitre-like lump in his throat while his hands fidgeted nervously with the inside button of his double-breasted jacket.

'Well, enjoy this an' a',' Ben answered, throwing a punch at him. He was afraid his fist would go clean through the other, so there was little or no force behind the blow. For all that the recipient staggered backwards till he hit the tiled wall with his spine, where he slid downwards, and was brought up short with his hindquarters resting in a gutter half-full of water. Ben held up his fist, looked at it wonderingly, then glanced back to the bloke on the floor. 'Noo – wad ye like tae have a wee talk wi' me?' he asked.

The little fellow, still wearing a scared look, shook his head in a negative manner, wiped a trickle of blood from white lips and levered himself unsteadily to his feet.

With a derisive snort and a contemptuous backward glance, Ben left the other to his own devices, and

146

returned to the bar. He was glad he hadn't been carrying a lot of liquor or he'd probably have killed that character. He was angry at Jenny too. She knew he didn't like her talking to strangers. But for obvious reasons he refrained from questioning her in front of their friends.

While filling his pockets with screwtops, he saw the little 'un, with the water dripping from the seat of his pants, join the blonde and her companion, who were now leaving the shop. It just showed you could never tell with women. Seated in the room, the blonde had appeared flawless. Now, viewed from the rear, in a walking position, you'd have thought one of her knees was cheese and the other was trying to eat it.

A couple of minutes later, Jenny and Mrs Sinclair left, followed by Jackie, and lastly, Ben. When he stepped into the darkness of the night he felt a heavy blow on the head that sent him to the ground, partly stunned. The bottle sped off at a tangent to smash against a wall.

One thought was making a valiant attempt to swim above the waves of numbness, while the suction strived to drown in: 'The wee bastart was gamer than I thought he was.'

A tramcar rumbled along in the distance, hurrying, as if the driver could finish his shift earlier than the scheduled time. A woman's voice screamed hysterically, as a boot landed bang in the pit of Ben's stomach, and now the waves of unconsciousness were crashing against the waves of sickness that were wracking his guts. His whole innards were a raging turmoil, and he was far too weak to raise an arm in defence. He had been sitting on his heels. The kick sent him over backwards, after which other boots rained on his body from all sides.

Someone bent over him, grabbed him by a lapel and slashed at his face with a razor.

Strange how a razor could look, not like something

concrete and therefore dangerous, but like abstract matter projected on a cinema screen, while all was darkness around, and there were only the boots to give thought to. The boots that kept striking you till every bone in your body felt like a bunch of firewood.

As he finally blacked out, his last remaining effort was expended in staying conscious long enough to take a bedimmed look at the face of the person who was bending over him. He closed his eyes, satisfied. There was no doubt who the character was – Flash O'Hara!

CHAPTER FOURTEEN

Ben woke slowly, grudgingly, in strange surroundings. All around him were beds. Beds and spotless linen everywhere. He was lying on a bed himself, and he didn't need the smell of ether and disinfectants to put him wise to the fact that he was in hospital.

From the corner of his eye he could see a large bowl of multi-coloured flowers resting on a polished table, and just beyond that an open window. A pair of pretty nurses were stepping smartly about the glistening floor, administering to their charges, and in some other part of the building an accordion band was breaking into the first bars of the signature tune of 'Music While You Work'.

He tried to figure what he was doing in dock. For a moment he couldn't recapture the train of events that had led to this situation. Then his brain began to function in a kind of staggering way, till his memory played a request recording of breaking glass, and he knew it was a screwtop, careering from his head to a wall. The kaleidoscope of boots and razor flashed before his vision, to end with a still that didn't go away, but stayed there to cause a festering sore in his brain. That still was a portrait photo of Flash.

Still thinking about the razor, he attempted to move his right hand towards his face, with the intention of finding out the extent of the damage to that area. The arm's progress was immediately halted, both by the excruciating pain that shot through him, and the bandages that were tightly bound around his body and arms, holding the limb close to his side.

Experimenting, he discovered that his left hand was free. He slowly raised it to his face, only to find that, apart from eyes and mouth, his features were completely covered. Talk about an Egyptian mummy? It had nothing on him in his present state, the only difference being that the mummy couldn't suffer the pain that coincided with any movement of Ben's body or limbs.

As he dispiritedly dropped his hand and relaxed on the soft bed, two men, who were obviously detectives, came ambling along the middle of the ward, side by side, hands in raincoat-pockets and fedoras perched on their heads.

'Well?' one of them asked as he reached his bedside. 'What's your story?' He spoke with an air of disbelief. He was used to negative information, garnered from attack victims in the city. His mate, with a gesture of futility, withdrew a notebook and pencil from his breast-pocket and flopped down on the only available chair.

'Ah wiz in a pub in the Soo' Side, havin' a drink,' Ben answered, as was expected, 'an' a crowd wired inty me when Ah wiz comin' oot.' He refrained from turning even his eyes towards them, but kept staring at the white ceiling above him.

'We already have that part of the story from independent witnesses,' the 'busy' interpolated in a sarcastic tone. 'Now we're expecting you to – enlarge a bit. To – name your assailants.' The detective smirked at his mate and added, 'If you can.' His mate adopted a hopeful look and sucked noisily at his pencil

149

in preparation.

Ben pleaded ignorant. He didn't need any polis to square this up for him. 'Don't know who it wiz,' he said. 'It wiz too dark tae see.' He glanced sidewise and observed the disbelief that dwelt on their faces. 'Straight!' he added.

The busty put on his 'you're-my-pal' look and wheedled, 'Come on now. Don't give us that.'

Ben noticed that the same fellow was doing all the talking. His mate might have been a mute. He just sat looking intently at Ben, without even the slightest flicker of his eye-lids. The other was still speaking.

'Tell us who it was,' he went on, 'an' we'll see that they get the book thrown at them.'

'Straight,' Ben sighed. 'Ah don't know.' He felt too weak to resist the policeman's pressure, but was determined to impart no information.

'C'mon then,' the busy persisted. 'Can you think of anyone who would be interested in giving you a doing?' A dozen names flipped over Ben's brain, but none of them came from his tight lips.

'If Ah could, Ah'd tell ye,' he muttered selfrighteously. 'Z'at no' enough?'

The busy said, 'Don't feel so sorry for yourself. Let us do it for you.' He glanced once more at his mate, who nodded his head slightly.

'We're just dying to feel sorry for you,' the talkative one said, then went as silent as his mate.

Ben was watching a lively sparrow that was hopping about on the open window-sill. He reckoned, due to the stagnant silence, that the detectives had departed, when the spokesman again made his presence felt.

'By the way, the wife was having a drink with you – wasn't she?' he asked, acting as if he had delivered a shrewd observation. Ben didn't get it. This strange change of attack.

'Aye!' he replied. 'How?'

'Yes,' the busy continued, while the other fellow sucked away at his pencil like a Red Indian with a peace-pipe. 'We got that bit of information from a Mr and Mrs Sinclair.' He stood silent for a moment, then barked suddenly. 'There was a little man who spoke to her in the pub?' But Ben was too old a hand to be surprised.

'Ah never noticed,' he muttered, turning his head once more towards the window and the bird, which had now been joined by one of its kind.

'Are ye sure?' the busy asked, and without waiting for an answer, 'Anyway, we'd like to question your wife about him. Where can we get in touch with her?'

Ben gave them the address of his room, since they would find out in any case.

'Oh – we've been there,' said the busy casual-like, watching Ben closely. 'She hasn't been near since you got the doing, which, in case you're not aware, was four days ago.'

He very nearly startled some important information from Ben at that, but, although Ben's brain was reeling with the impact of the statement, force of habit helped him to keep his mouth shut in the presence of the police. As it was, his teeth were grinding in his head, and the coppers knew it, but he didn't care. They could go to hell and back.

A sympathetic grin appeared on the detective's face as he leaned across the foot of the bed, and the chair at Ben's side creaked protestingly as the silent one shifted his fourteen stone, in preparation for getting to his feet. And what feet. His heavy brogues looked as if they had been launched in John Brown's yard.

'Well—,' the speaker said, 'we'll leave you and love you, but I think you're making a bloomer. Think it over. You could do with a bit of help.' Ben eyed him coldly, but he added undeterred, 'You know where to find us.'

The two sparrows flew away, and the busies also,

151

while Ben gazed in hatred at their retreating backs. They disappeared through the door at the end of the ward, and a doctor took over on Ben.

During the ensuing weeks, the physical pain of the knitting of Ben's broken bones and the healing of his facial wounds were only equalled by the mental anguish he suffered. He knew there was but one explanation for Jenny's disappearance, and it wasn't by any means of foul play or abduction. Wherever she was, and whatever she was doing, she was a willing participant, and he didn't need to puzzle over the identity of the person she was with. The man who was occupying her time, while he lay here helpless, was the same man who had left him with a face like a Karloff character.

He did wonder, however, whether the whole thing had been planned, or if it had been pure coincidence, that of all people to be waiting outside the pub it should be O'Hara. He was just as curious as the policeman regarding the identity of the little man, and his conversation with Jenny. It seemed to have some connection with the trouble outside.

Anyway these questions were never answered for him (or for me). Not that it matters a great deal. The outcome would probably have been the same no matter what the circumstances.

The first time the quack allowed Ben a mirror, he nearly went off his chump when he saw the damage. But, after the initial shock, a form of insanity kept him sane, if that doesn't sound too cryptic. An emotion which spelt the beginning of the end for Ben McNulty. A malignant, all-consuming hatred for Flash O'Hara. And, funnily enough, Jenny, the guiltiest contributor to his troubles, faded into comparative oblivion in his twisted mind. To him, she was now a complete nonentity. He had only lost something that he had never had.

Ben didn't send word of his hospitalization to his

152

mother and we didn't hear anything about it until later. Sinclair and his wife stayed away, presumably with an allergy to fighting men and their troubles. So he lay in that white bed for weeks, without even the solace that a visitor can bring the sick, while his arms, ribs and upper leg healed, until, at last, the day arrived when they discharged him, weak, but ready for revenge.

The kindness of the doctors and nurses had done nothing to dilute Ben's hatred for his fellow-humans. Some of the other patients had, at the sister's instigation, made overtures in his direction, only to watch their friendly words flow over him like water on a duck's back. In the early days of his incarceration he had grown a hard shell that had become more impenetrable with time, and, beneath that shell, his soul was being burned up by the fires of vengeance.

At least four of O'Hara's chinas were easily identifiable and he was determined to sort each one, or die in the attempt.

He left the Royal dressed in the same clothes as he had worn on the night of the assault. One of the nurses, without being thanked, had very kindly mended a couple of small tears in his suit, and sponged and pressed it to the best of her ability. Traces of Ben's blood were still evident in the faint rusty-brown stains that decorated the cloth, and, if he had had a bag over his head and face, he'd have looked quite respectable.

When he arrived at his digs, he found that it was as the detectives had said. Jenny hadn't been around and the room had been re-let to a married couple with three kids, and the landlady, who was generous enough to serve him a meal, had a few personal belongings in safe custody. Her man was on the 'Buroo', she explained, and they needed the room money.

She pointed to a bundle of Jenny's clothes that lay in

a corner. 'Whit'll Ah dae wi' them?' she asked.

'O'Hara must have had plenty o' cash tae buy her new claes,' he mused. Then told her, 'Leave them there in case she comes for them. Ah don't think she wull, but she might. If she dizny, ye can dae whit ye like wi' them.' He continued to attack the food.

While the woman alternately sympathised with him, and reiterated her previous diatribe on the character and conduct of the young females nowadays, Ben heard not a word, and prepared to leave.

With his battered suitcase in one hand and, under the other arm, a little battery wireless set he had bought a few months back from a hawker in the Bridgegate open-air market, he bade the landlady good-day and clumped downstairs, his last link with an errant wife severed.

A dealer in the Cowcaddens gave him ten shillings for the radio, and he travelled over Govan way to see Bandy Johnson.

In the street and on the tram he was naïvely unaware of the furtive glances that were directed at him, until, as he rose to disembark, his suitcase collided with the head of a small boy who was accompanied by a drab-looking young woman who had another infant in her arms. The boy turned around, trying to force some tears to his eyes, though the case had done no more than glance off him. When he got a look at Ben's coupon he didn't need any encouragement for crying. He yelled blue murder while his mother prepared to do battle for him. Then, when she also had taken a look at his face she changed her mind.

Ben ignored them completely, pushed past the clippie who was collecting a fare and jumped off the tram.

Bandy was at home when Ben called.

'Gawd stiff me!' he ejaculated on sight of Ben's face. 'What happened tae you?'

154

'Ah ran inty a bit o' trouble,' Ben answered shortly.

'Ye didny hauf. Ye look as if ye'd run inty a wa',' Bandy joked, then bit his tongue on seeing Ben's changing expression. 'Who done it?' he gulped.

'Some o' that bloody Dagger mob, the bastarts.'

Bandy was silent for a moment. 'Well, if it's a hander you're lookin' for,' he said, 'ye don't need tae ask twice.'

'It's no' that, Bandy, but thanks onywey,' Ben said as he laid his case down in a corner. 'If Ah need wan, Ah'll let ye know.'

'Och, that's a' right. Ah'm wi' ye onytime,' Bandy replied.

By this time Ben was comfortably ensconced in an armchair by the fireside. The house was a room and kitchen, sparsely furnished with old-fashioned pieces, but spotlessly clean, which fact, to Ben, was surprising, since he knew that Bandy was unmarried, and he had lived alone for the past four years, since his mother had died. His father was the original unknown soldier and Bandy's mother had never mentioned him.

Bandy opened a packet of Woodbines that rested on the mantelpiece, and, after they had lit up, Ben told him the sorry tale, ending with a request for a couple of weeks' kip, till he got things squared up, as he put it.

'Ah wiz gaunny get fixed up in wan o' the models,' Ben explained. 'But Ah've goat tae have somebuddy tae talk tae. Either that, or Ah'll be gaun' aff ma chump proper, an' Ah don't want onythin' tae happen tae Ah get ma hauns oan that bastart O'Hara an' ese muckers.' He turned to face Bandy. 'Efter that,' he said, 'Ah don't gie a "donald".' Venom literally poured from his emotion-moistened eyes, as he nervously opened and closed his fist, rubbing his fingertips on the palms of his hands.

'He's in a helluva state,' Bandy thought as he watched him, 'and it's no wonder – being left with a coupon like that.' Ben's face would make most people turn away in horror, even in Glasgow where a fair number of scarred faces are to be seen.

Bandy told Ben he could stay, but, at the same time, he decided that he would avoid Ben's company as much as possible. He didn't like everyone to be looking at him, and how could you avoid it if your constant companion was a fellow with a face like a fish supper.

He gave Ben the use of the room and the few pieces of furniture that were in it. The bed was exceptionally comfortable, covered with a spotless patchwork quilt, and Ben was quite satisfied.

Occasionally Bandy drank a pint with Ben, but always left him as soon as possible and he wouldn't see him again till the small hours of the morning. Most of the time Ben spent roaming the streets of the Gorbals in search of his enemies. In vain he patrolled the district, failing to encounter any of them, so that he began imagining things. He thought that the word had gone round that he was in the vicinity, and that everyone was informing against him.

In fact there had been some talk, a certain amount of speculation as to how things would go when the antagonists met face to face. At the street corners, in the pubs and around the bookies' boards, there had to be some topic of conversation. It might be Celtic and Rangers, or it might be how the hot-pot favourite for the three-thirty got beat, or, depending on the character of the conversationalists, it could be a discussion about who was 'inside', who had done what 'job' or what 'job' was worth doing. But when other subjects had exhausted themselves, and sometimes before that, someone would say, 'Ah wun'ner whit O'Hara'll dae when him an' McNulty get thegither.'

Indeed, in the local phrase, Ben was the 'talk of the wash-house'.

One night he was in a boozer in Crown Street,

when an old friend of his father's appeared on the scene.

Ben was standing in a corner by himself when a bit of a commotion started at the other end of the bar, next to the door. He looked uninterestedly in that direction. He could hear the waiter's voice raised in anger. 'You're not on – Ah telt ye. You're barred, an' that's it finished.'

Another voice was shouting, 'Ya baw-faced bastart. Bar me, wad ye? Ah'll redd the bloody shoap wi' ye, so Ah wull. Come roon this side an' Ah'll wrap wan o' your stinkin' pints roon your fat neck.'

Ben amusedly watched the waiter charge towards him, hurry through the little opening and back along the other side of the counter, his fat buttocks bouncing till it seemed they were about to fall to the floor. Suddenly the grin disappeared from Ben's countenance. He had edged away from the bar and could now see the waiter's opponent. It was Limpy Meikle, who had once been a china of Ben's old man. Ben hadn't seen him for years. He hadn't changed much. There he was, close on seventy, with a wooden-leg, and he still had the cheek to throw his weight about! Ben dived along the bar just as the waiter grabbed Limpy by the shoulder and pushed him towards the door.

'A minute, Fat-ass,' he shouted, waving his open razor.

The waiter stood stock-still, mouth agape, while Limpy shrugged himself free, then he suddenly struck out at the fellow's chin. Down the fat fellow went on his ample back. Ben didn't stand on ceremony. He stood on the waiter. Literally. Right on the fellow's face, Ben ground his heel. The waiter squealed like a pig, and Ben and Limpy walked out, with an old crone taking up the rear.

Further along the road they entered another pub

and the old fellow 'stood on his hands'. 'Three "jags" an'
three beers,' he ordered. They carried the drinks into a
little room at the rear of the shop.

While Ben and the woman were seeing off the wine,
Limpy was praising Ben's prowess as a fighting man.

'Ye certainly showed that fat bastart whit's whit.
Jist like your aul' man used tae dae. He didny staun'
for ony nonsense.' He gulped down the red wine and
took a sip of beer. 'Mind ye,' he said, 'Ah wiz jist
gaunny gie it tae that yin masel'. Ah wadny have been
long in takin' him tae the cleaners. Big mug, that yin.'

Ben wasn't listening to any of Limpy's conversation.
He was studying the third occupant of the room.
Suddenly he spoke to Limpy.

'Where did ye dig up that aul' cow?' he asked, and a
grin twisted his lips when he saw the tears trickle
from the corners of her wrinkled eyelids.

'Here – that's nae wey tae talk,' Limpy cried
indignantly, placing his arm around the woman's
shoulders.

'Whit are ye takin' the spur at, ya sully aul' bastart,'
Ben laughed half-crazily. 'It's no' ma fau't you're
runnin' aboot wi' an aul' wine-moppin' bun.' A throaty
cough broke off another giggle, and Limpy rose
unsteadily to his feet.

'See here—,' he said, pointing an admonishing
finger in Ben's general direction, while the woman
gazed up at her knight in shining armour. 'Ah'm no'
havin' this. Ah knew ye when ye were a smile oan
your maw's cheek. An' watched ye growin' up.' He
illustrated his words by holding his hand out, palm
down, and raising it, while he paused asthmatically for
breath. 'This is the furst time Ah've seen ye for years,'
he continued in a hurt tone, 'an' a' ye can dae is make
remarks aboot ma wumman. Well, Ah'm no' havin' it,
so ye can jist turn it up.'

Ben couldn't make it out. Imagine the aul' yin giving
him such cheek! Him that sorted Shooter Gunn and all

those other hard-cases. Him that Flash O'Hara had needed to be mob-handled to sort, and here's an old wine-mopper shouting the odds at him! He too, got to his feet.

'An' whit are ye gaunny dae aboot it?' he asked, his brows lowering till they met. 'How are ye gaunny stoap me?'

'Ye can get tae hell oota here, onywey,' Limpy shouted, oblivious to the danger, aware only of the tear-riveleted face of the woman at his side and the light of admiration that was now in her tired eyes. '*Get*, bloody sharp an' a' if you're smart. Don't try tae bluff me. Ah can see you're a yella bastart.'

Crazy Ben didn't need any more. He pulled the razor quickly from his pocket and drew it down Limpy's cheek. The woman gave a sort of sobbing moan as Limpy flopped down on the seat. Foolish lady. Ben turned towards her, said, 'Here – you get this stitched an' a'. It'll be a' the wan journey,' and slashed the razor across her face.

Without a sound she joined her champion on the seat, and, when the head-case took another look, he saw that both of them had fainted, or worse. You never knew what shock could do to elderly people. For one partly sane fraction of a second, Ben wondered if he regretted his actions, but it was only a fleeting thought, effortlessly dismissed, and he found that his main concern at present was his own safety.

Looking through the glass top of the partition, Ben perceived that the few customers and bartender hadn't noticed anything. Cold-bloodedly, he wiped the razor on the woman's coat, dropped it in his pocket and left, with no more than a casual glance at the faces turned towards him as he passed.

Out on the street, his feet prudently hurried him off to safety at the quickest pace possible without actually breaking into a gallop. Ben's day of reckoning was slowly drawing nearer but he was too crazy to know.

CHAPTER FIFTEEN

That week-end brought a piece of luck in his direction: bad or good remains a matter of conjecture. He had signed on the 'Buroo' at Golspie Street, and, when he called there on Friday morning, he was told there was no money due. He expected this set-back and had planned accordingly.

Bandy lent him a dollar, so he jumped into the first boozer he espied, had a couple of pints, then proceeded to a little workmen's restaurant near Govan Cross, for a bite of dinner.

The place was full of workers from the nearby shipyards who were on their meal-hour, but he thrust over to a solitary seat in a corner. A pretty red-haired waitress in a flowered overall appeared at his side as if by magic. He glanced up at her and gaped. Facially, she was a dead-ringer for Jenny. For a moment he actually thought it was she, then, on reflection, he decided that her type was easily duplicated.

'Well – are ye gettin' your eyes filled?' she asked as his gaze roved down her shapely body and stopped at her legs. She suited the short clothes she wore. If Cyd Charisse's trams were worth a million dollars, as reported, this bird could have lent Lord Nuffield a few bob. Again he looked at her face.

'For a minute Ah thoaght ye were somebuddy else,' he breathed when his lungs began to function properly.

'An' where did ye meet me before?' was her sarcastic rejoinder, 'Wiz it the River Era?'

'Aw, don't start giein' me ony patter,' he said, scowling and peering around self-consciously. But he needn't have worried. The others were too busy eating. 'Ah wadny touch ye wi' a ten-fit pole wi' crap oan the end o' it. Get me a plate o' totties-an'-mince,' he ordered.

'Who dae ye think you're talkin' tae?' she said angrily. 'Ye canny talk tae me like that, ya—.' There, her inventory stopped. She had already seen expressions such as Ben wore as he now looked up at her. A 'nutter'! And his face brooked no arguments. She walked away and was back in no time with his order, without making further comment.

When he'd eaten everything but the plate, the girl brought him a soggy mess that looked like yellow distemper, and tasted about the same, but was listed as custard. There was supposed to be stewed apple present in the concoction, but he must have taken too big a swallow and missed it.

When he was finished he sat smoking, sipping at the three-leaf shamrock tea and, through the large plate-glass window, watching the hurrying workers jumping on and off trams and rushing in all directions in a frantic effort to have an extra five minutes in their homes while having their mid-day meals.

At last the girl returned and told him that would be one and sevenpence. His own penury, and the girl's nether limbs made him feel ambiguous. He had half a crown left. He handed it to the girl. She glanced at him expectantly. He rose to his feet, told her to keep the change and left, while she bestowed a dazzling smile on him.

Outside, in passing, he glanced through the window and saw her lean over the table to retrieve a soiled plate. There will be no further comment on his thoughts. A man's thoughts should be his own. With some kind of smile doing its best to brighten his face, he went on his way.

About two in the afternoon he made his way to the Public Assistance Office. This is when fate took a hand. Just as he turned the corner, whom did he see coming out of the 'Means Test' but one of O'Hara's

161

pals, a fellow with a nose like a pin-cushion, one eye missing with an ugly scar around the empty socket, and more hair on his eyebrows than he had on his head. You couldn't make a wrong identification here. There were no two people quite like him.

The fellow was counting money which he had probably been paid inside, and was so engrossed in the task that he failed to notice Ben's presence as he turned along the street, with Ben following at a reasonable distance, his 'Means Tests' visit temporarily postponed.

Hairy-Eyebrows halted at the corner, and Ben peered unseeingly into a newsagent's window, while the other crossed the street after allowing a van to pass. Further along Hairy-Eyebrows turned a corner and Ben almost broke into a gallop in his eagerness to get him into sight once more.

Ben was wondering how to set about the One-Eye-Care-For in broad daylight, without repercussions, when he noticed the direction which they were following, and hope arose in his human-kindness-milkless breast. It looked as if the fellow was playing right into Ben's barrow.

A satisfied smirk appeared slowly on Ben's face as he followed his quarry down Plantation Street, across the main drag and over towards the hoists which descend to the entrance of the tunnel beneath the Clyde. This tunnel is utilised mainly by traffic, since it disposes of a very roundabout route between the north and south sides of the river. Because of river traffic there are no bridges below the city centre. It's a sort of Severn Tunnel in miniature, and to Ben it seemed an ideal spot for an attack.

Ben put a spurt on and boarded the lift with a lorry between himself and his prospective victim. The attendant looked at Ben's face and hurriedly turned his head away as he pulled the grill down, and the giant wheels started to turn, leaving Ben's stomach suspended somewhere above his head.

With the sudden change from daylight to semi-darkness, Ben peered over the tail-board beside him for quite a bit, before he was able to discern the shadowy figure of the other occupant. For a moment, he felt a distinct urge to deal with One-Eye there and then, but he controlled himself in the presence of the occupied lorry, and consoled himself with the thought that in a minute or two he would have his quarry all to himself.

The hoist stopped with a jolt at the bottom of the shaft, but he remained behind, while the lorry-driver put his charge into gear and drove away, by which time the other fellow had a bit of a start. Then Ben hurried past the attendant in charge of the bottom end, and sped into the kerbstoned, circular cavity.

After covering a distance of about one hundred yards, he heard the sound of footsteps in front get even louder as he increased his pace. However, he wasn't getting it all his own way. The fellow in front was also speeding up, and Ben, as he hurried along, vainly trying to muffle his hollow-sounding footfalls, knew that One-Eye had tippled. Guilty conscience, or something, was urging him to escape the following feet.

Suddenly Ben broke into a run just as the other did. Knowing just how much he was out of condition after his convalescent sojourn, and therefore somewhat surprised, he realized he was gaining, for he could now see the fleeing figure in front with its long draped jacket jutting out near-horizontally, like some be-cloaked character from a comic strip.

On Ben ran, without noticing the speed at which the circular, porthole-like wall lights flew by him, like dismembered heads floating in the darkness, while the respiratory pains tore at his chest and the nervous butterflies fluttered around in his stomach, panicking at the thing that was beyond their control.

163

One-Eye took a fleeting glance over his shoulder, and appeared to draw energy from some new source, for his feet seemed to fly over the ground without actually coming in contact. However, it was a futile effort, for Ben also was speeding on borrowed power: the agility that comes to limbs when the brain goes awry.

Ben had his razor out now, and, as he leapt desperately, his victim turned, cosh in hand, and let out an unearthly yell, which wasn't surprising. An underwater tunnel can be a dismal, eerie enough place at any time. The simple fact that countless gallons of water are pressing on all sides can be a bit of excitement to many nervous people. The strange noises that go on above, and all around the curved walls, with their minutely interlaced rivulets of dampness; the half-light that glows without much evidence of brightness; and the feeling that here, if anywhere, one is completely cut off from the outside world; all these help to build up the somewhat grotesque atmosphere. Hence the reason why children always find it a thrilling, if awe-inspiring, excursion to visit the tunnel, even on an occasion when there are lots of people about.

In the present case, there was also to be seen, leaping out of the shadows, the horrible mess that Ben called a face, and the gleam of the razor-blade as it sped towards One-Eye's head. No wonder One-Eye screamed.

The terrible victim dropped to the ground in helpless fear with the impetus of the first blow, while Ben, a demented gleam in his eye, alternately laughing and cursing, slashed at the sprawled figure like a Chindit cutting creepers. Then, suddenly, he ceased, and looked about him as if surprised to find himself here. With an automatic movement of his arm he wiped the bloody razor on his victim's jacket-lining and discarded his own raincoat which now resembled

164

a butcher's apron. After a moment of indecision, he turned on his heels and ran like hell for the Finnieston end of the tunnel, leaving an out-of-action O'Hara member lying against the wall.

He left the tunnel without any untoward encounter and found himself once more on the street, dodging among the constant stream of traffic, horse-drawn and petrol-driven, that is ever-present on the cobbled roads of the dockside.

When he got back to Bandy's cane, and had a look at himself in the mirror that hung over the sink, Ben couldn't make out why he hadn't been pulled up. His unkempt hair and nervously twitching face were spotted with blood, like 'jops' from a red-leader's brush, and his jacket-sleeve was slit from elbow to cuff. 'The One-Eye-Care-For must have had a belt at me with that cosh,' he thought as he did his best to clean himself up a bit.

Bandy came in just as he was changing into the only other jacket he had, a somewhat decrepit-looking garment. Ben saw the early edition of the 'Times' in Bandy's hand, grabbed it and eagerly scanned its pages.

A look of disappointment spread over his face as he finished his task and angrily threw the newspaper from him.

Bandy, with understandable curiosity, asked, 'Whit are ye lookin' for?'

Ben laughed the angry expression from his face, but as Bandy watched he didn't think that his smile was much improvement on his scowl.

'Ah goat wan o' O'Hara's muckers this efternin,' Ben grinned. 'Ah caught up wi' 'im in the Tunnel an' gied 'im it right.'

'Cheeses! Ye didny put 'im right oot the gemme did ye?' Bandy ejaculated, looking askance at the bloody scarf that was draped over the chair-back.

'Ah don't know,' Ben sighed as he flopped down on

165

the chair, the effects of his expended energy now showing. 'The wey he wiz lyin' when Ah left 'im, Ah wadny be surprised.' His demeanour plainly said, 'I couldn't care less.'

'Gawd a'mighty,' Bandy protested. 'Dae ye want tae get yursel' topped?'

Ben sat for a moment choking over his words, then composed himself.

'No' before Ah get every wan o' they bastarts,' he said, almost in a whisper, and yet with a vibrant note in his voice. 'Particularly O'Hara. Ah don't mind swingin' for him.'

But, as he turned away, Bandy could see, from the corner of his eye, his lodger's hand, as it moved up to finger the collar of his shirt just about the spot where the knot would break his neck.

Bandy started to make a pot of tea and Ben rose to his feet.

'Ah'm badly needin' a drink o' somethin' stroanger, how aboot subbin' us a few bob?' he asked, and, after pocketing Bandy's offering, added, 'See ye later.'

Bandy nodded silently and Ben left. Just as well. The more Bandy saw of his lodger, the less he liked the situation.

A newsvendor at the corner accepted the proffered copper and handed Ben a later edition of the paper. He ducked into a boozer, four doors away, and anxiously scanned the paper cover to cover. Nothing! Not a damned thing! Funny. There wasn't even a mention in the stop-press. A reasonable period had elapsed and the papers should have the story by this time. Apart from learning just how much damage he had done, he wanted Flash and his chinas to know exactly what was coming to them. Hence the urge to see his handiwork mentioned in print.

Ben was a bag of nerves, and, in an effort to calm himself, he got stuck into four gills of 'scud' in no time, with disastrous effect.

The 'head was away'. He leaned over the bar and grabbed the publican, a short barrel-chested individual with a chubby face, and two strands of greying hair plastered over a high forehead which extended to somewhere near the nape of his neck.

'You're gaunny gie me a five-giller tae cairry oot, withoot me peyin',' he spluttered, the saliva dripping from his lower lip on to the dishcloth that the barman held in his hand, resting on the counter. 'Are ye gled?' he asked, leering drunkenly.

The publican turned as white as a shilling on a sweep's rear, reached over to the gantry behind him, handed over a bottle without a word and stepped back with a sigh of relief as Ben released him. A couple of fellows who stood around the other end of the horseshoe-shaped bar must have seen the incident, but made not the slightest move to interfere. Ben patted the bottle lovingly, saluted the publican with two fingers, receiving a nervous nod in return and staggered out.

He roamed the streets of the Gorbals aimlessly, occasionally dodging up a close to have a suck at the wine-bottle, till his mind was so befuddled that no coherent thought dwelt there – apart from the ever-present subconscious urge to get hold of another Dagger member.

Another hour and three-quarters and five gills of wine later, Ben was stumbling along Norfolk Street when he saw Jakey Torrance, another of O'Hara's handers, coming out of a chip shop with a fish supper in one hand, a bottle of lemonade protruding from his pocket and a young woman hanging from his other arm.

Jakey was enveloped in a jacket so long that, if he were to fall, his feet would have been removed from the ankles, and Ben didn't think much of his taste in women either. She was a drab creature with a poor figure, but she had a couple of points in her favour.

The sweater that she wore beneath her unbuttoned coat helped to stress these points. That was all that Ben noticed before a red mist crept over his already bedimmed eyes.

He crept along like a stalking tiger, all the time hugging the wall, till he was no more than a few feet from the couple who were still blissfully unaware of his presence. The glow from the chip-shop door split the darkness, like some not very strong searchlight with a square lens, and the man and woman stood talking, making no effort to move out of its rays into the surrounding darkness which might have meant a chance of escape or at least a measure of safety.

Ben edged nearer till he could almost have put out a hand and touched the woman's arm, then halted for a moment, gloating. He drew the razor from his pocket and dived at Jakey, who made a half-turn in time to catch a blow on the cheek, then screamed flat soprano, while his girl danced about like a hen on a hot girdle, yelling blue murder. She made a grab at the lemonade bottle in Jakey's pocket but Ben ignored her, for, just then, a loud cry drew his attention to the chip-shop door.

Just inside, Jenny stood, and although Ben couldn't distinguish the features of the form that was fast coming from that direction, he knew it was Flash. It all added up. Then he became cold sober. There could be no slip-ups here.

In the same second as Ben spotted his approaching antagonist, the girl threw the bottle, and it smoothed down his sidelocks as it flew past his head. He braced himself for the attack, but before he and Flash could get to grips an unexpected interruption occurred. The sound of breaking glass as the bottle hit the ground was still in his ears when he received a tremendous push from behind and he fell sidewise to the ground. Glancing upwards as he dropped he observed the unmistakable blue uniforms of the two policemen who had joined in the barney. He also noticed that they had their batons out. No joke when one of those came in contact with your skull. It was time he wasn't here. The odds against him were increasing.

He rolled along the pavement as one of the grass swung his baton, then sprang to his feet and ran like hell around the nearest corner, just in time to see a four-seater black Ford car slow down to take the corner just opposite.

He jumped on the running-board, with the policeman at his heels, held the razor to the face of the lone occupant, and said, 'Get crackin' – bloody sharp tae, or ye'll be loosin' an ear.'

'Yes, sir!' the driver gulped, and quickly pressed his foot on the accelerator. The car jumped forward, its power suddenly unleashed. The copper leapt and grabbed at Ben's jacket, only to be knocked aside as Ben swung his free arm.

A couple of blocks further, and Ben jumped off at a crossing, telling the driver, 'Don't be stoappin' tae talk tae ony polis, or Ah'll cut your heid aff an' hit ye in the face wi' it.' He laughed crazily.

The driver gave an emphatic negative nod and sped on, looking neither to left nor right, glad to be out of it with his throat still intact.

Glancing backwards Ben could see no sign of the police. He dropped the razor in his pocket, pushed past some spectators who hurriedly made way for him and, to be on the safe side, dashed up a close, where he negotiated some back-courts, clambering over railings when he encountered any, and emerging in another street. Only then did he breathe freely.

Using devious routes, he directed himself back on to the main road, well clear of the danger area, and boarded a Govan-bound tram.

CHAPTER SIXTEEN

As Ben walked along the street he saw an approaching figure on the opposite pavement. It had 'busy' written all over it. Ben hurried up the close and plunged upstairs, taking them three at a time, motivated by the hunted-man complex that tells you that every copper on the beat has spotted you for who you are. He rattled the door impatiently while his lungs gasped for air.

Bandy wasn't pleased to see him when he barged through the door.

'Ye look as if ye'd been rakin' middens,' he said, pointing to the dust and mud on Ben's clothing. 'Mair trouble?'

'Ah goat anither wan o' them,' Ben answered exultantly. 'Ah nearly goat O'Hara tae, but the grass came oan the bloody scene an' Ah had tae blow masel'.' He flopped down on the chair. 'But don't worry. Ah'll get 'im yet. Ah know where tae go an' look for 'im noo.'

'The wey it's gaun ye'll have tae dig up some mair claes. A' the wans ye've goat are covered wi' blood an' muck,' Bandy said, pointing once more to the dirty clothes, but Ben didn't bother to answer.

Bandy was standing looking at him with mixed emotions. At times he felt sorry for Ben. He'd had some hard knocks, most of them deservedly. But you could never tell what was going to happen next with a character like Ben. Especially in the state he was in at present. Maybe, if Ben heard the latest, Bandy mused, he would blow himself down to England or somewhere else out of the road, and that would be beneficial to everyone concerned, except maybe a few policemen who were keen on promotion. Anyway it would be a load off Bandy's mind.

'Wan o' the coppers grabbed ma jaiket,' Ben was saying, 'but Ah jumped oan the runnin' board o' a motor an' made the driver take me oot it.'

'It'll no' make much difference,' Bandy replied fatalistically. 'They're oan your top onywey.' He threw a newspaper over to Ben. 'Have a look at that,' he told him.

At that time most of the papers were full of tactical errors, strategic advances and glorious victories, but this particular sheet was opened at an inside page and folded there. Ben read the banner headline – SLASHING IN TUNNEL – under which it said: 'A razor-slasher seems to have gone berserk today in the tunnel which passes beneath the River Clyde at Plantation. "It is the worst case of slashing seen for years," one of the city's medical officers has stated. William Shirra, aged twenty-six, of Ballater Street, Gorbals, was found lying in the tunnel at approximately half-past three this afternoon. He was bleeding profusely from several wounds in his head, face, arms and body. He was immediately rushed to the Victoria Infirmary where he is being kept alive by the administering of blood transfusions. The police are keeping constant surveillance at the bedside, and are confident that the victim of this murderous attack, when he recovers consciousness, will be able to name his assailant . . .'

There was more, mainly concerning the victim's family, and their statements as to 'How quiet a boy William is'.

Finally there were a few scathing comments on the characters of people who committed such crimes. Seemingly, there had been a spate of such incidents in recent weeks.

There was also a recent photo of Shirra. Ben studied it closely while Bandy studied Ben's expression.

Maniacal or diabolical, or something they called it in books that Bandy had read.

Crumpling the paper between his hands, Ben said, 'Ah hope the bastart snuffs it,' and threw it from him into a corner of the room where it re-opened, like a piece of silk, to show Shirra's one eye staring up at them accusingly. 'Ah hope he dies,' Ben repeated fervently, glaring at the corner where the newspaper lay.

'Then it'll be a murder rap,' Bandy commented. 'Ye'll have had it.'

'No' if he dizny regain consciousness,' Ben answered, but Bandy could see a lot of flaws, and, with the same purpose in mind as he had when showing Ben the newspaper, he quickly brought the drawbacks to Ben's attention.

'Mibbe somebuddy'll mind seein' ye comin' oot the tunnel,' he suggested. 'They wad be able tae gie your description.' Ben pursed his lips thoughtfully but said nothing. 'Whit happened the night?' Bandy asked. Ben, in the floweriest of language, told him the story, while Bandy listened silently to the end, a look of consternation appearing on his rugged face.

'Stiff me!' he exclaimed with Ben's last words. 'D'ye think the polis are stupit or somethin'? They can put two an' two thegither an' get four jist the same as onybuddy else.' Ben looked up at him but still kept his peace. 'They know that Shirra, Torrance an' O'Hara are a' chinas,' Bandy continued. 'An' they'll connect the barney the night wi' the caper the day.' He was pacing up and down the floor like a High Court lawyer, emphasising each point by thumping a fist into the open palm of his other hand. 'Them two polis that ye met the night'll no' forget your face. No' only that – mibbe Torrance'll shop ye,' he added, pleased with his oratory powers, and satisfied that this brilliant afterthought would swing the argument, but still prepared to say more if need be.

'Tae hell wi' him,' Ben answered with a shout as he, too, jumped to his feet. 'An' the coppers an' a'. Tae hell wi' the whole bloody lot o' them. Ah'll get that rat O'Hara before they get me. That's a' Ah want. Efter that Ah don't gie a "monkeys" – .'

Looking at him, slightly hedgy, Bandy realized that Ben had definitely 'done his nut' by this time. Sane people didn't have saliva running from the corner of the mouth, to drip from the chin. The shock of his injuries and his wife's infidelity had been aggravated by the strain he'd been under during the past few days. And Bandy wasn't quite happy about his own position. It was not a pleasant prospect – a crazy man for a room-mate – even for the short period that Ben could stay a free man. Yet Bandy was hesitant about asking him to leave. Nobody wants to antagonize a 'nutter'. For the first time in his life Bandy wished the police would pay his house a visit. It now seemed the only manner in which Ben's ominous presence could be removed. Yet, as the thought struck him, Bandy knew, deep down, that he could never 'copper' Ben. He had never shopped anyone in his life, and he couldn't start now. He'd hate himself all his days, if he did.

But he needn't have worried. The seeds of doubt he had planted were taking root. His problem was already being solved for him.

Ben started pacing around the room, a crafty look in his eyes, while he muttered in a quiet undertone that Bandy strained to hear. 'They jist might come here lookin' for me. Ye never can tell.'

'Jist whit Ah wiz thinkin',' Bandy cut in. Ben looked at him quizzically. There was something about that look and the electric atmosphere that accompanied it that made Bandy gulp nervously.

'Ye didny tell them Ah wiz here, did ye, Bandy?' he asked.

'Cheeses wept, Ben!' Bandy exclaimed in a hurt

173

tone, conveniently forgetting his thoughts of a moment before. 'Ye know me better than that.'

There was a power-cut in the atmosphere.

Ben was nodding silently without taking his eyes from Bandy's.

'That's right, Bandy,' he answered as he administered a pat on the other's shoulder, accompanied by his version of a friendly smile. 'Ah know ye wadny shop me.' Then he added as an afterthought, 'But some-buddy else might – mibbe some o' the neebours – eh? Ah better no' "anchor". Dizny dae tae stey too long in the wan place. Ah better blow.' So saying, he opened the door and made his exit from Bandy's life without as much as a 'Cheerio'.

Bandy sat looking at the closed door for a minute, silently wishing Ben all the luck he needed, while deciding that he was glad to see the back of him. He lifted the tea-pot from the hob and started to brew up.

CHAPTER SEVENTEEN

A car was trundling along the Govan Road as Ben emerged from Neptune Street. He raced in pursuit and jumped aboard, violently pushing the clippie in the process.

She said, 'Here – mind whit you're daein'. There's nae room onywey. Ye'll have tae get aff.' She raised her arm till it was in line with his chest.

The tram slowed down as it reached another stop and a young fellow came running down the stairs from the upper deck. Ben looked at the clippie. She removed the obstructive arm.

'A' right—,' she said, '—wan upstairs.'

Ben nodded, turned his back on her and went upstairs. He was seated before he noticed who was sharing his pew. It was Maggie Murphy. She was 'half-smugged'. He felt like a slaughterhouse porter shouldering a side of beef when she threw one of her enormous arms around his neck and mumbled whiskily, 'Hello, Ben, ma darlin'.'

He shuddered and muttered, 'Aye, aye.'

'Ah see you're in a wee bit o' trouble,' she whispered at the top of her voice.

'Trouble? Ah don't know whit you're talkin' aboot,' he grunted irritably, vainly trying to remove the boa-constrictor that was doing its best to strangle him.

'Come oan, son, who're ye tryin' tae kid?' she coaxed, forcibly retaining her armlock. 'There's no' much gets by big Maggie. Ah heard a' aboot it. Ye can tell me straight enough.'

'Ah tell ye Ah'm no' in ony trouble,' he persisted.

'It's a' right,' she continued undeterred, while Ben scrutinized the other passengers for signs of snoopers. 'Ah'm alang wi' ye as faur as that O'Hara mob are concerned. They're a shower o' "chanty-rasslers", an' he's the biggest layaboot o' the lot.'

Maggie took a drag at a Woodbine that peeped between her gigantic fingers, and went into a fit of coughing that only ceased when the conductress had collected a few fares, including Ben's, and returned to her platform. Ben had then decided that the only persons who were near enough to overhear the conversation were too drunk to care, so when a little of the lobster-colouring had faded from Maggie's face, and she had gained enough breath to wheeze a few words, he allowed her to continue.

'They came up tae ma hoose at the "demand",' she said with an incongruous air of indignation. 'An' that yin O'Hara tried tae get fresh wi' me inty the bargain.' Now she was letting her imagination run away with her. Bad enough as he was, Flash would have to be awful hard stuck to chase up Maggie, and, if Ben knew her, the man who made a pass at her was inviting a ravishing. Fancy attempting an all-in wrestle with

175

twenty-stone-worth, Ben thought with a shudder.

'Ah hope ye gied 'im it right,' she hiccupped, and handed him a whisky-bottle which she had produced from the folds of her voluminous coat. 'Have share o' ma rations,' she offered.

There was about a gill remaining in the bottle, and half of that when Ben had taken one gulp and handed it over to her to finish.

'You're a good boy,' she muttered between belches, patting his shoulder-blade, while one huge breast pressed hard against his arm. 'You an' me could have some rerr times thegither, couldn't we? Eh?'

'Perish the thoaght,' Ben mumbled, but Maggie thought he was agreeing with her.

'That's right, terr times,' she repeated, while she shoved some limp, sweat-soggy hair back from her forehead. 'We can have a right good terr when ye get ower your wee bit o' trouble.'

The tram had crossed the Clyde and was threading its way through the city centre, its axles screeching protestingly as the wheels took the bends. The streets were crowded with people emerging from late-running theatres and cinema shows, who were hurrying for homeward-bound conveyances. Ben watched them without seeing them. His mind was otherwise occupied.

'Ah'm gaun' tae the coffee stall,' Maggie announced, as if imparting a valuable piece of information. 'Where are you gaun'?'

Ben got to his feet and looked once more at the other passengers around them. 'Ah'm gaun' a message, Maggie,' he said. 'Ah'll see ye later oan. Don't be talkin' too much.'

'Ye know me, Ben, ma boy. Hear "sweet", see "sweet", say "sweet", know "sweet"—' and Ben trotted downstairs, as she slowly went through the miming ritual of the three wise monkeys.

Ben had reached the conclusion that Maggie's shack

was as good a place as any in which to spend the night, but he didn't wish to hang around the city with her. She was a very conspicuous personage, even in semi-darkness, and he wanted to lose himself among the crowd for the present. When he had allowed her sufficient time to get home he would pay her a call, and maybe buy her a drink to keep her in a good mood. There were other ways, but he didn't have the stomach. However, there was a slight drawback in regard to the alternative. He had only about four bob in his pocket. Such a sum of money would hardly buy a drink for a sparrow, and Maggie was no sparrow. He would have to dig up some gelt.

At the Broomielaw coffee-stall, he dallied over a gritty hot dog and a cup of muddy tea, in the hope that some moneyed acquaintance would appear on the scene. No luck! He had stood there close on ten minutes and the only other customers were two 'brass' and a 'stickman'. Ben couldn't afford to stir up more trouble with a bit of 'demand'. Anyway the night was young and the girls' purses would be pretty empty. The takings for the early part of the evening were always spent on alcohol which the stickman shared, part of his payment for the dubious protection he afforded them, and for soliciting an occasional client, where that kind of approach seemed better.

One of the girls looked at Ben shrewdly, sizing him up, then turned away to continue the conversation with her confederates. Ben smiled grimly to himself. She had, for a moment, considered him as a prospect. If she had known who he was and what was in his mind, she would have taken a 'canary'.

He threw away part of the hot dog and drained his cup, handed it to the attendant and received his deposit back, looked around despondently and decided to move on.

The girl had a closer look at him as he passed the trio, and, instead of crossing the street towards the city centre, he wandered along idly to the centre of the bridge, where he leaned on the parapet and let his mind drift like a piece of wood on the muddy waters that raced beneath him.

He shivered as he remembered acquaintances who had been fished from the dark depths. Some who, for no obvious reason, had, according to the inquest verdicts, thrown themselves from one of these bridges. He could understand that, too. Things piled up on you, and if you weren't strong enough, and prepared to prove to the world just how strong you were, the world could crap on you. He wondered what it would feel like to make a hole in the water, as the witty boys termed it.

A wet spot touched his cheek unnoticed, followed by another on his eyelid, then quickly the rain splattered against his hat brim as he drew it down, and continued to gaze at the swiftly moving water.

A small white hand laid on his arm roused him from his reverie. He raised his wet face. 'Hullo, Ben,' said Susie Divers.

Ben rested his weary eyes on her face. She was beautiful, he thought. Standing there like one of them paintings of Joan of Arc or somebody. Those paintings that he'd seen when visiting the Art Galleries as a child. Always looking for dirty pictures. But Susie didn't look dirty. Just now, with the rain making a shimmering silken fringe of her hair, she appeared as a nymph, whose comings and goings would be influenced by the misty drizzle which enveloped them.

What had he ever seen in Jenny?

Looking at the girl in front of him, he fervently wished he had his life to live over again, then immediately wondered if things would be any different. Probably not. He would more than likely make just the same mistakes. And the biggest error of all? Well – Jenny undoubtedly had something for him that other women didn't. He couldn't define it, but knew, even at this moment, that it was there.

Still, Susan had plenty too, and all in the right places. Anyway, what was the use of thinking about it? It would soon be all over. He felt it in his bones, along with the Scotch mist that was seeping through his clothes.

'Hullo, Susie,' he said, with little animation, although the words brought to mind an old song. Once more he turned despondently towards the river. Farther down the water he could discern the dark hulk of a steamer. One of the Irish boats. And farther still, on both sides of the river, were the myriad wharf-lights of the Glasgow docks, and here and there, the illuminated portholes or navigation lights of some ocean-going liner. For a moment his imagination took him aboard one of those ships, and strangely enough, Susan with him.

'Whit's up, Ben?' Susie asked, still retaining her grip on his arm. He shook his mind free of its voyaging as a dog dries its fur.

'Och, the usual, Susie,' he replied with a watery travesty of a smile. He would never have admitted it, but he was feeling extremely sorry for himself. 'Gelt—,' he explained, '—or the want of it.' Susie's motherly instinct was exerting its influence, as with all women. Ben knew by her expression that this was the case, and proceeded to try to take advantage of it. 'How are ye fixed?' he asked.

'Ah've a coupla quid,' she admitted doubtfully, 'but Ah'll be needin' it.'

'Dae ye need it the noo?' he persisted, wearing a look of salvation.

'Naw! No' jist this minute – but Ah'll be needin' it for the week-end. Ma aul' man threw me oot the hoose a while back, an' Ah'm in digs noo.' She imparted the last piece of information, proudly, as much as to say, 'I'm a big lassie now.' Ben couldn't agree more.

'Oh! Are ye? Whereaboots?' he asked. Not that he really cared, but he had to keep the conversation going.

A sort of foundation for the appeal he was about to make to the girl's generosity. Besides, the information might prove useful in some way.

'Charlotte Street. At – at the Gallagate end,' she answered with a trace of hesitation, obviously anticipating Ben's next question. That wasn't worrying him. He went right ahead and put it to her.

'Ony chance o' me gaun' hame wi' ye the night?' he asked eagerly. He hadn't a doubt what the answer would be, since he knew that Susan held him in very high regard. He was extremely disappointed when she replied in a negative manner.

'Oh, naw! Ah couldny,' she said, not in the least insulted by the suggestion. In fact, she actually seemed pleased that it had been made.

'How no'?' he persisted, although he knew by her demeanour that there must be a good cause.

'The landlady wadny wear it,' she muttered in a disgusted tone. 'Ah tried tae slip a fella in wi' me wan night, an' ye shoulda heard whit Ah goat. She'll take a' the "bungs." Ah gie her, affy whit Ah get fae the men, but she's hedgy aboot takin' ony chances 'ersel'. Dead windy aboot gettin' done for keepin' a kip shop.' Ben stood quietly listening, purposely creating an impression of more despondency than he felt. When Susan had earlier mentioned money she had disposed of that emotion.

'Ah know where we could go if we had jist a wee bit mair money,' he told her, as if the idea had struck him. 'Ah'm expectin' a turn the moarra, an' Ah could gie ye your cash back.'

Susie didn't hesitate for a moment. She laid hold of his arm, firmly.

'C'moan up tae the St Vincent Street stall an' Ah'll see whit Ah can dae,' she said in her best business-like manner.

Passing the nearby stall they were thoroughly scrutinized by the two 'brass'. One of them was dead peeved that she hadn't used her initiative when she had the opportunity. You couldn't afford to pass up a customer on a quiet week-night, especially when it was wet, she told herself. The stickman was reflecting on the whack he'd missed.

Going up Renfield Street, they passed a little fat bloke who wore a greasy-looking soft hat and had old-fashioned pince-nez glasses perched on the end of his blob of a nose. He stood at the edge of the kerb, back to the road, and ogled Susan suggestively as she passed. A little further on she stopped and commanded Ben, 'Go up tae the stall an' get yoursel' a cup o' tea. Ah'll be back directly.'

Ben glanced back at the little fellow who was still watching them intently, then leaned over towards Susan and said in an undertone: 'Ah'll go at the "tail-up", an' we'll tak' the aul' bastart for ese lot.'

'Naw, Ben!' she protested vehemently, fear imprinted on her pretty face. 'Ah don't fancy that gemme. Ye get plenty o' time if you're caught at it.'

'Aw c'moan, hen,' Ben coaxed. But she wasn't having it.

'Naw! Definitely! Ah'm no' havin' onythin' tae dae wi' that caper.'

'Hell!' Ben muttered angrily, but he strolled away just the same. He knew which side his bread was buttered. It was her pigeon and he didn't want to push his luck. She was carrying the rent book.

Susie minced away in the other direction, hips writhing sinuously, and high heels clicking on the wet flagstones. Still farther away, the lecherous-looking individual was becoming animated, stepping forward to meet her, an elated look on his fat face, with his eyes tearing the clothes from the girl. They walked arm in arm down the street to disappear into one of the many lanes which intersect the buildings around the city centre. When Ben looked backwards before turning into St Vincent Street, there was no sign of the others.

CHAPTER EIGHTEEN

Ben spent a couple of minutes scrutinizing the crowd at the stall before he decided that Maggie wasn't around. He ventured over to the dimly illuminated counter and bought a cup of tea. Not much more than a quarter of an hour had passed when Susie joined him in a shop door. She took a twenty Capstan from her handbag, put a cigarette in his mouth and one in her own. As she leaned over his hand for a light, from the corner of her carmined lips she said, 'Ah've goat anither poun'.'

'A "wanner"?' Ben repeated. She grinned and nodded. There was not the faintest sign of self-consciousness in her demeanour, and Ben, thinking on why the old layabout had given her the money, couldn't understand how she could be so cold-blooded about it, or perhaps that is the wrong expression. He shook his mind clear of these thoughts and nodded. No skin off his nose.

'Okay,' he said gruffly. 'We'll hing aboot for a wee while. We canny go tae this cane jist yet.'

A short time later Ben and the girl were finishing a cup of coffee. There was a bit of commotion taking place at the corner. Two 'brass' were trying to tear each other to pieces, while the resident midnight news-vendor was refereeing. From what one could gather, one lady had stolen a Yank behind the other's back, and now the other lady was yanking a stole from the first lady's back. And you take it from me, Solomon would have backed a deuce in trying to solve this problem, for they would have taken half a man apiece, and still fought over who was to get the most interesting part – the bottom half – with the money-belt.

Ben brushed aside a gentleman who was about to

182

proposition Susie. The fellow took one look at Ben's coupon, then took a powder.

'C'moan,' Ben said, taking Susie's arm. 'They sully bitches'll bring the grass oan the scene wi' their cairry-oan.'

They were turning the far corner into Hope Street when they heard a female voice screaming, 'Who's a durty cow?' The pot was evidently calling the kettle black. This precipitate remark was followed by the crash of breaking glass. Plate glass at that. One of the shops was short of a window, if nothing else. There were plenty of thieves hanging around there, waiting for just such an opportunity. Ben could have done with a turn but he didn't want to take a thief's chance on that night, so he kept going, down past the Central Station and into Argyle Street.

They spent a short time at the St Enoch stall, before Ben decided that Maggie had been allowed enough time to reach her home.

'C'moan an' we'll get crackin',' he said to Susan. She broke off the conversation she was having with another girl, and they left. At such a late hour, there was no public transport, and a taxi was an extravagant luxury they could ill afford, so they walked slowly over to the Rutherglen Road.

Susan halted on the stairs, directly beneath the flickering gas-light on the landing. 'Wait an' Ah'll gie ye the money, Ben,' she said, moving a hand towards the neck of her white silk blouse.

'Never mind, hen. Ah'll get it masel',' he said, and, without further ado, began to explore the inviting hollow between her breasts, while she, in turn, grabbed and kissed him. There's just no accounting for women. This was one case where love, or something, was blind. Ben was slightly out of breath, but looking forward to the rest of the programme. They broke off their clinch, and continued the climb.

Maggie answered the door.

'Hullo, shweetheart,' she greeted Ben, then glanced shrewdly at the girl. 'C'moan in.' Then, after a drunken giggle, 'Take off your trooshers an' make yourshel' at hame.' That might have sounded humorous, coming from some other woman. From Maggie's mouth it sounded disgusting. Ben shuddered off the feeling.

'Ah'd like tae stey here the night, an' buy ye a drink,' he said, while he studied her blubbery mouth in an effort to guess at the words her lips would form. 'Wad three quid cover it?' he asked.

She must have been preparing for bed when they knocked at the door, for she never let anyone see her without her multicoloured false teeth, only removing them at the last moment. She knew she wasn't as good-looking without them. She stood for a moment, considering, while she contemplated the girl's trim youthful figure.

'Maggie makesh it bargain night 'cosh she likesh ye,' she giggled, and showed her misshapen gums with a leering top lip. 'Mind ye,' she added, laying a hand on his upper arm, 'if the lashie hadny been wi' ye, it mighta been gratish night.' Perish the thought, Ben told himself. 'Never mind,' she continued. 'Anither time.' She put a huge hand on each of their shoulders and gave them a gentle push. 'Go inty that room at the end o' the loabby,' she told them. 'No' the wan oan the right, or ye'll be gettin' your heid in your haun'sh. There'sh shomebuddy in there in the middle o' shomethin' the noo.' Another drunken laugh. 'The wan right faishin' ye.'

They followed her instructions, and were seated in two wicker-work chairs when, in a minute or so, Maggie joined them, with a half-bottle of her fire-water and three glasses.

Susie didn't take much, but the other two made up for it, and in no time the bottle was empty, at which stage Maggie left for bed, remarking that the bed-springs in this room were the strongest she could find,

184

and not to break them.

Maggie's laughter was silenced by the closed door, and an awkward pause reigned for a couple of minutes before Ben broke it impatiently.

'Ah think we'll get inty kip,' he said, and Susie nodded her head.

He sat watching her undress, and, for the present, controlling his reflexes, while gradually the problems that beset him took flight. When she had removed everything but her skin a warm glow had permeated through his veins, and that was attributable to more than the poteen from Maggie's bottle. He rose from the chair, lifted her like a child and placed her gently on the bed. She lay there unmoving, watching him, while he himself excitedly stripped off, and in no seconds flat he had joined her.

Before his mind sank completely in the deep pools that were Susie's eyes his last conscious thought was concerned with the probable appearance of the owner of the voice that filtered through the wall of the other room. It was saying, 'Och, don't dae that. That's tickly.'

Ben would have bet anything that the lassie next door just couldn't compete as far as his own partner's good looks or technique were concerned. Susie's bed-side manner was far better than any doctor's.

Much later silence enveloped the house like a cloak, only to be broken by the asthmatic wheezing sound that Maggie emitted while asleep, while the very walls seemed to vibrate in time. But Ben lay there oblivious. Unaware, too, that half of his friends, if such they could be called, were being turned out of their beds by the police, and that the 'models' (the lodging-houses) and the coffee-stalls were now being methodically but belatedly searched.

CHAPTER NINETEEN

Ben woke first. He lay completely relaxed, the door of his mind locked, for the present, against his problems. Beside him, Susie was prostrate, breathing regularly, and wearing, surprisingly, the most angelic of expressions. One of Ben's arms was cradling her head, wispy strands of her hair was tickling his nose, and one of her dimpled arms was thrown across his bare chest. With his free hand he extracted, and lit, a Capstan from the packet that lay on the chair. Pulling the nicotine down into his lungs, he closed his eyes and thought of nothing.

When the dog-end was burning his fingers, he stubbed it out on the matchbox and gently roused Susan by simultaneously fondling her breast and kissing her cheek. At first the only response he got was the parting of the moist lips on an ecstatic smile. He kissed her again, this time on the lips. She opened one eye slowly and regarded him. The smile stayed put, only more so.

'You still here?' she laughed. 'Ah thoaght ye'd ha' left after ye goat a' ye wantit.' She placed a little hand over the one of his that rested on her breast. He kissed her once more.

'Too mony ither nights tae think aboot,' he replied, 'tae leave ye the noo.'

She looked up at him with a mock-angry frown that was belied by the light of happiness shining from her eyes. 'An' who says there's gaunny be ither nights?' she asked. Then added with a laugh, 'Whit aboot that ither lassie, Maggie, through the wa'?'

Ben sniggered in agreement and said, 'Never mind Maggie. Ah'm sayin' there's gaunny be ither nights. Dae ye think Ah'd let ye aff as easy as that?'

'Ah still think ye should gie Maggie a wee break,' she kidded.

'Aye – on her leg. Look, hen – it's nourishment Ah want – no' punishment. Naw! Whither ye like it or no', you're stuck wi' me, an' that's that.'

'An whit if Ah decided no' tae have onythin' else tae dae wi' ye, efter ye soilin' ma virginity?'

'Ye wadny get leavin' me!'

'An' whit wad stoap me?'

'Ah wad an' you wad,' he replied earnestly. 'Ye think too much o' me, an' Ah'm the same wey aboot you.' Both his arms were around her, pressing her naked body to his.

'You're only sayin' that because it's true,' she laughed and kissed him soundly.

The banter continued while they both got dressed. They had one last passionate clinch which Ben almost forgot to break up, then they left Maggie's house surreptitiously, to call at a nearby café.

They were seated at a table and had ordered cheese rolls and teas when Susie gave Ben half a crown from some loose change in her pocket, and he went to a newsagent's next door, where he bought some cigarettes and a 'Daily Record'. When he returned the girl was munching ravenously at her roll. He sat down and laid the paper beside his plate.

He had the tea-cup to his mouth, taking an experimental sip, and was twisting the paper open, when, with an explosive splutter, he soaked his shirt-front. Staring up at him was a photograph of himself. A copy, in fact, of an old one that was lying around his mother's house. Beside it the words were jumping around and he found it extremely difficult to unjumble them.

Susan stopped chewing and looked at him questioningly.

'Went doon the wrang way,' he excused himself, simulating a cough. She looked doubtful for a moment, then with the slightest shrug of her shoulders she dismissed her thoughts and continued with the job in hand. Ben absent-mindedly lifted one of his rolls and took a bite while he perused the words in front of him.

The column stated that the police believed that one, Bernard McNulty, whereabouts unknown, could help them with their enquiries in connection with the previous day's slashings. The man, Shirra, who had been assaulted during the afternoon, had since died in the early hours of the morning. Another man, John Torrance, who was a close friend of the deceased, had been brutally slashed late last night. The police had evidence pointing to the fact that both crimes were perpetrated by the same person. This man was dangerous, and the public were asked to co-operate fully with the police in their endeavours to apprehend him. A detailed description followed here, and Ben's eyes glanced over the words, but his eyes got stuck at the part further down where it stated that the police had obtained a deposition from Shirra before he died. The whole thing was footed by five words printed in large letters, more in keeping with a headline. It said: 'HAVE *YOU* SEEN THIS MAN?'

The 'ba' was up on the dyke' proper.

Ben swallowed the roll without mastication, gulped down the tea and said to Susan. 'Ah've goat tae hurry away, hen. Ah'll mibbee see ye later oan.' He got to his feet.

'Mibbe?' she retorted, a spark of anger igniting her eyes. 'Ye said ye were gettin' a turn, an' giein' me back ma money.' Ben silently cursed his stupidity while she added, 'Whit aboot a' the patter ye've been giein' me, an' where are ye gaun', onywey?'

'That's whit Ah'm gaun' tae see aboot,' Ben improvized. 'Ah forgot tae tell ye. Ah've tae see the bloke at eleven o'clock.' It was now a quarter to the hour on the café clock he was looking at. 'Don't worry aboot the money,' he assured her. 'Ah'll see ye later oan, an' then ye'll see ma patter's been true.' She took hold of one of his hands, ignoring the stares of some of the other customers. The stares that were causing the sweat to break on Ben's brow. He expected a voice to cry out, at any moment. 'That's the fellow in this morning's paper.'

'Ye know it's no' the money, Ben darlin', that Ah'm worryin' aboot,' Susie said, looking up at him beseechingly. 'You're gaunny blow me out.'

'Naw, Ah'll no', hen. Ah'll see ye later.'

'Where?' she asked doubtfully.

'In the Oswald Street amusements,' he answered, mentioning the first place that came to his mind, 'at – at four o'clock.'

Susie let go of his hand, slowly, grudgingly, and he turned and walked out of another friend's life, while she sat staring at the door as he closed it behind him. She continued to gaze unseeingly while her pupils became damper as her feminine intuition got to work.

Back to Maggie's he went, glancing nervously at each passer-by for signs of recognition, forgetting in his fear that the mass of scarred tissue that he wore below his hair was unrecognizable as the face of Ben McNulty as the newspapers depicted it. He knocked incessantly for a full minute before he heard Maggie approaching, shouting.

'Awright! A'right!' she was saying. 'Ah'm comin'. Haud oan your dicky for a minute. Ah'm comin' as fast as Ah can.' He heard her fumble at the door, cursing because she couldn't find the handle.

When she saw who it was, she turned away and left him to close the door. He followed her into her own room, or the kitchen as Glasgow folk prefer to call it.

'Have your ither visitors left yet?' he asked her warily, while she spread herself on a kitchen chair that stood beside the table. As she looked at him quizzically, he idly wondered, with one part of his brain, if the chair legs were making indentations on the linoleum.

'Visitors?' she queried. 'Aw, them? Aye! Furst thing this moarnin'. He dizny like tae be seen leavin' here. Word might get tae ese wee wifey.' Her laugh grated on Ben's nerves, but he let it pass. 'How? Whit's up?' she asked watching him intently.

Ben said nothing, but, with a stagey, dramatic flourish, threw the open newspaper on the table in front of her. For a moment she peered short-sightedly, lips pursed, her head swaying from side to side like a Wimbledon spectator. Then:

'Gawd a'mighty!' she ejaculated, an amazed look on her face as she tore her eyes away from the paper to confront him. 'Ye've made a right mess o' things. Whit

189

the hell did ye want tae go an' stiffen 'im for?'

'Look, Maggie, never mind that,' Ben said. 'It's done an' nothin' can be done aboot it, but Ah'll need a bit o' smother-up.' He sat down facing her. 'Ah want tae anchor here tae it's dark.' Her expression conveyed refusal. 'Whit Ah meant tae dae,' he told her, 'an' whit Ah did it for, dizny maitter noo. The point is, that it's happened an' it canny be changed, an' Ah'll need tae stay oot the road o' the grass.'

'Och, ye canny stay here, Ben,' she protested, shaking her huge head, her graveyard teeth showing as she bit her lower lip petulantly. 'They bloody coppers wad put me the whole road if they goat hauf the chance. That's just whit they've been waitin' for.' There were giant beads of sweat on her brow as she considered herself as an inmate of Duke Street prison. She had been there a few times during her younger days, but she knew that, nowadays, she couldn't last the pace. For one thing she carried too much weight for a con. For another, she suffered from all sorts of ailments, which she knew would be aggravated by the rigid conditions of prison life, and above all, by separation from the booze. She couldn't face that.

'Naw, Ben – ye'll have tae leave,' she finished, laying her large hands palm down on the table in a gesture of finality, and looking up at him with lowered brows.

'See here, Maggie—,' Ben said, pointing a warning forefinger at her face, 'Ah'm no' leavin', an' ye can like it or lump it. Ah've nothin' tae loass noo, so there's no' much ye can dae about it.'

Maggie was staring at him, her face now tinted with the first shades of fear. For all her wealth of experience, it was something new to be threatened by a maniacal murderer.

'Ah'll leave when Ah think it's dark enough, an' naebuddy'll be ony the wiser,' he said in a commanding tone that brooked no argument.

'Whit aboot the lassie that wiz wi' ye a' night?' Maggie asked, with an air of having pulled an ace from her capacious sleeve. 'She might send them here.'

Ben shook his head exasperatedly.

'Naw – she's a' right – Ah think,' he said. 'Onyway – she dizny know Ah'm here. We left aboot ten o'cloak an' she dizny know Ah came back.'

Maggie sat considering for a moment. She'd have to take the chance. She could always tell the police that she had been intimidated into acceding to Ben's wishes. He was a good fellow at heart. He would go along with her on that story. Anyway, he was in no mood to be baulked. Better to string along with him and see what turned up.

'Awright, Ben, you're on,' she said resignedly. 'Ah don't fancy it, mind ye, but ye can stay. Ah haveny much choice onywey. Have Ah?'

'That's right, Maggie. Ye haveny,' Ben agreed.

He strolled over to the fireside chair, and settled for the long wait till darkness fell. He hadn't a clue what he was going to do then, but darkness meant a measure of safety, and he would decide then.

CHAPTER TWENTY

I was surreptitiously reading the paper, and, before I could close it, Isa was glancing over my shoulder. I waited expectantly for a completely feminine hysterical outburst. I was wrong. Isa was made of finer stuff.

She simply asked, 'Oh Bill – whit'll we dae?' This obviously without expecting an answer, since there was none possible.

'There's no' much we can dae, hen,' I said, drawing her on to my knee. 'Bar keep close tae your au' wife. She's takin' it bad.' We both listened to Mrs Mac potter about the room. 'Still,' I added, '— she's hidin' it well.'

She was. Especially, after the way things had happened. It was like this.

Isa and I were still lodging with Mrs McNulty and we had all been wakened, the night before, from a sleep such as I had never experienced in the old days of excitement and worry. Not realizing immediately the portent of the repeated heavy knocking on the outside door, I glanced drowsily at the clock on the wall. It was three o'clock in the morning, and, contrary to the popular song, we hadn't danced a step. We had been sleeping, soundly. As the mists of my sleep drifted away from me, the idea struck me that there was only one type of person who knocked in such a manner at such a time.

I hopped from beneath the warm blankets, ignoring Isa's grunted protests. While I was dragging my trousers, hastily, up my legs, she was asking, 'Whit's wrang!' Only then did she hear the hammering at the door. I might tell you that Isa could sleep her brains into train oil.

'Who's that at the door?' she asked irritably, as if it were my fault someone was knocking us up. 'Imagine at this time o' night.'

'How the hell dae Ah know,' I answered shortly. 'It sounds like the polis, but Ah'll be able tae tell ye when Ah go an' open it.'

As I left the room I heard her withdraw the sheets from her body, shivering with the sudden change in temperature as she did so.

Needless to say, it was the police. I stood gaping at them, then Mrs Mac joined me, a belligerent look replacing the worried one when she saw them. Although she was entirely law-abiding she disliked police. She was wonderful. Many another woman, especially one up in years such as she was, would have gone all hysterical. Not her.

When one of the policemen said, 'We'd like to speak to Bernard McNulty, missus. We have a warrant for his arrest,' she just set her jaw in a grim line, and answered angrily:

'Ye needny look here for 'im. He's nae son o' mine. Hizny been near this hoose for donkey's.'

A detective put an apprehensive hand against the door-panel, although none of us had made a move to close it. 'Do you mind if we look around just the same?' he asked.

'No' at a' – go ahead,' Ma said. 'But ye could save yoursel' the bother.'

She turned her broad back on them and shuffled into

the kitchen, with the two police behind her. Two others tried to push past me into the room. I halted them by the simple expedient of leaning against one wall of the lobby, with my hand pressed against the other wall.

'Ma missus is in bed in that room,' I told them. 'An' you're no' having a look.'

'Would you tell her to get up and come through?' one bloke asked. I was saved the bother. Isa joined me, rubbing her eyes sleepily. When she spotted the policemen she was startled wide awake. We went into the kitchen and allowed the coppers to carry on their search.

When we entered we found the other two police making an inspection there. We walked over to the fireplace and stood on either side of Mrs Mac. Isa placing her arm around her mother's shoulders. Just then one of the grass found the photo of Ben that was hidden behind a calendar on the mantelpiece. Isa and I knew of its existence, but we never mentioned it for we had been told that it had been burned. You can't blame a mother for a white lie.

'We'll take this with us if you don't mind,' the copper said, and without waiting for permission he put it in his pocket.

'Makes nae difference tae me,' Ma replied with a not very convincing shrug. 'Ah didny even know it wiz here.' She hesitated for a moment, then asked, 'But – whit dae yese want ese photy for?'

'We'll be getting the public to help to catch your son,' he told her. His attitude added, 'They should prove more helpful than you.'

I thought to myself, 'These coppers must be hard-cases – expecting a mother to hand over a son to the law.' Ma was quick to take him up.

'The public? Yese must want 'im bad. Whit are yese after 'im for?' she asked, apprehension causing a quiver in her voice.

The police were leaving now, but the last one halted with his hand on the handle of the door.

'Murder!' he stated simply. 'Sorry, mum,' and closed the door behind him.

But he didn't take the noise with him. The knell of doom that reverberated from the walls, repeating over and over again just one word: 'Murder!' For a moment time stood still.

Mrs Mac was motionless, as if paralysed by the shock. She gazed blankly at the wife and me, then stumbled 'ben-the-room'. I detained Isa when she attempted to follow. Daughter or no daughter, I had an idea that this was one time when the poor soul would rather be alone.

Isa cried a bit, too, and I did my best to comfort her. The whole thing just demonstrated the different densities of blood and water.

I found out later that the policeman's statement was not quite accurate. Shirra was not quite dead at that moment. But the finest medical opinions had assured the police that the victim would definitely not last the night. So his words were only a little premature.

Later, when Mrs Mac returned to the kitchen, she turned her red-rimmed eyes towards us pleadingly, but what could we say? There were no words. I thought it better not to mention Ben at all, and Isa seemed to be of the same opinion for she said not a word. Almost in silence we put her to bed.

Over on the other side of the city there were others who were experiencing different emotions. There were two people cooped up in a one-storey house. One was a man, the other a woman. That night and all the next day they were there. While Ben sat in Maggie's cane waiting for daylight to fade, they sat no great distance away, bickering and silently praying that night would never come, or at least until the police had got their man.

Flash was suffering from the shakes even more than Jenny. With her, there was a glimmer of hope somewhere in her subconscious that, because of what she had meant to Ben, he would refrain from assaulting her seriously. Not so with Flash. He had read the morning paper as I had. He knew that the headlines would make Ben more desperate than ever, if that was possible. For once in his life Flash regretted the kind of existence he had led. The quiet fellows could walk around without a care to-day, and here he was afraid to venture over the door, for fear of being murdered.

But Jenny, who decided that anything was better than sitting about the house arguing, left him there that night, while she paid a visit to the Crown Cinema along the road.

A fair amount of fading sunlight managed to filter between the tall tenements and the smutty haze that hung over the city. Nevertheless, as Jenny approached each close, her pace slackened apprehensively, with the ever-present fear of being confronted by an insane, murderous husband.

When she at last reached the cinema, she hurried inside with a sigh of relief, and squatted between an old woman who kept muttering to herself and a young couple who were trying to outdo the screen lovers.

She sat through one film without the least idea of what it was about. Her hands refused to stay at peace, and consequently her handkerchief was in shreds. Her eyes kept swivelling from side to side, and she smoked incessantly. The local chemists were certainly being done out of laxative sales as far as Flash and Jenny were concerned.

There were a couple of vacant seats behind Jenny and she couldn't help but inspect them now and again to make sure they were still unoccupied. The trouble was, when she turned her head towards the neckers she drew herself a couple of glares, and, when she twisted it in the other direction, the old woman tried to start a conversation on the merits of the film hero, or a wordy condemnation of the villain. Jenny was in no mood for social contacts with daft old women.

She sat halfway through the second feature, and could stand it no longer. She rose to her feet as someone on the screen burst into song about how rosy the world looked today, and a cynical grin flickered weakly at the corner of her mouth. The young couple came up for air and drew themselves up in the their seats to let her pass, obviously glad that she was leaving. Near the end of the row, some fellow pressed his knee into her rear, and she half-turned to slap his face, but reconsidered, then edged into the carpeted passage, without taking any action.

When she got to the foyer she had a fit of the shakes. Hell! It was so dark out on the streets. How was she going to get home? Ben might be lurking around there. She didn't want to meet the madman unprotected. Not that Flash would have been much use in that line. He was even more frightened than she. And him supposed to be a hard man!

Out of the cinema came three faces she knew, and she breathed a sigh of relief. A 'butty': Flash's younger brother, Dick, and two of his chinas. Safety in numbers.

She hurried over to them, her lips parted in a wide smile which would have looked good on that poster – the one about the toothpaste that makes your gums healthy.

'Ah never was so gled tae see onybuddy in ma life,' she said, gripping Dick's arm.

'Well,' Dick replied with a smirk, 'that makes two o' us,' and stood watching her expectantly, while his friends slid their eyes up and down her trim frame.

'Wad ye leave me up tae the hoose?' she asked, turning her eyes towards the malignant darkness. She thought he might refuse, but she needn't have worried.

'Sure!' he replied, placing his hand over hers, which still rested in the crook of his arm. 'But Ah'd raither take ye up tae ma ain hoose. The wife's in hospital, ye know.'

That was just the injection that Jenny needed to restore her morale, which had been flagging somewhat during the last few weeks. When Jenny's morals deteriorated, her morale always jumped a peg. Flash's brother had as little scruples as she herself had. It was nothing to him to steal his brother's woman. Well, that suited her. She was getting a bit fed-up with Flash. Thought he owned her, he did. And they were always bickering. Morning, noon and night. And Dick's face had the same handsome characteristics as his brother's, without being marred by any chibmarks such as Flash had. He was quite a fellow . . .

Using all her feminine wiles, she looked up at him, enraptured, as if he were Frank Sinatra or somebody, and

196

pressed his arm against her soft yielding breast, saying, 'You're on, sweetheart. Let's get crackin'.'

Dick was all smiles now. 'Come on,' he said and marched out of the foyer into Crown Street, shoulders pushed back and hands in jacket pockets. Straight into it he walked, with his hands in his pockets, and no chance to ward off the blow when it came, and that was soon enough.

The crowd around the door scattered – Jenny screamed – Dick hit a note that was almost a high C as the razor tore at the side of his neck, and he dropped to the ground, writhing and kicking. Ben glanced around him, and saw Dick's two friends standing in the foyer gaping. He took one step towards them and they ran like hell back into the cinema as fast as their legs would carry them. So much for the handers.

Ben seemed undecided what to do next; then Jenny screamed again, so drawing attention to herself, the silly bitch.

Ben turned from the figure on the ground and automatically drew the razor across her cheek. The noise that Jenny now made was indescribable. Compared to the previous screams this was supersonic. Her good looks had been destroyed and she was half-crazed by the thought. Ben looked at her puzzled for a moment, then at the razor in his hand. He looked as if he was going to take her in his arms to comfort her, but he didn't

He stooped for a moment over the now-still form on the ground, then, as if he'd just remembered he had a train to catch, he turned and ran towards Gorbals Cross.

Ben dodged all over the city that night, half of the time completely unaware of which direction he was taking. Looking for the streets with the least traffic, afraid to use any means of transport, suspecting every passer-by of having recognized him and hurrying away to find a policeman, he was ready for dropping when he found himself in London Road, up near Celtic Park. In a spur-of-the-moment decision, actuated by a desperate need to get off the streets, he turned down Kinnear Road, hugging the wall on the side where there are no houses.

This side of that particular street is flanked by a wooden sleeper fence about seven feet high, which borders a railway embankment.

When Ben had gone two or three hundred yards, he glanced around quickly for signs of onlookers. There didn't seem to be any, and, quick as a flash, he was over the fence, and dropping on the wet grass.

Lying there, oblivious to the dampness that was seeping through his clothes, taking a much-needed breather, he was unaware just how much commotion he had caused in the city. I suppose, in a way, it might have pleased him to know . . .

For instance, Maggie's shack got a turnover. They were very shrewd about it, too. No heavy police knock here.

Maggie was sitting at the table, splitting a bottle with two of the 'Tims' and giving them her worries. She was telling them about Ben being there all day.

'In fact,' she said,'he jist left aboot a quarter-an-hour before yese came up.'

'An' where is he away tae, noo?' one of the blokes asked.

'Chrise knows, an' he can go tae hell in a haun'barra as faur as Ah'm concerned,' she retorted indignantly. "Magine the cheek o' it – threatenin' tae dae me?' Then pursing her lips thoughtfully and leaning over the table towards them she muttered confidentially, 'Ye know – for a minute Ah thoaght he wiz gaunny get at it wi' me.' She nodded in agreement with herself. It was one of the few non-alcoholic hobbies she had, to indulge in an occasional bit of wishful thinking.

The two blokes smirked at each other, not realizing that Maggie drunk observed more than either of them sober, in spite of her small eyes.

'Jist a minute, youse,' she said, anger bringing a blood-pressure twinge to her flabby face. 'Are yese tryin' tae take a rise oota me?' She got to her feet, pointing a fat sausage finger. 'If yese—.'

She halted in the middle of her admonitions, ear cocked in a listening attitude. All three of them heard the repeated knock. Maggie's door really needed a commissionaire to answer the numerous callers who stood at it, but her nerves were in such a state she forgot all that.

'Mibbe that's him back,' she whispered, fear making her flesh shake like a jelly. 'Are yese stickin' by me if he starts onythin'?' They both shook their heads from side to side, in a wordless negative. She glanced from one to the other and tried a bit of bribery. 'Ah'll gie yese a good drink buckshee after ese away,' she pleaded, but they weren't having any. One of them did his spokesman act, with a demonstrative palm.

'You're not on, Maggie,' he said. 'Whit dae ye think we are? McNulty's runnin' aboot daft, chibbin' hauf o' the people in Glesca, an' you want us tae stick wur necks oot for a drink. Well, you're not on. Dig yoursel' up anither mug.' Maggie was about to protest, to persuade, but changed her mind and hurried away to answer the now impatient knock at the door.

She opened the door slightly and had it pushed in her face for her trouble. As three of the detectives rushed past her, she started crying, her eyes closed tightly so that the tears seemed to be oozing from the large black pores of her face. One of the other policemen stood beside her.

'We got a tip that Bernard McNulty was here,' he told her.

'Ese no' here,' she wailed. 'Ah wadny have him here.' She turned angrily on him and cried, 'Whit right have youse goat tae rush inty people's hooses?'

'A search-warrant,' was the blunt reply. 'Want to see it?'

The three busies came along the lobby. One was escorting an elderly man and a half-naked young woman. The other two had a grip on Maggie's boozing friends.

'We've plenty of evidence of other things here, but no McNulty,' the leader said.

'Ah never selt them ony drink,' Maggie averred, forgetting her tears. 'Ah gave them it for nothin'. Ask them an' they'll tell ye.'

'That's funny,' a policeman said. 'They're after telling

us a half-bottle of your stuff cost them fifty bob.'

She turned on the culprits, opening her mouth and emitting a tirade.

'Ya sully-luckin' bastarts! Whit ye tryin' tae dae? Get me done? Ya stupit—.'

The busy cut short the remainder of her oration by grabbing her arm, turning her round and pushing her towards the door. She struggled in vain to release herself.

'Alright, alright, turn it up,' he said. And then to his mates, 'Come on – bring them all down to the station.'

They trooped downstairs, closing Maggie's door behind them, and pressed past the gaping neighbours, some of whom licked their lips in anticipation when they thought of the booze that might be hidden in Maggie's house and how easily the door would be opened later. It would be a long time before Maggie opened it again, if ever, since factors didn't fancy such goings-on. In the squad car down on the street, she shed some real tears, thinking about it.

Then there was Bandy's cane. It, also, was turned over, although he was a bit luckier. They had nothing on him, and, of course, he was left in the house. Except for the inconvenience of having to emerge from the bedclothes to answer the door, and the unfriendly remarks he had to take from the police, it was no bother.

Bandy wondered where they had got their information, but, after puzzling over it for a quarter of an hour after the police had left without reaching any conclusions, he decided it could be anybody or nobody. Maybe they had found out that he and Ben had been friends, and just paid him a visit on the off-chance.

He also wondered whether, in his heart, he wished Ben luck. Enough at least to escape his hunters. One thing for certain. He never wanted him back here. He'd seen enough of the Ben fellow to do him a lifetime.

Anyway, he mused, no use meeting trouble halfway. Better to let it slide from his mind. He slithered under the blankets, picked up from a bedside chair and became engrossed in a cheap soft-back book with a lurid glossy cover, an improbable title and an even less probable author's name.

Mrs McNulty too had another visit from the police, but, apart from the fact that I didn't like the way one of them looked at Isa and that I told him so, in the floweriest language that came to my mind, nothing untoward occurred. But I knew I wouldn't forget that joker's face, or his expression when he heard me.

Where Isa is concerned, I honestly don't flare up over nothing, but this guy was one of those pretty-prettys that any normal married man, and most single ones, hate the sight of. A proper ladies' man.

He had one of those black pencil-lines of stubble on his upper lip. A relic of Clark Gable's heyday. And to this day, I'd gladly forfeit a week's pay to knock his moustache up among his hair and get away with it.

Anyway, some of his more decent mates broke it up before it went too far, and they left empty-handed.

Do you know, I never dreamt that there were so many coppers' narks in the city. The grass knew of practically every move Ben had made since he had left hospital. They, themselves, must have kept tabs on him to a certain extent. Not enough to prevent him doing the damage he had done to other people, and himself, but sufficient to make their now frantic search even more like a Cook's tour. Everywhere that he'd been, they went.

They even went upstairs to visit the Divers' abode. At least, that was their intention, but they only got as far as the door, for, of course, Susan wasn't there, and her old man was lying drunk elsewhere. Where the hell they got their information regarding the association between Ben and Susan was a mystery to me.

Some other nark whispered in their ears for half a dollar, and a certain house in Charlotte Street was inspected. Since Susie was out on business, it proved another unnecessary journey, the only result being that, when the girl finally returned much later, she got her 'walking papers'.

'Get yoursel' anither place for Friday night,' she was told. 'We don't want ony trouble wi' the polis here.' As Susie had told Ben, they liked the money but they didn't like to take any of the risks.

The police also questioned old Limpy and his 'case-up' regarding the razor they had walked into recently. Said they had 'information'. Might have been. Then again, it might have been just a good guess. Limpy and McNulty Senior had been tried, convicted and served time together on several occasions in the distant past. This, the police records told them.

Abiding by the law of the street-corner, Limpy told them the information they had was all they were likely to get from him, in not so many words.

The police didn't like this kind of talk, but they ignored him and turned to his woman, with an equal amount of success. She was every bit as stubborn as her man, and the grass finally gave it up as a bad job.

A room in Parkhead was visited, and one in Garngad, where the garrulous landlady told them that Ben used to give his wife an awful time of it, and she didn't know what the lassie saw in him, and these young fellows were something terrible nowadays. The detectives managed to escape at last, wondering how often she had to be wound up.

All this bother, and nothing to show for it – yet. But the police are nothing if not persistent, and Ben's ticket was punched. A one-way ticket at that. And he was practically at the terminus, and didn't know it.

He half-sat half-lay, drowsing, on a clump of damp grass, surrounded by soggy slag ashes behind a fence of sleepers, while his name passed from lip to lip, and people couldn't get arguing, about Celtic or Rangers, or discussing the new 'wean's claes' or the holiday destination at the 'Fair', without somebody bringing up the timely topic – Ben McNulty.

CHAPTER TWENTY-ONE

It was around eleven o'clock that night, or maybe half-past. My memory is not sure of the smaller details during that particular day.

Anyway, Mrs McNulty, Isa and myself had been sitting around the house all evening, not saying much, and doing very little except twiddle our thumbs, I had taken the day off work to stay with Isa and her mother, mainly to be with the older woman when my wife found it necessary to run an errand. Needless to say the day had been a drag.

I was listening for the newsvendor who comes around the streets with a midnight edition of next day's paper, and we were having a cup of tea before going to bed, when there came a rather furtive knock on the door.

As usual, the ordinary check-key had been left in the lock until the last moment, and most of the neighbours were in the habit of turning it and entering, without waiting to be summoned. That was the kind of house Ma's was. Open.

Consequently none of us moved, but, when the knock was repeated, I rose from my chair and the other two did likewise.

Isa said, 'Dae ye think it'll be the polis again?' With the words, the tears were welling up in her eyes as she gazed fearfully at her mother. 'Surely no' wi' a knock like that.'

'There's wan wey o' findin' oot,' I answered shortly and turned the handle, while Isa opened her mouth to make an angry retort. We were all rather on edge. Her mouth stayed open like a dead cod's for there, on the doorstep, stood Ben. His hair was like straw hanging out of a midden, and his jacket and right sleeve were soaked in blood.

'Maw,' he said, 'Wid ye let me in fur a minute?' He paused and repeated. 'Jist fur a minute?'

I stepped aside so that they might face each other. He steadied himself with a hand on the lintel supports of the door, and said, 'They'll be comin' tae take me away directly. They'll soon catch up wi' me.'

I saw unbelievingly that the look on his face was one of pleading. Ben pleading – I never thought I'd see the day!

His mother stood and stared at him, her face working with conflicting emotions. She was obviously about to refuse his request, when I nodded my head towards her urgently. I felt at this moment that, if Ma didn't allow him a short period of sanctuary now, she would regret it for the rest of her life.

A heavy silence enveloped us, while we all stood looking from one to the other, to finish with three pairs of eyes resting on Mrs Mac's suspiciously moist ones.

She shrugged her shoulders continental-like, and turned away to face the fireplace, in all probability to hide those tears that were so near. I half-felt like crying myself, and one look at Isa's face told me that she too was about ready.

There was a feeling of foreboding that seemed to enter the door behind Ben, as he staggered into the kitchen to collapse on a chair. I closed the door. The malignant aura settled around us, while we three stood around the table, looked at each other unable to think of anything to say, then stared at Ben till he broke the silence.

'Thanks for lettin' me in, Maw,' he said, but he was looking at me. He seemed puzzled about something. His next words gave me an idea what it was. 'Ah wany o'been surprised if ye'd chased me, after whit Ah done tae the three o' yese.' None of us ventured to agree with him, or otherwise. 'Ah haveny a freen' in the world,' he continued blankly. 'Ye see – Ah've killed a fella.'

He rubbed his hands and held them, palms outwards, towards the fire, a singularly strange action since the night was a particularly warm one in June. Funny thing is, I, too felt a strange chill in my bones. Maybe it was because it was the first, and only, time I ever heard anyone use those particular words. In real life, I mean. It's different when Robert Mitchum or Burt Lancaster use them.

Isa had her arm around her mother, but she spoke over

her shoulder to Ben.

'We know,' she answered. 'It wiz in the papers the night aboot that fella Shirra dyin'.' But I knew Ben had something more to tell us. For one thing, the blood on his jacket was obviously fresh. His eyelids rose a shade in surprise, then drooped again.

'Ah forgot a' aboot him,' he said. I wondered how anyone could be so absent-minded as to forget about taking a man's life. But he spoke again, elucidating a little. 'It's no' him Ah'm talkin' aboot,' he muttered in a low hopeless monotone. 'Ah gave it tae a bloke ootside the Crownie, the night.'

Well, that was that. It was out now, and no wonder he'd forgotten about Shirra. There was a new notch on his razor. I wondered if Flash could be the victim. I knew Shirra and Torrance were chinas of his. Ben lowered his head into his hands, and rested his elbows on his knees.

'He wiz alang wi' Jenny an' Ah hit 'im wi' a razor,' he said, and some irreverent inner part of me was pleased that my deduction was correct. I smothered the feeling and concentrated on what Ben was saying, watching him run nervous fingers through his damp hair as he spoke. 'Ah goat 'im oan the neck an' the blood splashed a'ower the shop,' he said; and I felt a queer stirring in the region of my solar plexus, for his tone could only be described as a whimper. One of his hands dropped back down to his face to grip his upper lip with forefinger and thumb, yet his next words were clear enough. 'It musta goat ese jugular vein,' he finished, and this time there was no doubt; there was a sob in his voice.

Isa had come nearer me, and was holding on to one of my front braces. I put an arm around her. I felt I could do with someone's arm around me, for my stomach was retching as I visualized the scene Ben was describing.

Mrs Mac stood, mouth agape, paralysed with shock. I drew Isa to me and placed my other arm about her mother. I thought she was never going to speak. At last – 'My God!' she cried, now unable to halt the tears that flowed down her chubby cheeks. 'Anither wan? Whit in God's name has went up wi' ye!'

205

When Mrs McNulty's strident tones had ceased we all waited motionless, as if any movement that disturbed the ensuing silence could bring further calamity. Then a hot coal in the grate shifted. It was like a signal for us to breathe again. Isa moved away from me. I lit two cigarettes and handed one to Ben. Isa filled a glass with water from the sink and fetched it to her mother. Ben opened his mouth to speak and I watched him grip the arms of the chair to control his shaking hands. He managed it, with a visible effort that brought new blobs of sweat to his damp brow, and forced his lungs to expel the tobacco-smoke in a thick cloud, to be followed by a cough. He spoke.

'Ah thoaght it wiz Flash,' he said simply, as if that was sufficient reason to alter the case to justifiable homicide, and that wer were the only jury he wanted to convince. I had an idea he was going to put up a good defence, but I could be wrong. I had been about the victim's identity. 'He was a dead ringer for Flash an' Jenny wiz hingin' oanty ese arm. When Ah seen her alang wi''im Ah wiz sae sure that Ah gied 'im it quick.' He stopped and looked up at me. 'As sure as Chrise Ah thought it wiz Flash,' he reiterated, again combing his hair with his fingers. He turned back to the fire. 'Then—,' he said, hesitantly, 'then – efter Ah done it an'he fell, Ah – had a look at 'im—.' He glanced up at me again, amazement in his eyes. 'It – it wizny him at a'. It wiz somebuddy else – but he wiz a dead ringer for 'im, an' he wiz lyin' there wi' the blood spewin' oot ese neck.'

Strange shadows that the fire threw were dancing over his face till it looked like something by Picasso. I followed his gaze to the grate and saw that the fallen coal was gushing fresh gas, and a growing flame was flickering from the crack. That's what I saw, but I wondered what Ben saw. An eerie train-whistle that blew not so far away disturbed both our reveries. Mrs McNulty stuttered something incomprehensible.

Here, uncontrollable grief took hold of her, and she buried her sobs on Isa's shoulder, while Ben sat staring in front of him, hypnotised by the leaping flames.

206

'Jenny ran away wi' 'im,' he answered calmly, as if the reason he gave was all the logic necessary. 'Efter he gied me this,' pointing to his deeply scarred face. He was like a man in the throes of a malaria bout. One minute shivering ague-like, sweating the next.

His face was in a bit of a state, now we had a chance to think about it. As Isa and her mother returned my glances I wondered if Ben ever thought of me while his scars were healing. My own face will never be quite the same, thanks to Ben.

'So help me, Maw,' Ben insisted. 'If he had o' left ma wife alane an' hadny gied me this, nane o' it wad o' happened.'

I reconsidered. Maybe Flash had gone over the score when he stole Ben's wife. I wouldn't have a great deal of affection for anyone who stole mine. Still, I was married to Isa, and he was married to Jenny. A great difference.

Mrs McNulty stepped over to him, pushing Isa aside. 'But, heavens above, Ben!' she stormed. 'Whit right have you goat tae go aboot killin'? Ye canny get oaf wi' that. Who dae ye think ye are? God?'

For a moment a strained silence reigned which I couldn't help but break.

'When did she leave ye, Ben?' I asked with, I hoped, neither sympathy nor condemnation in my voice, since I wasn't sure which sentiment I was feeling. I was trying to be a proper disinterested jury-type.

Slowly, but methodically, he told us of the few happy weeks he had spent since he and I had last met, omitting of course, the occasional skirmish that he had been involved in. Then he gave us a résumé of the events that led up to his 'tanking'. The sing-song pub, the drink with the Sinclairs and the argument with the wee nadger in the toilet. The crowd waiting for him outside the boozer, and the awful drawn-out weeks he had spent in hospital, all the time knowing that Jenny was living with his worst enemy.

While he spoke I felt a sudden pity for him, when I considered the physical and mental torture he must have gone through

Mrs Mac and Isa sat listening to his tale. Isa was showing constant signs of distress, but her mother's face was inscrutable now and I couldn't tell how she felt about the matter. When Ben finally finished she spoke, and there was a hint of motherly compassion in her voice.

'Well, son,' she said, 'ye brought a loat o' that oan yoursel'. Ye know whit the text says: "Be sure your sins'll fun' ye oot." That's the way it always is.'

Ben was looking at his mother with an expression that I hadn't seen there in all the years I had known him.

'They're the truest words ye could fun',' she told him. 'Ye canny live the way you've been livin' withoot it comin' back oan ye.'

At that moment, as if on cue, an unmistakable heavy knock sounded on the door.

'That's them for me,' Ben commented unnecessarily, rising to his feet with an effort. He looked so tired. Maybe of life. He gave Isa and me a wry smile and turned to his mother.

'Maw—,' he said. 'Before Ah go – Ah want tae ask ye – can ye forgive me for a' the trouble Ah've caused ye. Ah'm sorry Ah had tae come here the night – but something made me come. Ye – ye deserve a better son than me.'

Tears were in his eyes now, and I thought for a moment he was going to go down on his knees. I hoped he wouldn't for I didn't want to see him like that. Not Ben. He didn't, but he continued to speak.

'Sittin' here amongst yese an' talkin' aboot it a', Ah've goat a loat calmer. That's because ye were here. Maw.' He took one of her hands in his and I was glad to see she didn't withdraw it. 'Ah should never have left the hoose. Never goat merrit tae that cow. But Ah can face whitever's comin' tae me, if ye say ye forgive me.'

I stood watching them hopefully, but in the background I could hear the police becoming impatient. I knew there would be others in the back court, and out on the street, watching the room and kitchen windows. The place would probably be chock-full of people waiting to see Ben being 'lifted', and hoping that he would do something spectacular, befitting his reputation, to make the incident worth telling to their grandchildren. Those people would wait all night, but not the police. *They* sounded as if they were ready to burst the door in. I turned to let them in, and heard Ben's voice behind me.

'Ah'll tell ye somethin', Bill, before ye let them in,' he said. I halted but kept my back to him. 'Ah always thoaght ye'd o' had the better o'me, if y'd o' startit. The quick wey ye gied it tae the Shooter fella wi' the gun in your gut took some beatin'.'

He stopped speaking, and as I covered the remainder of the distance to the door, I wondered why he had said that, and I told myself that Ben's words were nothing more than patter. He could eat and crap me any time.

As I threw open the door, and the first of the policemen hurried past me to halt on the threshold of the kitchen, Mrs Mac threw her arms around her son's neck, letting his wet face rest on her ample bosom. The coppers looked as if they didn't quite expect such a scene. They thought they would have a mess of trouble to deal with.

There were two uniformed constables and three plain-clothes man. They all crowded together watching us like an audience at a play, all of them registering regret. Trouble would have meant headlines and publicity, whereas, instead of a real hard case with a razor in his hand, here was a big boy crying on his mother's breast. I felt like telling Ben to draw his razor and prove to them just how right they had been in the first place. One of them walked over and faced Ben.

'Well – we finally caught up with you,' he said, his thoughts of a moment before transmitted in his voice. Ben took umbrage, momentarily the old Ben once more.

'Aye – only 'cos Ah let ye – ya monkey,' he spat out.

'Listen, you. You're a big boy now, and it's time your brain grew up,' the busy said, ever so sure of himself, and I wondered once more if Ben still had his razor in his pocket. Much more of this and I could see the detective's demeanour suddenly being changed. He looked Ben up and down insolently while his mates stood and watched. They thought they might as well be home in bed. They would find out different if Ben started. The detective spoke to Ben again, using the same tone.

'I told you once that you'd need help – remember?' The look of recognition slowly appeared in Ben's eyes, and the busy continued. 'That's right – the hospital. Well – it'll never be any truer than it is at this moment. I think it's about time you stopped playing the hard case. Those days are over for you. You've used your razor for the last time.' He took hold of Ben's arm and gabbled the formal sentence of arrest.

I didn't like the copper's tone, and, while he frisked Ben for the razor that didn't seem to be there, I told him so.

'There's nae need tae talk tae 'im like that. You're here tae arrest 'im. No' tae make comments oan the rights or wrangs o' whit he did.'

I was surprised at myself. Usually a look from a copper is enough to send me to the stairhead 'lavvy', yet here was I, throwing my weight about. Maybe it was intuition for, as the policeman turned angrily on me, I got a proper look at his coupon for the first time. The fedora he wore had blocked my view up to this point, but this was one fellow I really wanted to have a fight with, jail or no jail. I'll give you three guesses and you can stop at the first one. Yes! it was the Brylcreem boy with the Gable moustache.

He opened his mouth to start on me, and I was about to do a very foolish thing – close it with my fist – when Ben intervened.

'It's okay, Bill,' he said. 'Ye know whit like his type are.' With his free hand he tapped his escort's chest and jerked a thumb at me. 'See that fella there. At wan time him an' me were chinas, an' Ah chibbed 'im wi' a razor – when Ah wiz drunk. See it oan ese face?' He looked at me with an expression I hadn't seen on his face for years, then turned to the busy and continued, 'Ah gied 'im that, an' diz he want tae see me swingin' at the end o' a rope? Ah don't think so. Know how? 'Cos he's goat mair humanness in 'im than you. You're talkin' aboot me an' ma chib. Dae ye think you're ony better than me?' The busy opened his mouth again to make a hot retort, but Ben wouldn't let him speak. 'Well you're no',' he continued. 'You're every

210

bit as hard a case as Ah am. Only, because o' that badge ye abuse, it didny come oot in ye the same as it diz in me. Wi' me it wiz a razor. Wi' you, it's the happy feelin' ye get when ye see suckers like me squirmin' tae get oot the trouble we goat inty, tae keep a bastart like you in a joab.' Ben should have been in politics. I never knew he could make such a long speech.

The busy gave him a shove towards the door, and one of his mates took over the grip on Ben's arm. They were leading Ben away, but before they got as far as the door, he turned again to me.

'Thanks for stickin' up for me, Bill,' he said, resisting the hand that was tugging at his arm, and added, 'You'll never know how sorry Ah am noo aboot a loat o' things Ah done, an' maist o' a', whit Ah done tae you.' It rang true, and without being capable of doing anything to prevent it, a warm glow stole over me. I smiled at him reassuringly. 'Honest, Bill, Ah'm helluva sorry,' he said, and I was glad. Glad we had met again before it was all over, and glad that the Ben I met was so different to the Ben I had known recently. As I said – I was glad. A dying man was making a last gesture. I didn't hesitate.

'That's all right, Ben,' I told him. His eyes took a strange new light. He leaned over, and, with Isa's co-operation, kissed her cheek, then turned away to the door. I patted his shoulder, and said, 'Best o' luck.'

'Thanks,' he replied, as he passed through the door, to be surrounded by the waiting policemen as they tramped downstairs. I spoke to the upstart busy when he took up the rear.

'Mind—,' I said, '—nae rough stuff wi' 'im when ye get 'im inside. If ye dae, Ah'll see that ye get done. Wan wey or anither.' He smirked, not quite sure of himself, and trotted downstairs, while I closed the door on the neighbour's face that was peeping from the slightly open door across the landing. Ben had gone out of our lives. This time for good.

CHAPTER TWENTY-TWO

Embarrassed, and not knowing what to do in the presence of two weeping women, I wandered 'ben-the-room' and lay back on the bed. It was just as well, for I had some thoughts I wanted to be alone with for a little while.

I still wasn't sure whether I could really forgive Ben, but I wouldn't have told him that under the circumstances.

I let my mind drift back a few years to the time when Ben and I were kids, and slowly analysed the relationship that had existed between us in those days. You never saw two greater childhood friends. At the same time I dwelt on the kindly fate that hides the future from us, and so safeguards the equilibrium of the youthful brain. It would have been horrific to have known what lay before us.

A rumbling sound broke the outdoor silence and I idly wondered what it was. Then, when it came nearer, and I was able to interpret it properly, more memories were added to the pictures on my mind.

A 'midden-motor' came along the street and stopped at our entry. I heard the clump of the midden-men's heavy boots as they trudged through the close with their large baskets of refuse on their backs, and it made a sort of sound-track to the film my brain was showing.

As long as I can remember, it's been a night-shift job. An unpleasant one too. Humping a large straw basket, loaded with all sorts of rubbish from midden to wagon, via each entry way. Night after night, in most weathers. That's the job. And they can have it. I wouldn't take it if they put me on tonnage and gave me Joe Louis and Floyd Patterson as mates. But some blokes stuck it for years. Old Paddy for instance.

I recalled the summer nights years ago, when Ben and I used to run around the streets till midnight, contrary to our parents' wishes. When the 'midden motor' drove along our street, we clung to it for a ride. One of the labourers was an Irish fellow, aged about sixty, who seemed as old as Methuselah to us. How the hell he carried the basket was a mystery to me, for there wasn't a speck on him.

He often used to share his breakfast with us, sitting against a tenement wall. He also gave us little mementoes he picked up in back-courts of better-class districts. You know how children amuse themselves with the strangest odds and ends.

I remember the rag-doll he gave to Ben, for his sister. Isa still has it, among her souvenirs.

The old midden-man might still be alive. At the time he knew Ben, he thought the world of him. I wondered, if he were still kicking and had read the case, what his sentiments would be, and that started a train of thought.

The other people Ben had encountered in his short life? No need to wonder how most of them would feel.

Davie the Dummy and Shooter Gunn – old Limpy and his woman, probably gloating. Jenny, who caused most of the trouble, and Flash, who helped a deal. Maggie, who at one time had nearly felt his razor, and, at another time, nearly went to bed with him, and had finished up in jail because of him. The publicans, the bookies who, at one time, had been getting the squeeze. I didn't think any of that bunch would shed a tear for Ben's demise. Apart from the small business men, whose only fault was the possession of money, they were all strictly Ben's kind of people.

But I wasn't so sure about Blaster. He had once said he would be there to see when Ben backed a deuce. Well – he couldn't back a bigger one than now. A murder conviction was the surest thing on the card, but I had an idea that, when Blaster attended the trial, and saw the mess that Ben's face was in, revengeful thoughts would disintegrate.

There was one other person – Susie. I had an idea she would take it bad. Say what you like about her way of life, but I thought, and still do, that she was a good kid, who hadn't got the breaks. If Jenny's path hadn't crossed Ben's, it's on the cards that he and Susie would have married and settled down.

But of course there are plenty of slum kids who don't

get the breaks, I philosophised. Sometimes, because they don't work hard enough for them.

Ben himself was like that. You see, he was really pretty intelligent, but he could never be bothered with any kind of studying. A good deal of brainwork, and he might have gone places, but he, with his infinite capacity for other things, preferred the pursuit of excitement, as the average slum-child does.

He was always forming groups, of which he must invariably be the boss. He would give them some outlandish name, such as the Black Hand Gang, or the Hooded Cobra Society, with a written set of rules and a membership card showing the appropriate title. Since Ben's constant spur was the accumulation of money in any form, nefarious escapades were numerous and the kitty was always in good shape. He even appointed a treasurer to look after this side of things, although when it came to any cut-up, Ben, as the boss, would get a bigger whack than anyone else.

He always made me his second-in-command, and, when asked by others why this should be so, his simple explanation was that I was his pal. To the Ben of that period, that was the best reason in the world.

Only in the very early stages was his leadership disputed, and in those cases the matter was quickly settled, when someone scampered off home with a bloody nose. And yet, surprisingly enough, he was not, at that time, truly a bully. In fact, on many occasions he proved himself quite the opposite, and had a fair reputation for protecting the smaller element at our school from their older aggressors.

When St Patrick's Day came around yearly, he and his gang took part in the Billy-or-a-Dan battles between schools, and I might add, a prominent part, so that, even at an early age, Ben was creating a reputation among people of his own tender years.

Hatred and bigotry lie easy in the breast of the young Glaswegian. Most of them, almost before they had been taught words other than 'Mammy' and Daddy', have instilled in their minds a special regard for expressions like Fenian and Pope, or King Billy and Orangeman, depending on their respective denominations. They unconsciously adopt an attitude similar to the one attained by the ordinary British bombed-out person, when the word Nazi was flung at him, by radio and newspaper. And that attitude remains with most of them, at least under the surface, for the rest of their lives.

We were no exceptions. What Ben's or my adult relatives neglected to preach to us, we learned, like our first sexual information, from the older lads at school, or the gang at the corner.

When you get hatred you get fights, and Ben was in his element in those fights. Even when we left school at fourteen and became, in our own estimation, working-men, Ben still liked to get in a fight, although there were reasons, other than religious ones, that could be used as an excuse. The wee hairys, for instance, used to cause a lot of barneys. They carried tales from one corner to another corner and they were wont to play two or more young fellows on a string at one time.

One night the fight would be in a cinema, and the innocent picturegoers would have to forgo part of their entertainment, or risk life and limb in a cinema seat, while a fight went on around them. Another occasion and the trouble would start in the showground on the Glasgow Green or the 'Sody Waste' and the police would have a job catching anyone with so many avenues of escape available. More often than not eruptions started at some street corner, particularly on the Twelfth of July when the Orange Walk took place.

But if Ben hadn't had religion to fight over it would have been something else. He was that type, as his career in later years proved.

I lay on top of the bed that Ben used to sleep in, and thought about the fights that Ben got into during that period, while the sound of the two weeping women slowly decreased in volume. Women weeping for a man who had stepped into one fight too many.

Finally the sobs stopped completely and I lay perfectly still, listening to the utter silence that fell – fell being the

215

operative word. It pressed down on me ominously, like some great weight being lowered on my body by a crane, trying to crush the life from me. The Corporation Cleansing unit had long since moved on to other parts, and outside not even the usual group of stray cats gave one little purr to cheer me up.

I wondered how long I had been lying here. I reckoned about an hour and a half had elapsed since Ben had left the house, and Isa had still not come through from the kitchen.

I rose from the bed, allowing the chill night air to strike my spine, while a penetrative shiver ran up and down its knuckles. I gave myself a mental and physical shake, and crept along the lobby, subconsciously noting the sound of heavy feet on the stair.

The two women were drowsing on the couch, and I lifted a blanket from the bed to cover them. I gently place it around them, watching the dreamy frown on my wife's tear-stained face, and, without disturbing them, returned to the lobby to go back to bed. This time beneath the clothes.

I was just in time to open the door to another heavy knock. I heard the sound of someone jumping to their feet behind me, startled from a bad dream by an unpleasant reality. For, standing with one foot in the doorstep, was another uniformed policeman.

'Is Missus McNulty in?' he asked. I glanced behind me, made sure both women were on their feet, and waved him into the house without answering. There was something stuck in my throat that was interfering with my vocal chords. I think it was my heart. Me and my premonitions.

The policeman looked extremely uncomfortable as he stood in the middle of the kitchen floor, bracing himself as if on parade, and about to have his unpolished buttons inspected. He coughed nervously.

Ma looked at him directly and asked, 'Whit dae ye want noo?' She looked ready to throw him out, and it wouldn't have surprised me if she had.

'Ah've some bad news for you, Missus.' He paused as if choosing his words. I didn't like the ones he chose. 'Your son is dead,' he said.

Just that. No fol-de-rols or flowery language with him. No messing about. Just, 'Your son is dead', but the words created more of a stir than Churchill's 'Fight on the streets' could have. Mrs Mac went stone daft and we had a hellava job trying to control her, as she tore her hair and screamed. I swear there were tears in the copper's eyes as he helped us to control the demented woman. Up till that time I had thought one of the qualifications for a policeman's job was a piece of concrete in your left breast.

Isa was so busy consoling her mother, that I don't believe that the copper's statement had sunk into her shock-numbed brain.

Finally we got the prostrate Mrs Mac into our bed in the room and Isa remained with her, while I went back into the kitchen with the policeman. He graciously accepted a cup of tea and while I made it, he gave me the details.

You see Ben had beaten them after all. He had taken the only chance he had got, and this is the way it happened.

When Ben and his escort left the house and were on their way downstairs he halted them, saying, 'Yese think yese are gaunny hing me, dae yese? Well, ye've backed a deuce. Ye'll never get a rope roon' ma neck. There's no' been wan made tae fit it.'

Some of the coppers gave him a push and he laughed a little hysterically as he stumbled down the remainder of the stairs, through the close and into the police 'drag' which stood at the kerb.

While the driver revved up and the others settled in their seats, the Brylcreem boy offered his prisoner a cigarette.

Ben told him, 'Stick it in your jacksy,' and closed his mouth grimly. During the journey Ben said no more, and an awkward silence reigned, which even the grass didn't feel like breaking. Then it happened.

For one moment the police relaxed their vigilance as the squad car emptied in the yard at Craigie Street Police Office. One couldn't blame them, for no one could have dreamt what Ben intended to do.

One detective was standing on the flagstones, having got out first. Another was behind Ben as he stepped out, and two others were disembarking from the driver's seat. With one blow, Ben put his head clean through the window and drew his throat swiftly across the jagged edges of glass. That was his 'out'. Of course, the busies tried their best to stop him, but the thing was done so quickly and unexpectedly, that it was really all over before they had a chance.

They rushed him to the Victoria Infirmary, but, with half of his throat torn away, he was dead long before they got there.

The policeman who was telling me about it, said that Brylcreem Boy, whose name he gave as Sergeant Bluish, seemed to be taking it bad, and he couldn't understand it. Evidently the sergeant had a bit of a reputation for being a hard man. I had my own ideas about the sergeant's reasons.

Anyway, Ben saved himself weeks of waiting, which could only be followed by one of two things. Death ignominiously, at the end of a rope – or spending the remainder of his years in the Criminal Lunatic Department at Perth, which is a doubtful lesser evil. Ben took a road he thought was better than either, and who am I to say he was wrong?

CHAPTER TWENTY-THREE

Ben's death and the circumstances surrounding it, were in the nature of a nine-days' wonder for the public, and although Isa, Ma and I never mentioned his name, I think he was constantly in all our thoughts.

The newspapers made a real spread of it. The month was June, the year 'forty-three' and the 'linens' were covered in War Correspondent articles and Reuter communiqués, but on that particular occasion the crime reporters got a break, and made the most of it. It got so that I felt sure that a Madame Tussaud's representative would call for some of Ben's old clothes.

Finally a major offensive that was taking place somewhere or other eclipsed the sensationalist tripe, and the newspapers topped pestering Ma for personal interviews to be entitled 'How I Gave Birth to the Razor-Slasher', and which were to be ever so remunerative.

Isa and I stayed as close to her mother as was possible most of the time. We even took her to the pictures with us, but it was a long time before she showed any signs of having enjoyed the films. We tried to avoid films with delinquent-son themes as we always had to get up and leave such a show. But we dragged her along anyway mainly because we daren't leave her by herself.

But all wounds heal partly, even though it does take time, and gradually life became a little more placid in the McNulty house.

One night, nearly three months later, I saw someone, and I think Ben would have been glad. Wherever he was, I could imagine a cynical smile on his face. I'll tell you why.

It was Flash I saw, and the point that would have been particularly pleasing to my late brother-in-law was the fact that Flash was lying under a bus which had just run over him. He was as dead as a mackerel. If only Ben had lived to see it . . .

When with the other curious passers-by, I gazed at the mess that used to be Flash, while the crowd jostled me mercilessly in an effort to get a better view, I had a strange feeling that Ben was at my shoulder. In fact, when an elbow dug into my ribs, I could quite easily imagine it was he, nudging me, and I waited to hear his voice saying, 'Have a look at that, Bill.'

Before they got the bus jacked up to remove the body, a photographer took some flashbulb shots of Flash as he lay there. He, too, was going to make the tabloids, even if only on the back page.

Jenny? I see her occasionally although we've never spoken. She has a fair idea that any remarks I might make to her would be other than complimentary, once I started, so she dodges to the other side of the street when I appear on the horizon.

She 'blew out' her fancy-man shortly after Ben's death, so she wasn't at Glasgow Cross the night Flash got his, but since then I have spotted her on the city streets, parading her greatly jaded charms for inspection. The brand that Ben put on her that final night and the life she had been living since have removed much of her attraction, but I think that her real disfigurement is the part of her rotten soul that is showing through the veneer. Nowadays, everyone seems able to discern what I saw, and Ben couldn't.

She drinks the meths like a spirit-stove, and she has plenty of time for thought, for a scarred face and methylated breath don't bring a select clientele to one practising the oldest profession. Business is invariably slack with her.

However, most nights her memories should walk unmolested, for the cubicles in the women's 'model' where she is reported to be staying are nice and quiet. It should only be a matter of time till the third corner of the triangle joins the other two, providing they all go to the same place. Each time I see her, I feel more certain it won't be long.

Myself? Isa and I are doing all right. Got a couple of kids – both boys. Nice kids, even though I say it myself. We still live with Mrs Mac, but we have our name down in the Corporation lists for a new house. I think I'm due one about the same year as my old-age pension becomes due.

It can't be too soon, for this house holds associations which I, for one, would rather try to forget. Besides I'd like to give my kids a better chance than the one that Ben and I got, and it's hard to do that when you live in the slums.

If we get the place, we'll take Isa's mother with us. She's wrapped up in her two grandchildren. But now and again I watch her sit with one of my kids fast asleep on her knee, and it's only too obvious that her thoughts have drifted back close on thirty years, and, mentally, she's holding another child on her lap.

I myself think of Ben quite often, and not always

charitably, I'm afraid. For although, for most of his life, I was reckoned his best friend, I think I grew to hate him more than many of his enemies. And yet he didn't die an enemy of mine.

It turned out that Blaster felt the same way about things.

I met him in the city one Christmas week. The wife and I were going around the shops looking for some toys for the kids. We hadn't a great deal of money, and were coming out of one of the department stores where we thought the price-tags were a trifle depressing. Blaster and I collided at the door.

'Oh, hullo, Bill,' he cried, looking very pleased to see me indeed.

He was a changed man, I thought, as I eyed up his well-cut tweed overcoat, hard hat and fine worsted suit. When my startled gaze wandered down to his feet, I was even more surprised. He had *spats* on! He laughed as he saw my expression.

'Ah always wantit tae wear spats, ye know, an' never could afford them.' Each of his hands was gripped on one of our arms. 'Ah think they make ye get dressy-lookin'.' He released my arm and took Isa's hand. 'An' this'll be the wife, likely?' and without waiting for a reply, 'Pleased tae meet ye,' he said, all but shaking the hand from her wrist. 'Good-lookin' wumman ye've goat, Bill,' he rumbled, scrutinizing her features closely, and my chest measurements increased by two inches. He paused for a moment, and I took my chance to get a word in.

'We're lookin' for toys for the weans,' I told him.

'Have ye a family then?' he asked.

'Aye! Two boys.'

'Ah bet if they've ony good points they take them aff their mither,' he joked, and I saw him wink slyly at Isa. 'Whit aboot comin' in wi' me for a cup o' tea?' he suggested, as he stepped aside to let two women shoppers pass between us. 'We seem tae be in the road here an' Ah'd like a chat wi' yese.' I nodded and followed, as he led Isa by the arm back into the store and upstairs to

221

the restaurant.

The place was chock-full of Christmas shoppers, but we managed to squeeze into a corner table, and, while the waitress left to fetch our order, Blaster and Isa made idle comments about the weather, the Christmas rush, the rising cost of living and life in general.

The waitress laid out our food and departed with a laugh, as Blaster made some crack or other which I didn't catch. He seemed to know her well. His appearance shouted prosperity, and I pondered on which safe he might have 'blown', but I wouldn't dream of asking him. He looked at me shrewdly with the expression of a thought-reader.

'How d'ye think Ah'm lookin'?' he asked, with a smile nullifying the slightly grim look the scar gave him.

'You're lookin' fine, Blaster,' I replied. 'Flush, tae.'

'Oh Ah'm no' bad off nooadays,' he agreed. 'Goat a good wee turn aff the coupon coupla years back, ye know. Over three thousan', it was.' I gave an appreciative whistle that turned curious heads on either side of us. 'Boaght a wee boozer doon in Partick right away.'

I couldn't help but wonder if the money really came from a football-pools firm, or whether that was a subterfuge to cover up a more questionable source. I knew he was the type who never failed to send his coupon away every week – had been trying them for years. Could be he had a coupon up. The blurbs say it can happen to anyone.

We yattered away, all three of us avoiding the subject of Ben. I had told Isa long before about the chibbing Ben had given Blaster, yet the silly so-and-so inadvertently mentioned my youngest boy's name – Ben – then bit off her words, and by so doing only made the situation worse. Old Blaster looked directly into her eyes reassuringly.

'It wiz hard lines oan Ben,' he said, turning his face to me, 'tae finish up, the way he did.'

'Aye—,' I said hesitantly. 'That – that wife o' his gied him a helluva messin' aboot. Nae kiddin'. You've nae idea.'

222

'But Ah have, Bill,' the old fellow said, 'Ah have. Ah used tae get a' the news ye know.'

Isa was looking at the old fellow and there was a damp film over the pupils of her eyes. 'Ah'm sorry—,' she stuttered, '– aboot – for whit Ben did tae – tae your face. He wiz—.'

She was ready to drown us both in a flood of tears when Blaster patted her arm.

'That's a'right, hen,' he said. 'It was an—.' I could see the word 'accident' forming on his lips, but it must have stuck in his throat, and he didn't say it. He knew he couldn't get away with that. 'Ah asked for it that time,' he finished lamely, so quietly that I had to strain my ears to hear the words. The white lie caused another awkward silence between the three of us, which Blaster broke with a forced heartiness.

'Well,' he said, 'this'll no' pey the rent. Ah'm keepin' yese back fae gettin' ahead wi' your shoppin'.'

He rose from the table, and, after paying the bill, followed us down and into the street where he gripped my arm.

'Ah really am sorry aboot, Ben,' he said. 'Tell the wife that.'

I turned around, but Isa was standing a little distance away, as women sometimes do, in case their menfolk wish to discuss ponderous male matters. 'Ah'll tell her, Blaster,' I replied.

'Aye! An' mind. If you're wantin' a drink, gie me a wee look up, eh? Onybuddy'll tell ye where ma pub is.' I nodded as he said, 'Here's ma caur comin'. Haveny boaght a motor yet. Couldny drive wan, onyway.' He laughed. 'Couldny drive a nail inty a bit of wudd,' he added.

I was opening my mouth to say something, but the tram was ready to pull away from the shop. Blaster said, 'Gie your boys a good Christmas,' pushing something hurriedly into my palm, and jumped aboard with a wave. I stood watching him with my mouth agape, as the tram rumbled away. He stood waving through the glass, until the tram had reached the next stop, and climbed up to the top deck. Isa came over to me.

'Whit did he put in your haun'?' she asked. Trust a woman to notice these things. Silently I opened my clenched fingers and both of us scrutinized the piece of paper as I unfolded it.

'A fiver!' I gasped, and took another look to make sure I was right. But I was wrong. There were two. I looked once more in the direction the tram had taken but could see nothing for the moisture that was in my eyes. I really needed that money.

I haven't seen Blaster since, but some of these days I'll go along there for a booze-up and a chat about old times. And Blaster will probably philosophise on the subject of Ben and head-cases in general. I may not agree with all he says, but at least we'll have a common denominator – one each of Ben's scars. My own ideas are somewhat muddled.

Many of Ben's worst crimes can be attributed to environment, the fickleness of a woman and the fact that there are men in any city who cannot, or will not, leave another man's wife alone: to whom a wedding-ring is a challenge. Flash's only reason for linking up with Jenny was too obvious.

But, make no mistake about it, and no one knows better than I. Ben was, first and last, that special product of the slums: A HEAD-CASE.

Yet who knows? If someone were to break my home, were to entice Isa away from me and my two kids – and maybe leave me face a network of ugly scars into the bargain – I, too, might one day become A HEAD-CASE.

THE END